£1·50

VICTOR SUT̶... ...n
War Museum ...g
experience in tradi̶tio̶na̶l ... ...ch
he has followed the routes of the eighteenth-century
wars. He was commissioned in Canada's Navy Reserve
and is a Board Member of the Canadian Sail Training
Association. His novels featuring Edward Mainwaring,
Royal Yankee, *The Golden Galleon*, *Admiral of Fear*
and *Captain Monsoon*, are written with authenticity, an
historian's eye for detail and a born storyteller's art. He
lives with his wife and children in Ottawa.

Also by Victor Suthren

The Black Cockade
A King's Ransom
In Perilous Seas
Royal Yankee
The Golden Galleon
Admiral of Fear

Captain Monsoon

Victor Suthren

CORONET BOOKS
Hodder and Stoughton

First published in Great Britain in 1992 by Hodder and Stoughton Ltd
First published in paperback in 1995 by Hodder & Stoughton
A division of Hodder Headline PLC

A Coronet paperback

10 9 8 7 6 5 4 3 2 1

British Library Cataloguing in Publication Data

Suthren, Victor
      Captain Monsoon
      I. Title
      813.54 [F]

ISBN 0 340 63839 7

Printed and bound in Great Britain by
Cox & Wyman Ltd, Reading, Berkshire

Hodder and Stoughton
A division of Hodder Headline PLC
338 Euston Road
London NW1 3BH

CAPTAIN MONSOON

1

The rain had begun in the dark, pre-dawn hours of April 19, 1744; it was intensifying now as the grey light grew in the east. The drifting curtains of the rain swirled and danced over the heaving, gunmetal surface of the sea, leaving the slopes and valleys of the heavy swells mottled by the countless craterings of the showers. The wind had been fitful out of the south-east, but was building now, sending dark rushes over the sea while a leaden, low ceiling of billowing black cloud raced off to the north-west.

Two hundred and twenty miles due east of Cape Masoala on the Madagascar coast, in the southern Indian Ocean, His Britannic Majesty's Ship *Pallas*, forty-four guns, rolled and plunged into the rain-pattered swells. The drifting sheets of rain obscured her form and then parted, like curtains, as she steered off to the north under reduced canvas. Her mustard and black hull pitched in slow majesty through the dark scene, the white tumult of the bow wave under her cutwater gleaming rhythmically.

A ship-rigged man-o'-war, *Pallas* was sailing under the sodden curves of her inner jib, foretopmast staysail, and single-reefed fore and main topsails. The courses and the topgallants were gathered tightly against their yards and on the mizzen, its topsail carried a single reef above the brailed lateen spanker. From the foretruck a Union Jack fluttered, matching the delicate, snaking red line of the commissioning pennant that streamed out from the main truck. On the ensign staff, the darkened, outsized shape of the Royal Navy's Red Squadron ensign curled and rippled, a startling palette-knife thrust of colour in a scene painted otherwise in shades of grey. There was little chill to the hissing walls of rain as the ship pitched and heaved her way through them, steering towards the inky northern horizon, or as close to that heading as the two drenched, oil-skinned helmsmen who grasped the great double wheel could manage in the corkscrewing motion caused by the swells. They sweated at their work under the critical eye of the tall naval officer in a voluminous sea cloak who stood braced to windward of the helm and its clutch of attendant figures.

Captain Edward Mainwaring, Royal Navy, commanding officer of *Pallas*, blew a drop of water from the tip of his nose. His plain black cocked hat, rimed with salt spray, was pulled down low over his eyes, and the front cock was running like a drainspout. He spat over the rail and turned to the nearest of the figures at the helm.

"If you please, Mr Hooke," said Mainwaring to the man who was the sailing master in *Pallas*. "She'll stand another reef in the topsails."

"Aye, zur." Hooke nodded and peered forward, looking for his mates. Though the heavy, cape-shouldered oilskins reached to his ankles, Isaiah Hooke was bareheaded, and his thick blond-and-pepper hair which was not captured in a long, tarry queue, was plastered wetly across his forehead and down his ruddy, stubbled cheeks. "Beloike as 'ow there'd be freshenin' wind astern o' this rain, zur. C'd come from any quarter."

Mainwaring nodded. "Aye. Call the people, then, if you please."

"Zur!" Hooke nodded to the sturdy figure of Isaac Jewett, *Pallas*' boatswain, who stood in spreadfooted readiness at the coaming of the fore companionway, pipe gleaming like silver in his black-palmed hand in the gloom. "Make yer pipe, 'swain!" Hooke barked.

But Jewett was already hopping nimbly down the companionway ladder, heading for the lower gun deck, his pipe a high, keening note that floated up through the gratings as he vanished below.

"D'ye hear, there! All hands, aloft t' reef tops'ls! On deck, there! Stir y'selves!"

"Where's Mr Howe?" asked Mainwaring, referring to the ship's first lieutenant.

"Below, zur. Oi've the watch whilst 'e's peerin' at the larb'd pump casin', zur. Not pumpin' th' bilges as she should. 'E's wiv th' carpenter an' 'is mates," said Hooke.

"Very well. I hope ye'll mind your sheets and tacklines in these winds, Mr Hooke. I recall a *pampero* that took us over to the gunports in the old *Diana*, on the Main."

"Aye, zur," growled the master. "Oi've no wish t' be tumbled arse over kit beloike o' that again. Oi've got Stewart wiv 'is lads posted t' th' pinrails, zur. A word, an' they're cut, afore we takes a knockdown, like."

Mainwaring followed Hooke's gaze, to where another squarish figure in a tarred short jacket and billowing duck 'petticoat breeches' was talking to a drenched knot of seamen at the pinrails. It was Alexander Stewart, the Glaswegian master's mate in *Pallas* and, in his own dour way, an equal of Isaiah Hooke in blocky authority.

Mainwaring was nodding, his eyes piercing and clear under the shadow of his cocked hat. "I'll hold you to that, Mr Hooke. If we swim, you'll owe my table a prime cask o' Madeira!"

"Done, zur!" said Hooke, an answering grin spreading over his weathered features.

Edward Mainwaring was taller than the burly Hooke, verging on six feet in an age when that was a remarkable size. Under the dripping cocked hat his hair was a kind of sundusted brown, tied back simply in an eelskin-wrapped queue. His long face showed clear strength, its firmness softened by the laughter lines around his mouth. Below straight black brows, his eyes were of a rather startling blue, and the long line of his nose would have been described as aristocratic were it not for the prizefighter's break in its arch. The figure under the sea cloak, in a sombre blue coat, waistcoat and breeches, with legs thrust into salt-whitened seaboots, was athletic, broad in the shoulder and slim in the hips. An easy grace to his carriage revealed to a practised eye the mark of a man raised to maturity in the forested wilderness of America with its moccasin-trod trails beneath towering white pine, and a buckskin-and-homespun life of vigour and free action. But a look into the watchful and perceptive blue eyes dispersed any suggestion that he might be sniffed at as a 'Provincial', as North American colonists were often termed.

Mainwaring was, indeed, an American, a native of the seafaring island of Martha's Vineyard, off the coast of Massachusetts. He had entered the Royal Navy through extraordinary circumstances when serving as a Provincial officer in command of an American topsail schooner which had been bought into the Navy. His subsequent career had been marked by a no less extraordinary series of dramatic events and successes that had brought him at a comparatively young age to the rank of post captain. And it had been through the direct interest of His Britannic Majesty, George the Second, that Mainwaring had taken command of *Pallas*; a command that might otherwise have been denied an officer of Mainwaring's background and lack of 'interest' in influential places.

Hooke had moved to the waistdeck rail, and cupped his hands to bellow.

"I'll have a single reef in the tops'ls!" he roared. "'Way aloft, there, topmen!"

As was the custom in the Royal Navy, all three topsails were to be reefed together. There was a rush of feet to the ratlines and the men swarmed aloft to the yards, agile and sure-footed despite the rain.

"Steady, all. Clewlines an' buntlines, now! Weather braces! *Lively*, Quintal, you thick-footed squid!" Hooke sent a stream of tobacco juice over the lee rail, eyes still aloft.

"Out wiv yer reef tackle! Up buntl'nes, now! Collins, ye be cap' o' that top! Lay aholt that toggle on th' fore! Light out to leeward! Roundly, there!"

The great topsails were lowered in order that the reefs could be tied in, and *Pallas* slowed and wallowed as the canvas thumped and ballooned aloft. But soon Hooke was bellowing for the topsails to be hoisted, the halyards to be belayed, and the bowlines 'steadied out'. *Pallas* lifted again as her canvas regained its power, and Mainwaring and Hooke exchanged a nod.

"She's easier, now, zur," said Hooke, wiping one paw across his streaming face.

"Aye." Mainwaring shook a cloud of water from his cloak. He fumbled under its folds for his watch, and peered at it. "Ye'll be setting the morning watch, so I'll go below, Mr Hooke. See that the first lieutenant comes to my cabin directly he arrives on deck."

Hooke put a thick finger to his brow. "Aye, aye, zur." He turned to the men at the helm. "Steady th' ship's 'ead, lads. Yer course be to th' nor'ard, not a-wanderin' about th' binnacle!"

Mainwaring wanted to go below not only because there was now a folio of orders he had authority – with the dawn – to open and read, but because he knew that Howe and Hooke had the ship's daily routine to begin, and he wanted to be out of their way. The matter of the pump worried him; he would get a report from Howe, briefly, before letting him get on with his everyday affairs.

The morning watchmen had gone on deck shortly before eight bells in the midwatch, and in the gloom and rain Howe had seen to the streaming of the log and the changing of the lookouts, before issuing instructions for the cooks to start their galley fires – and for Jewett to roust out the 'idlers', or men who slept all night. He had also had the carpenter called, a large-nosed Hampshireman named Fennell, for his usual first task of sounding the bilge wells. That was when the problem of the pump had been discovered. Hooke would send the off-duty watch below for a bit more oblivion in their tightly-packed hammocks while setting the watchmen to scrubbing and stoning *Pallas*' white oaken

11

decks. Mainwaring had dispensed with calling the ship to
Quarters this morning, having received a 'horizon clear'
call from Howe at first light; now the boatswain's mate,
Turvey, was busy at his daily rigging check, every lashing
and seizing that had caught his eye and required work being
inspected now to see that it was done. It was, in short, the
ordered beginning of the ordered day of a British warship
at sea, and as Mainwaring went down the ladder, gripping
at the rail as *Pallas* heaved under him, he noted with satisfaction that the work, at least to the eye, was being done
well. Even the landsmen and pressed men had changed
from sullen, seasick or despairing wretches in terror of
Jewett's rattan into sunbrowned workers with some sense
of what they were about, able more often to put a hand on
the proper line or manage to cross a pitching, wet deck
without tumbling into a heap in the scuppers. Their appearance too had improved in the sturdy white duck and blue
wool that Mainwaring insisted upon as dress for *Pallas'*
ship's company. No uniform existed in the Royal Navy, not
even for officers, although pressure was afoot to grant a
uniform to sea officers much as the French and Spanish
already did. Men wore what they could, or what they could
purchase from the 'slops' maintained by the ship's purser;
for the most part this meant a crew in every possible vari-
ation of clothing, as often ragged and ill-fitting as not.
Mainwaring had insisted on the purchase of bolts of white
duck canvas and blue wool, paying for it himself when the
purser protested at such expense, and had ordered the men
to make up frocks, petticoat breeches, 'trowzers' and 'fear-
nought' jackets from the material, directing Howe to ensure
that those who proved to be competent tailors were excused
all other duties until each man in the ship was dressed to
Mainwaring's satisfaction. The clothing gave a smart and
seamanlike look to the ship, but more importantly, Mainwaring knew, it would save him the loss of prime seamen
from exposure and weather – men *Pallas* could not afford
to lose.

Yet even with the relentless gun and sailhandling drills he had forced on the ship since the Lizard dropped astern so many, many weeks ago, *Pallas* was still not to Mainwaring's mind the taut, capable man-o'-war that he knew she had to become.

He swung off the half-deck ladder and ducked down the after companionway, his heels thocking on the steps as *Pallas* rolled with a roar under him, and he put out his hands against the passageway sides to steady himself as he moved aft, feeling the thin partitioning that formed the cramped and airless officers' cabins flex under his touch. He reached his own cabin door, where a pox-scarred sea-regiment sentry stood leaning on his Long Land musket. As the man stiffened into the Position of the Soldier, Mainwaring grunted at him and went in.

The low-beamed cabin was lit with a warm glow from the lanterns that swung on hooks below the deckhead, one over the box bunk in a corner and the other above the broad trestle table and leather-covered settee which stood in front of the slanting windows, or stern lights, that ran across the width of the ship's stern. Mainwaring shrugged out of the sodden cape and hung his dripping cocked hat on a peg behind the cabin door. Then he bellowed for Willis, his servant. Another small door, leading forward on one side into Willis' dark little cabin, opened, and the man scuttled in like an anxious, wizened old shopkeeper.

"B – beg pardon, sir. I – didn't hear ye come in."

"The devil you didn't," grinned Mainwaring. "Turned into your bunk for some extra snores, I'll warrant. Hang up that cloak and fetch me some coffee, and quickly, before I decide to make you a foretopman."

The little man paled. "C – coffee, sir. Right away, sir." He made off, his small face creased with worry, to rattle cutlery in his dark burrow.

Mainwaring listened for a moment as water dripped from his cocked hat on the peg behind his cabin door on to the painted canvas deck covering. The sound was like blood dripping from a ghastly wound, and Mainwaring shivered slightly. Then his eyes flicked to his desk, and to the small wooden casket on one corner.

"Time to open Pandora's box, I should think," he murmured, feeling for a small key in his waistcoat pocket. In a moment he had opened the casket and was lifting out a fat, wax-sealed folio of papers that outlined the fate of *Pallas* – and that of Mainwaring and his men – during the next months. Addressed to 'E. Mainwaring, Pallas Frigate' it bore a simple, carefully-penned instruction that the folio was not to be opened until *Pallas* was in the Indian Ocean above a south latitude of twenty degrees.

Pursing his lips, Mainwaring broke the seal and opened the folio. He began to read, his brows knitted in deep concentration.

"Good Lord!" he breathed.

A knock sounded on the cabin door, and James Howe stepped in. He doffed his own cocked hat in a welter of droplets, and he was wearing a heavy, cape-shouldered oilskin that reached to his ankles but did not obscure the slim straightness of his figure and the determined set to his shoulders. His hair was mid-brown, simply dressed back, and his clear grey eyes in a solemn, thoughtful face were regarding Mainwaring with a mixture of friendly concern and professional deference.

"Well, James," said Mainwaring. "The damned pump."

"Not as serious as I feared, sir. The casing cracked on one side near the head, but Chips says he can fit in a caulk that'll hold till he can get up a new casing. I've got him on it now. I think it's that leak for'rard again, the one that first sprung at Saint Helena."

"But can the flow be gained upon?"

"Aye, sir. Fifteen minutes pumping a watch will do it. But we'll have to careen her before too long, sir. Only way to get at it."

"All right. As and when we may, James." Mainwaring

14

rubbed his brow. "The great guns. When next do you plan to exercise the people at 'em?"

"Four bells in the forenoon watch, sir, if you'll concur. Thought we'd set out a cask again. Have 'em fire at a mark. They've advanced their rate of fire quite well, actually, sir. That Welsh cutthroat of a gunner says he's put the fear o' God and himself into them."

"Very well. And I'll give a Spanish dollar to the gun captain who first strikes his mark."

"Aye, aye, sir." Howe's eyes dropped to the papers in Mainwaring's hands. "Orders, sir?"

"Yes. Take a chair, James." Mainwaring sat himself and read through the carefully penned sheets again, while Howe waited. "It's a bit of a job, all right, James," said Mainwaring, looking up.

"Sir?"

"It's the French at Mauritius – the Ile de France they call it. The governor at Port Louis there is an energetic fellow named La Bourdonnais. It appears the formal declaration of war between ourselves and the French has led him to some rather remarkable undertakings which we are meant to investigate."

"Nothing more specific than that, sir?"

Mainwaring smiled. "Indeed, James. As soon as this La Bourdonnais received word of the declaration of war, he apparently impounded and pressed into His Most Christian Majesty's service every barge and scow unlucky enough to be near Port Louis. He's armed them if they had no guns, trained their crews if they hadn't any knowledge of how to fight – in short, he's put together a formidable little squadron."

Howe looked surprised. "I wouldn't have thought a remote post like that would have had the resources, sir."

"Nor I. But this fellow's been the governor since 1735, and according to this he's fortified the harbour, fitted up a proper dockyard, and amassed a hefty quantity of stores."

"Are his intentions known as well?"

Mainwaring turned to the document's third page. "The French want to attack us in India, it seems." He bit his lip in thought. "Damned formidable enemy, out here. Their Lordships feel his most likely action will be to appear off the Coromandel coast and Pondicherry. Madras is likely the target, if they can besiege the place before the monsoon shows up and blows 'em off to loo'ard o' Ceylon. The French commander ashore at Pondicherry is one M'sieu' Dupleix. This La Bourdonnais fellow's first task is to work with him."

"What other of our ships are here besides ourselves, sir? Apart from the Company vessels, is there not a small squadron at Madras?"

"Aye, James, but a damned weak one. The list of vessels here is not impressive. And if I read between the lines, they're not well led. The Commodore's someone I don't know. Peyton." He paused. "Quite simply, we're to try to observe La Bourdonnais' squadron and dog 'em when they put to sea. If it's clear they've shaped course for the Coromandel we're to join Peyton and add ourselves to his squadron."

Howe frowned. "Sounds more like a job for a light-footed frigate, like old *Diana*, sir, wouldn't you say?"

"I would. But –" and here Mainwaring tapped the orders "– there's one other thing. The French have sent out a line-o'-battle ship to Port Louis. She sailed from L'Orient about two weeks before we cleared the Lizard. *Achille*, seventy guns."

"Seventy? Christ!" murmured Howe.

"Indeed. And *Achille*'s meant to be the flagship of whatever squadron La Bourdonnais has scraped together. Given that he will have commandeered a season's worth of *Compagnie des Indes* ships – fifty guns, most of 'em – he could have, with *Achille*, enough to blast poor old Peyton into so much firewood."

"What would that mean, sir?"

"Simple enough, James. The French take Madras while

still holding Pondicherry, and it'll be the slow death of damned near anything English in India – and the end of all that wealth that gets barged round Good Hope and back to England. Simply put, we'd lose the bloody Indian Ocean to the French. We'd end up like the Dutch, trotting along in someone else's shadow whilst dreaming of past glories."

"Damned grim scenario, if you ask me, sir," said Howe, after a moment. "What's Peyton got?"

"That's not made clear here. Maybe a forty-gunner, and a brace or two of twenty-fours and sloops. I don't think he's got anything to stand in the line against *Achille*."

Howe nodded sombrely.

"The wording of these orders is noteworthy, James," went on Mainwaring. "And you'll need to know all this, in any event. Listen. '. . . And upon your determining the Position, Course and Composition of the Enemy's forces, you shall not engage the former nor in nowise put at Risk the Vessel under your command, but shall repair to where you may effect a Juncture with Commodore Peyton & shall place yourself under his Command, upon apprising him of the Intelligences you have gathered; the better to produce a superior Concentration of Force as shall achieve with greater assurance the End we seek . . .'"

"Bloody hell," breathed Howe. "You mean we can't fight the buggers?"

"At first wording, that appears to be what we are being told," said Mainwaring. "The idea is to add us to Peyton's overall weight of broadside, rather than splintering ourselves to bits against *Achille* alone." He paused, his expression glum. "If you ask me, it's more bloody preoccupation with the damned Fighting Instructions. Lie in the line, no independent action. That sort of thing." A light seemed to flicker in his eyes. "What's our victualling state, James?"

"Fair to good, sir. The fresh produce and greens we took aboard at the Cape will be done in about a week. But the water's still sweet, and we've enough biscuit and salt provisions for a good two months, if need be."

"No cases of ship fever as yet?"

"No, sir."

"Good." Mainwaring stood, and cleared away a sheaf of papers from his desk before unrolling a dog-eared and watermarked chart. "Look here, James. If our reckonings on easting are worth a damn – and there's no guarantee of that, mind – we should be here, about a hundred leagues nor'west o' Réunion Island. Madagascar's off there to larboard, and on our present course we should raise Tromelin ahead within a day or two."

Howe had come round to frown down at the chart. He tapped it with one long finger.

"That puts us well to loo'ard o' Mauritius, sir. Devil of a beat back up to it, laying sou'west like that."

"You know, James, were I this fellow La Bourdonnais, I'd know that with the south-west monsoon his best track to the Coromandel would be the old Portugee one, like this." Mainwaring picked up a small, stiletto-like knife and traced a circular track westward from Mauritius. "Westward to Tromelin. Then a broad reach up through the Madagascar waters towards the Seychelles, with any number of sheltered harbours at hand as long as he kept off some damned reef: Agalega, Providence, Farquhar, Platte, even the Comoros, if he found himself blown into the Mozambique Channel. Then, north o' the Seychelles, he'd have the full monsoon for the run to the Coromandel."

"Yes, sir, but what –?" began Howe.

"Sorry, James. I was musing rather uselessly that with Peyton's squadron at hand, a patrol line between Diego Suarez and Agalega could be created. We could spot La Bourdonnais and be nipping at his heels before he even cleared Madagascar waters."

"That's assuming he sailed your track, sir."

"Always a risk, that sort of thing," smiled Mainwaring. He narrowed his eyes. "But we are without Peyton's ships, and our orders are clear enough. We must find out what La Bourdonnais intends."

The eyes of both men found the inked outline of the island of Mauritius.

"Mauritius, then, sir?"

"Aye, James. Wear around to windward, and harden up on a tack that will take us to the nor'rard of the Cargados Carajos shoals – there. I'll give ye a compass course presently. We'll beat as we must till we're well to eastward of 'em, and then run down for Mauritius."

"Once there, sir?"

"We wait and watch, James," said Mainwaring, setting down the little knife. "We see if the admirable M'sieu' La Bourdonnais has his fleet ready to sail, and if *Achille* has joined him. Our orders are to inform Commodore Peyton of what we find, and we will of course do that."

Then he smiled slowly at the first lieutenant. "But there may be a way, or ways, in which we can be a bother to La Bourdonnais, before we must run off to find Commodore Peyton."

"I'm sure you'll think of something, sir," said James Howe, with a grin.

Twenty-seven hours later, *Pallas* was tacking hard to the north-east against a brisk east-by-southerly wind that broke whitecaps from the dark blue of the long, lifting swells. Unlike the previous morning, this was a day of crystalline blue skies, with white cotton puffs of cloud in even rows hurrying westward over a blue, sun-washed sea. The mustard and black of the ship's paint gleamed wetly as she pitched and lifted through the white-foamed sea, the equally startling white of her underbody flashing now and then as the ship heeled to a particularly strong gust. *Pallas'* sails were wet and spray-mottled almost to the reef points of her sharply braced-up topsails, but she was carrying all working sail, and under her taut and quivering canvas the ship hurried on her course like a living creature, leaving a broad track of foam behind her over the heaving surface of the sea.

To James Howe, who had the watch, the roar and rush of the sea, the creak of *Pallas'* timbers, and the mixed sounds of the rigging's sonorous hum counterpointed by the rippling snap of the great ensign, were pure music. He grinned to himself, and was still grinning when he touched the front cock of his hat to Edward Mainwaring as the latter appeared up the windward quarterdeck ladder.

"Bit more to our liking, I'd say, James?" said Mainwaring. He was in simple linen small clothes and a docked linen coat of Spanish cut, with his feet thrust into well-oiled boots. Hatless, his brown locks were blown round his cheeks by the wind, giving him an oddly boyish look.

"Aye, sir! The old girl beats like a wherry!"

Mainwaring reached the windward side of the spray-darkened quarterdeck, motioning for Howe to stay with him.

"I've plotted on our course from the bearing we had on Tromelin last night. With what the chip log says we're making, we're perhaps a dozen leagues due west o' the Cargados Carajos shoals. But our easting – or westing – could be far from what I've reckoned. Have the lads keep a sharp eye aloft for breakers."

"Aye, aye, sir. I doubled them aloft at dawn. Enemy waters and all that."

Mainwaring nodded. "Good. What's the state of the ship?"

"Steering east-nor'east, starboard tack, sir. Jib, fore-topm'st stays'l, courses and tops'ls, mizzen spanker. Change o' the watch in half a glass, sir." He staggered a little as *Pallas* lunged with a roar under him. "The watch below is securing the gun deck, sir. I exercised the larboard battery. Excuse me, sir." He looked over his shoulder at the helm, where two splay-footed seamen were gripping the great double wheel under Isaiah Hooke's displeased glare.

20

"We've a board to make to windward, Mr Hooke! Those lads need a firmer grip, if you please!"

"Aye, aye, zur!" growled Hooke, over the roar of wind and sea, and began a *sotto voce* commentary to both helmsmen that soon widened their eyes in fright equally as it intensified their efforts.

"Very good," said Mainwaring. He squinted aloft. "That Deptford maintops'l has too shallow a roach, to my mind. A merchantman's cut would be –"

"Deck! Deck, there!" The foretop lookout was shrieking down at them, his voice cracking over the wind roar.

Mainwaring cupped his hands. "Deck, aye?"

"Sail, sir!"

"Where away?"

"Broad on the larb'd bow, sir! Ship's t'gallants, sir!"

Mainwaring spun, looking for Hooke. "Mr Hooke! Who's your best man to know a vessel's cut and rig?"

Hooke strode forward. "My mate, zur. Stewart. Read 'em loike a book, 'e does. Froggy hulks, Dons, the lot."

"Get him aloft, now! I want to know the identity of that ship!" Mainwaring cupped his hands again, squinting up at the foretop. "D'ye see colours, there!"

"No, sir, nought!"

The blocky form of Alexander Stewart was at the run towards the main shrouds, in response to Hooke's bellow. As the Glaswegian swung up off the rail over the shear pole and began to climb, Mainwaring called to him.

"Read her for us, Mr Stewart! Friend or foe, read her!"

"Aye, sir!" In a few moments of sweaty effort the Scot was at the futtock stave, out over the futtock shrouds with an ease Mainwaring envied, and into the nest of the maintop. It was not long before he was leaning out to bellow down at the anxious figures on the quarterdeck.

"She's French, sir! French man-o'-war, belike!"

"Hardly what we needed at present," Mainwaring muttered through his teeth. He cupped his hands again. "Are ye certain o' that, Mr Stewart?"

"Aye, sir! Ye canna mistake th' topm'sts, sir! Even, they are. An' white sails, not like our'n. Steeve o' th' jib-boom, too, sir!" There was a pause. "Bourbon pennant at th' foretruck, sir!"

"Bad luck, sir," offered Howe.

"Too bloody true, James. We're not ready to fight, yet!" Mainwaring spat off to leeward. "If she's only a *Compagnie des Indes* ship –"

"Deck, there!" Stewart's voice carried down. "I ken th' look of her, sir! She called at the Cape when I was on th' beach there!"

"*What* ship, man?"

"She'd be *Neptune*, sir! Fifty-gunner, an' a prime vessel, tae boot, sir!"

"Oh, Lord." Mainwaring squinted at the white shape on the horizon. "It never ceases to amaze me how, in the name of Christ, they can tell all that."

"It's a skill, sir," said Howe. "The best ones only have to see a t'gallant over the horizon and they'll recognise any one of a hundred ships. Topmast size and rake, the jib-boom steeve – it's almost a language to 'em."

Mainwaring nodded, cupping his hands. "Mr Stewart? What course does she steer?"

There was a pause, and *Pallas* lifted and plunged down with a roar over a swell. Then Stewart's voice sounded again.

"She's turning, sir! Hauling her wind, she is, an' steerin' t' cross our bows, sartin!"

Mainwaring sprang to the binnacle, his mind working as he looked quickly from the swaying card to *Pallas*' plunging bowsprit, then off to the distant French vessel, now an uneven oblong of gleaming white bright against the blue of the sky.

"Yes. Constant bearing. She's closing, well enough," he said to Howe. "Damn!"

"What d'ye wish to do, sir?"

Mainwaring stalked spread-legged up to the weather rail

again. He kept his voice low to avoid being heard by the helmsmen as he turned and looked intently at Howe.

"That finishes our damned element of surprise, James. She'll report us at Port Louis, or elsewhere. We've no choice but to fight her. But damned if I think we're ready!"

"We've exercised the gun batteries every day, sir –"

"And still fire broadsides like a ship's company of washerwomen, James!" Mainwaring shook his head. "Not your fault, James. Christ knows you've been driving them enough. We simply needed more time to turn this work-house rabble into a fighting crew." He squinted at the distant French vessel. "The test has come too soon, is all!"

Howe stepped closer. "Sir, we could tack away from her. Hold our distance until nightfall."

Mainwaring looked into his friend's eyes. "James, you know we can't. We must take her." He smiled lightly. "And fighting the French is why we're here, isn't it?"

"Yes, sir," said Howe. "Yes, it is."

Mainwaring's mouth became a tight line. "Very well, then, Mr Howe," he said, his voice assuming a formal tone, "call the sea-regiment drummer. And beat to Quarters, if you please!"

A small lad of perhaps eleven years, with a tight, frightened face under his tall mitre cap, arrived on deck wrestling his drum into position against the push of the wind. At a nod from Howe he pulled his sticks from his shoulder carriage, lifted them horizontally in a gesture to his upper lip, and began an energetic beat. The deep thump of the unsnared drum penetrated the roar of wind and sea, and its effect on the ship's company of His Britannic Majesty's Ship *Pallas* was nothing less than dramatic.

Another thunder rose above the crunch and hiss of the bows against the sea, and the drummer's beat; the sound of hundreds of running feet throughout the ship. As with every British warship, *Pallas* had its Watch and Quarter Bill, a laboriously-penned list posted throughout the ship, usually above the gunports, where the men messed on the gun deck. This gave each man a place and a duty for every major task: a man might find himself listed as part of the foretopsail crew in sailhandling; midships oar in the captain's gig; trail-tackle man on number three gun, starboard side upper-deck battery, at Quarters; and for boarding, to muster at the foremast foot under the command of the gunner, Evan Davies. The letter 'T' against his name on the Bill indicated his boarding weapon would be a tomahawk, the vicious-looking little tool the Admiralty referred to as a boarding axe. The drumbeat now sent each man to his assigned post at Quarters and there was a deadly efficiency to the seeming tumult of chaotic movement.

Pallas carried twenty eighteen-pounder guns on her lower deck and twenty nine-pounder guns on her upper deck. Abaft the mizzenmast foot on the quarterdeck – the wheel being forward of it – the ship carried four six-pounders, slim guns eight feet in length, and thus a foot shorter than the nines and eighteens. To these forty-four guns came a rush of crews, quick and competent veteran seamen alongside excited and wide-eyed novices. Each gun crew was led by its captain, an experienced seaman who would give the necessary orders for the loading and handling of the gun. It was also the gun captain, his rank marked by the great priming horn worn slung over his shoulder, who primed the great guns and who would fire them with the smouldering match of the linstock. And this he would do on the order of the officer who paced, sword drawn, along the line of guns in the battery which was his responsibility.

The ship greeted each day with her guns loaded and shotted, but secured for sea. Now, as the members of each crew arrived in a rush at their gun, they cast off the restraining seizings on the trail and side tackles, pulled out the tompion which sealed the muzzle like a plug, and took up their positions on the falls of the tackles, ready to heave the guns forward into their run-out position. Meanwhile the gun captains had primed the vents of the guns and had taken smouldering matches from the notched edges of the water tubs that had been thumped down behind each gun, moments after boys had skittered past scattering sand on the deck for traction. These matches they twined round the staff of their linstocks, fixing the glowing tips in the stocks' metal jaws, then holding the linstock to one side, ready to arc down and fire the guns. At a barked command the gunport lids opened, lifting like so many red-lined eyelids, and then Evan Davies' call of "Run out!" set the gun crews straining at the side tackles, the trucks squealing as the guns thrust out through the ports.

Mainwaring had ducked below as the drum had begun its thump, snatching his sword and cocked hat from his cabin seconds before a clutch of sweating seamen bearing the knocked-down partitions of the officers' cabins had burst in to stow them in the great cabin. Now he had regained the quarterdeck, and he crammed his hat down over his eyes, buckling on his sword belt as he looked for Howe who was already pacing in watchfulness behind the larboard row of upper-deck nine-pounders. William Parker, the youthful third lieutenant who made even Stephen Pellowe's blond good looks appear aged, had command of the starboard nines. Below on the lower, or gun deck, Stephen Pellowe commanded the larboard eighteen-pounders, seconded by *Pallas'* senior midshipman, a cheerful lad with the poetic name of Simeon Weatherby, who commanded the starboard guns. With the experienced and trustworthy gun captains manning the heavy eighteens, Pellowe and Weatherby would be kept out of trouble, only needing to react to Mainwaring's overall gunnery commands, relayed by messengers from the quarterdeck and men stationed at the companionways.

Already the ship's boys, grubby urchins for whom Mainwaring had become akin to a god, were arriving at the guns with replacement cartridge in leathern buckets, their eyes wild with excitement. They had been sent off by the gunner, Davies, and his mate, Quintal, as the latter two made ready cartridges far below in the gloom of the filling room, hung about with the wetted felt curtains intended to shield the powder from fire. The boys squatted like pinched-faced little crows on their cartridge buckets by the shot garlands of their guns, ready to leap forward as soon as the guns fired and the loading process had begun.

With a clumping of heavy shoes on the after companion-way, *Pallas*' company of sea-regiment infantrymen – increasingly called marines, after the French *Troupes de la Marine* – appeared in a dense mass from below, and were led up on to the quarterdeck just abaft the mast. There, the growls of a swarthy, halberd-wielding sergeant named Fell pushed the soldiery into three elbow-touching ranks across the quarterdeck, facing forward. They stiffened into the Position of the Soldier, swaying as *Pallas* rolled beneath them, their feet planted for steadiness a shoe-sole length apart. They carried their muskets on the left shoulder, grasped by a hand over the comb of the butt, right hands hovering over the black leather of the cartridge boxes hanging at the right hip. Different from the more rollicking seamen, they were silent, even taciturn, with pox-scarred and gunpowder-tattooed faces that had a hard look. They wore tall mitre caps, and their hair hung unbound to their shoulder with little pretence at a queue. Their full-skirted coats were brick-red, as were their breeches, above long white canvas gaiters that rose from their thick-soled shoes to above their knees. The bulky cartridge box was held by a broad buff belt from the left shoulder, and the double scabbard of hanger and bayonet on the left hip hung from the buff waistbelt.

Even as the company shuffled into the dressing, the marine lieutenant, Antony Beresford, had materialised up the ladder from the waist. His hair, by contrast, was queued neatly, and he wore a gilt-edged cocked hat. He was slim, with pale, watery eyes, and there was a languor to his movements as he acknowledged Fell's halberd salute with a lift of his hat.

"Pwime and load, if you pwease, Sergeant Fell," Beresford whined, and even with the tension of the moment, Mainwaring had to turn away, if only to keep from laughing. Beresford's childish voice was the butt of much wardroom humour, Mainwaring knew, some of it cruel. But there was little to complain about in the bearing of the soldiery, and nothing at all in the brisk slap and movement as they moved through the ritual of priming and loading the long Tower muskets known affectionately as Brown Bess. As Mainwaring watched, the little drummer fell in gravely on the right flank, still wrestling with his deep drum against the force of the wind.

Scores of other men were busy about the ship at tasks that had nothing to do with the ship's weaponry. At the wheel, the helmsmen of the watch had been relieved by two of *Pallas'* most experienced hands, Winton and Jackman. Isaiah Hooke's bellow was sounding forward as he hurried the sailhandlers along to their pinrail or fiferail stations. The topmen were aloft, ready to clew up canvas to the fighting set of topsails, headsails and spanker, and they were joined in their rush up the ratlines by men Stewart had sent aloft to rig chain lifts on the yards, to prevent them from crashing ponderously to the deck. Others with them, on fore, main and mizzen, were shaking out the enormous, fishnet folds of a netting that they quickly and ingeniously secured in place above the upper deck as a protection against falling wreckage and gear. When the men below had poured on deck at the first beat of the drum, they had borne up with them their tightly-rolled hammocks. These they had thrust in a U-shape, bend uppermost, side by side into the double row of nettings that circled the upper deck, affording a kind of barricade that would protect the crews at the long guns from musketry fire from the deck, though not the tops, of the enemy vessel. But there would be no refuge from the killing flight of the flying shot and the terrible splinters they produced except in the dim bowels of the ship, and Beresford had stationed musketmen at the hatchways with orders to put a ball into any man who ran below from sheer fright.

Mainwaring was squinting at the growing shape of the French vessel, spreading his feet as he did so against a particularly sharp pitch of *Pallas* into the spray-shrouded blue shoulders of a swell. He gestured to Howe who came back up on to the quarterdeck.

"Frenchman's still on the larboard tack, James, and still carrying his canvas. D'ye think he means to close and turn away, after making our colours?"

"Doubtful, sir," said Howe, tugging at a cuff. "I'd say we'll see him clew up his courses directly. Wait for us to come down on him."

"Yes." Mainwaring pursed his lips thoughtfully. "It'd be like them to give up the weather gauge. Shoot us to bits as we close." He moved to the waistdeck rail. "At Quarters at last, are we?"

"Yes, sir," said Howe, wincing. "Fourteen minutes from the drumbeat. Not bad, sir, for a raw crew."

"Not good enough, is what you should be saying, James." Mainwaring kept his voice low. "We'll have to do it in half the time." He cupped his hands. "D'ye hear, there! Gun captains! Double shot your guns, if you please! Pass the word, there!"

"Look, sir!" said Howe. "The Frenchman's clewing up!"

Mainwaring's gaze snapped up. About four miles away now, a little over a league, the French warship was close enough for the blue and tan paint scheme of her hull to be clearly visible below her snowy white canvas. On foremast and mainmast, the great quadrilaterals of her courses were crumpling upwards to their yards under the rhythmic pull of many hidden hands at the clewlines and buntlines. Sunlight gleamed on the hull as it turned, and the French vessel moved into the wind, her tall topsails going aback with a visible tremor against the topmasts.

"I'll warrant the hands aloft on her yards appreciated *that*," laughed Mainwaring, without humour. "Heaving to, as you said she would, James. The Frenchman wants us to –"

A pink flash showed on the French vessel's side and as a grey cotton-wool ball of smoke puffed into existence and was as quickly torn into shreds by the wind, a thump sounded over the sea and wind roar. Part way towards *Pallas*, a thin, glittering geyser shot up from the dark swells as the shot struck.

"Clear enough. The man's challenging us," said Mainwaring. "Stand to your battery, James. I'm going to close with him, and we'll engage him presently!"

"Sir!" Howe made off down the ladder, his coattails flying behind him.

Mainwaring was scanning for Hooke. "Mr Hooke!" he barked. "We'll fall off on to a reach! Sheets and braces, if you please!"

"Aye, zur!" came Hooke's booming reply.

Mainwaring was already beside Winton at the great double wheel, eye on the compass cards in the binnacle. He watched, waiting until he saw that Hooke's sailhandlers were ready.

"Ease away, Mr Hooke! Up helm, Winton. Let her fall off. Not too much, now. Ease her, ease her, steady! Steer nor'west by north!"

"Nor'west by north, aye, sir!" repeated Winton, his broad hands slapping the spokes of the great wheel as it turned.

"Sheet home, Mr Hooke!" cried Mainwaring.

Pallas lay over to the wind, which was abeam now, and began to roar ahead in a startling increase of speed. Blocks squealed aloft as Hooke's sailhandlers made short rhythmic jerks in sweating up the halyards an extra inch, or in time-worn fashion hauled in the lee sheets seemingly too far, then checked away until a curt word from Hooke or Stewart signalled that the perfect curve and set had come to the loose-woven flax sails that drove *Pallas* through the sea.

Mainwaring clutched his way up the deck to the weather

29

rail as *Pallas* heeled before a gust. He looked up at the still, swelling arches of white canvas above him and noticed again what most sailors saw, that there was a similar beauty in the lines of a wind-driven ship's sails and the lines of a woman's body. Like many in his calling he had an awe for the beauty of both – and equally painful experience that the admission of that awe could be dangerous if ill-timed and ill-considered. Battle at sea killed a vessel and its beauty, and it was not good to dwell too heavily on that thought only moments before the commencement of such destruction.

He peered forward, past the lifting and plunging finger of the jib-boom. The French ship was half-visible behind *Pallas*' straining headsails, still hove to and pitching slowly, the neat battle clew of her canvas complete. From both the foremast and mainmast trucks white Bourbon ensigns were streaming now to join the one at the ensign staff, and as Mainwaring watched the remainder of the French vessel's gunports opened like dark eyes along the ship's side towards *Pallas*.

Waiting, thought Mainwaring. *Just waiting. Knowing we never shrink from a fight!* His eyes narrowed. If *Pallas* bore straight in on this course, she would pass the French vessel either across the stern or the bows, which meant a chance to rake her fore and aft. But as soon as *Pallas* was within range – and her guns still not able to bear – the French vessel's full broadside would have three, perhaps four opportunities to smash at *Pallas* as she closed in. The fifty-gunner might have long eighteens or twenty-fours, and would fire high, in French practice, for *Pallas*' rigging. The English vessel could be an unmanageable hulk unable to manoeuvre before getting off a single round in reply.

Unless . . .

Mainwaring sprang to the wheel, casting a last look at the waiting *Neptune*. The French vessel was no more than half a mile ahead now, *Pallas* having closed the gap between the ships with dramatic suddenness, and that distance was narrowing rapidly.

"Mr Hooke!" he bellowed, clutching at the binnacle box as *Pallas* lunged over a huge swell. "Ease away, all! Winton, up helm! Let her fall off!"

"Fa – fall *off*, sir?" said Winton, staring.

"Damn your eyes, man, *do it*!"

"Aye, aye, sir! Up helm, sir!" His face a mask of perplexity, Winton spun the great wheel, and *Pallas* wallowed, lifting her stern galleries to the wind that now bore in over her quarter. Blocks squealed anew as Hooke's men scrambled to trim sail.

"Midships!" barked Mainwaring. "What's your ship's head now?"

"A half north. North, a half east. North –"

"Steer due north!"

"Due north, aye, sir!"

Mainwaring swung round. *Neptune* was clearly visible broad on the windward bow, and *Pallas* was angling down astern of her, widening the angle of fire for the guns of the French broadside.

Try to remain hove to, my lad, thought Mainwaring.

Howe was up the quarterdeck ladder in a bound, his sense of propriety momentarily gone. "Sorry, sir. But are ye *giving* him the windward gauge? Christ, he'll –!"

"I am doing exactly that, Mr Howe!" said Mainwaring, his eyes hard and his voice like steel. "And your place is with your guns, if you please!"

Howe saw the look on Mainwaring's face, and abruptly realised what he had done. His face reddened.

"Aye, aye, sir!" he said, and was off down the ladder.

Mainwaring's eyes flicked from the compass card to the French vessel as *Pallas* rushed closer, the sea boiling like a cauldron under her forefoot. The French vessel still lay hove to, pitching in slow grandeur.

But now the angle that Mainwaring had opened made it impossible for the Frenchman's guns to bear, and *Pallas* was rushing in to deliver a raking broadside into *Neptune*'s stern galleries if the French vessel remained as she was.

"Stand ready, both batteries, there!" Mainwaring called through cupped hands. "Larb's and starb'd, keep your matches hot!"

He squinted at the French vessel, now frighteningly close. *How long?* he wondered. *How long until his nerve cracks?*

There!

"Deck, sir!" a hand was shrieking from aloft. "She's backin' 'er 'eads'ls, sir! Fallin' off, she be!"

Mainwaring's eyes narrowed. The fifty-gunner was turning, her hull gleaming wetly in the sunlight. The French captain was not going to sit waiting and let the English vessel so unexpectedly give up the windward position, and thereby pass astern in a position to rake. He was turning his ship to keep his guns bearing on *Pallas* and in a moment those deadly, red-muzzled bores would explode with a cloud of shot and flame as they found her, downwind and exposing her flank so nakedly.

"Helm *down*, Winton! Haul your wind, Mr Hooke! As tight to windward as she'll make! Lively, now!"

Pallas lifted and plunged with a roar into the blue-green swells, rolling deeply as her great wheel spun and she swung round into the wind, which suddenly was singing again in the shrouds and setting the reef points to tapping. As Winton caught her turn and steadied her, the sailhandlers were hauling like madmen at the braces and sheets, and within moments the ship was punching up into the sun-coppered, whitecapped swells, with garlands of spray wisping up over her bows as she forged into the wind.

Mainwaring bounded over to the leeward rail, ducking to see under the foot of the maincourse. The French vessel was still falling off the wind, and from the wild tumult on deck, it was evident the ship would not be under control for some moments yet. As the English vessel now bore, *Pallas* was going to pass dead across the bows of *Neptune*, the French vessel so toweringly close that under her cloud of gleaming canvas the painted figure of the sea god, grasping a trident, was visible lifting and lunging under the jib-boom, painted eyes in a painted face glaring fiercely at *Pallas*. On the French decks Mainwaring could see men staring as *Pallas* rushed closer, then scrambling for the pin-rails as a rotund officer in blue and scarlet on the quarter-deck before was shrieking orders to a clutch of grey-clad French marines in a voice that carried to Mainwaring's ears.

"My compliments, m'sieu'," murmured Mainwaring, "but you are too late!" He took a deep breath. "Mr Howe! Mr Pellowe! Stand by! Gun action, larboard side!"

Pallas heeled to a gust, leaping and thundering down in a crunching burst of spray that shot up in glittering clouds and swept in a pattering shower down *Pallas*' decks, drenching the men at the guns.

A moment more. Only a moment –

"Now, lads!" Mainwaring barked. "*Fire!*"

And as *Pallas* lifted and plunged across the bows of the French vessel, barely fifty yards off the lance tip of her jib-boom end, *Pallas*' larboard side exploded in a ragged thunderstorm of pink flashes and boiling smoke. Howe's gun captains arced down their portfires, the pink huff leaping from the vents, and then the long guns were firing with sharp, savage bangs that deafened Mainwaring, the concussion punching at his chest like blows from a man's fist. Again and again the nine-pounders fired, their sharp crack a high harmony to the deep boom of the eighteen-pounders. Within a few moments, a vast, maintruck-high wall of smoke had leaped into being between the ships, and rolled off downwind to envelop the tall form of the French vessel. Now the slim quarterdeck six-pounders fired, with sharp, ringing reports, making Mainwaring wince involuntarily.

But there was no time to pause. *Pallas* must be kept away from the deadly French broadside and her own starboard batteries had to be brought to bear.

Mainwaring scrambled to the wheel past gun crews working with feverish energy.

"Braces and sheets, Mr Hooke! We'll fall off the wind, to starboard! Put him on our quarter! Put your helm to larboard, Winton!" he roared. "Stand by, starboard batteries!"

As the huge, drifting cloud of *Pallas'* broadside smoke enveloped the French vessel like a grey-white shroud, *Pallas* swung in long, ponderous heaves off the wind, her canvas rumpling and thumping aloft, lines whiplashing and snaking in a wild welter until the ship was round, her canvas thumping out now into hard, still curves, the starboard batteries almost ready to bear as the ship moved into the still world of the downwind sail.

As she did so, *Neptune* surged clear of the great cloud of *Pallas'* smoke, frighteningly close, not bows-on to *Pallas*, but turning off the wind as well, swinging so that her blue and tan hull and its line of gaping, red-lidded gunports bore on *Pallas* from only a few hundred yards away

Mainwaring stared for an instant at the dramatic sight of the fifty-gunner looming majestically out of the smoke and turning in ponderous grace to present her broadside. Here and there in the white, towering cloud of canvas, holes gaped where some of *Pallas'* shot had flown high. But was there no other damage?

"She's damned well untouched!" breathed Mainwaring.

In the next instant he bellowed the order for the starboard battery to fire, his words drowned out as the guns thundered. The long eighteens erupted into a rippling line of explosions, twenty-foot pink flames leaping out like lances from the gunports, the roiling, thick smoke suddenly there along *Pallas'* side, obscuring again the French vessel. Now the nines and sixes were barking, and the gun crews ducked and sweated into their frenzied loading drills even as the black-barrelled, ochre-painted guns recoiled with savage force against their breeching lines. As *Pallas* lifted and fell over the swells, the sea boiling under her stern below the huge, rippling ensign, the guns banged out again, this time in an almost simultaneous thunderclap of a broadside that seemed to shift *Pallas* sideways under Mainwaring's feet.

"Christ, lads, we're a-doin' uv 'er!" exulted a sweating hand at one of the quarterdeck six-pounders, until silenced by a snarl from the gun captain.

Then *Pallas* was rolling on, the enormous clouds of smoke rushing up and swirling round the foretopsail and on over the bows, and sweeping off to engulf the tall shape of the French vessel. Mainwaring sprang to the starboard rail, wincing inwardly as the thought struck him that now, in the next instant, was the moment for the Frenchman to fire, for a broadside to explode along *Neptune*'s flank, sending a storm of shot into *Pallas* at murderously close range. If the French gunners were not fools, *Pallas* was ready to be struck, as her people worked in panting fury to reload their great guns. It might all be over in the next instant –

"Deck, there! Cap'n, sir!" The voice was ringing down from the men stationed in the foretop. "She's struck, sir!"

"*What?*"

"Aye, sir! Strikin' 'er colours. Look thar, as she draws clear o' th' smoke, sir!"

Mainwaring stared as *Neptune*, standing along before the wind on a track parallel to *Pallas*, emerged in a flash of colour out of the wall of smoke. The French vessel was virtually unharmed aloft, but the hull bore shocking evidence of the force of *Pallas*' broadsides. The starboard cathead was carried away, and several holes gaped in the forepart of the ship. A ball had shattered the channels of the foremast shrouds on the visible side, and the lanyards and deadeyes were a welter of snarled tarred line that looked liable to give way at any moment, weakening the still-straight topmast. Along the full length of the tan and blue hull, great gouges and marks, and ragged holes at every level from the waterline wale to the rail, bore mute testimony of the brutal impact of a score of flying cast-iron shot. Aft, the visible quarter-gallery windows amidst their gilded carving were smashed.

Mainwaring's eyes narrowed. Only God knew what horror the flying shot had wreaked within the bowels of the ship, both with their own hurtling passage or because of the vicious flying splinters they produced. Most of the gunports still held the muzzles of run-out guns, but here and there a gunport lid was down, as if its line had been cut or the tenants of the gloom within had closed themselves away, unable to face the storm of shot striking at them.

As Mainwaring watched, the French vessel's anchor sagged with a thumping crash as the larboard cat tackle gave way, and the great black hook hung at a bizarre angle, held only by one fluke caught in the forechains below the smashed channel.

But aloft, the still curves of *Neptune*'s canvas remained arched out before the wind, untouched, unmarked. Above the sails, fluttering from the foretruck, the white Bourbon ensign was sinking to the deck, its great companion on the ensign staff crumpling to the transom rail and being gathered in. On *Neptune*'s deck Mainwaring could see a welter of wreckage and gear, the scattered rubbish of a fire-swept ship's deck. Here and there huddled bodies lay, and round them in seeming chaos milled seamen and grey-clad marines. The figures of officers, in blue and scarlet, moved among them, shouting and gesticulating, swords flashing in their hands.

There was a clump on the waistdeck ladder and James Howe arrived at Mainwaring's side.

"Your leave to join you, sir?" he asked.

"Of course, James. What d'ye make of that?"

"Damn me if I can say," Howe marvelled. "After all the threatening manoeuvre, he didn't fire a shot, sir."

"Yes, bloody peculiar. Think we simply damaged him too heavily to reply?"

"Hardly likely, sir. The French aren't cowards, not unless their people are pressed landsmen. By the look of

36

that mob, that may be the answer, sir." He paused. "Look, she's rounding up. Heaving to, I'll warrant."

Neptune was turning ponderously away now, her canvas aloft rumpling in long dark waves as she curtseyed slowly round until her great foretopsail went aback with an audible whump against the foremast. The ship lay waiting, lifting and falling slowly with all the majesty of a great seabird afloat on the swells.

"Mr Hooke!" Mainwaring barked. "We'll bring her into the wind and heave to! Braces and sheets, if you please!" He turned to Winton. "Down helm, Winton. Bring her round."

"Aye, aye, sir!" The spokes slapped in Winton's broad hands as the wheel spun. With a great rumbling and booming of canvas and rattling blocks, *Pallas* dipped round, the sea whooshing under her windward counter, until she too lay pitching, head to swells and wind, her topsail pressed hard aback.

Within a few minutes both vessels were positioned in gun range of one another, barely five hundred yards apart. On *Pallas*' quarterdeck Mainwaring looked at Howe and Hooke, who were standing in attendant watchfulness with Beresford in front of the swaying line of sea-regiment men. *Pallas* was still ready for action: everywhere in the ship the gun crews waited, clustered round their guns, their eyes flicking from the shape of the French fifty-gunner to the figures on the quarterdeck, their expressions wary and mistrustful.

"Oi dunno, zur," Hooke was saying, with a lancet of tobacco juice over the lee rail for emphasis. "Oi don't loike th' look uv it, zur. 'Ee struck too easy. Fancy a fifty-gunner, strikin' to th' loikes uv us wivout a gun firin'? Shallow waters, says oi, zur."

Mainwaring nodded, his eyes on *Neptune*. "I know, Isaiah. But he's waiting for us to make a move. Well, gentlemen, what will it be? What do you think, James?"

Howe's eyes were narrowed. "Could be genuine, sir. His

people may be weakened by the scurvy or a flux. Or he may have no stomach for a fight, to put it simply. Not the first time they've struck without a decent set-to."

"Yes. But usually one gun at least. The honour of the ensign, and all that." Mainwaring pursed his lips. "Very well. We'll see what the fellow's about. Call away the yawl, Mr Hooke. You'll come with me, James." He cupped his hands. "Mr Pellowe, sir! Ye'll have the ship. Keep a clear eye on us. At the first sign of trouble, broadside him! Whether we are clear of him or not! Understood?"

Stephen Pellowe had appeared at the companionway foot. He touched the front cock of his hat gravely, a concerned expression on his youthful features. "Aye, aye, sir. Keep a weather eye, if I may say, sir, will you?"

"That we shall, Stephen. Never fear."

Fifteen minutes later, the little four-oared yawl boat, with Mainwaring in the sternsheets, Howe at the tiller beside him, was dancing over the swells towards the bulk of *Neptune*, which lay pitching slowly as the boat approached. At the yawl's oars were a quartet of Mainwaring's older and more experienced hands: the wiry pair of Slade and Sawyer, the Irishman Shanahan, and Evans the muscular Welshman.

Evans, who was stroke oar, threw a quick look over his shoulder at the French ship's run-out guns.

"Bloody trap, to my mind, sir," he murmured, catching Mainwaring's eye.

"Eyes in the boat, Evans," said Howe, shifting his grip on the tiller. "And mind you keep silent."

"Aye, Bandy, yew talk too –" began Sawyer, who was second stroke, only to be cut off by an oath from Mainwaring.

"Damn ye, this is no skylark! *Keep silent!*"

The men dropped their eyes guiltily and put their backs into the rowing.

"I'll take the tiller, James," said Mainwaring quietly. "Stephen still keeping our guns bearing?"

Howe looked over his shoulder. "Aye, sir. I told him to give fire if the Frogs shot at us in the boat, as well, sir."

Mainwaring raised an eyebrow. "Damned cutthroat of you, James. We'd best pray they hold their fire."

Now *Neptune*'s side was looming ahead, a sloping wall of painted wood rising and falling slowly, the waterline wale clustered with barnacle. High above, faces were lining the rail, looking down at the six Englishmen without expression, bayonets and cutlass blades glinting beside them. Mainwaring felt his heart beginning to pound within his chest. What on earth had he got them into?

"Bows," he ordered, swinging the yawl to range in under the line of battens that rose away up the ship's side. "Way enough. Toss your oars. Hook on, there, Shanahan. Lively, now!"

In the next instant they were there, Shanahan reaching with his boathook for the irons of the main chainplates, the other men throwing the blade ends of their oars vertically and holding them dripping between their knees, the looms resting on the floorboards beneath their feet.

"Keep a good grip, Paddy," said Mainwaring, as the boat lifted and fell against the relatively still wall of the ship's side. "James, I'll go aboard alone. Wait for me here."

"But, sir –"

"No questions, James. If this is a trick, better that only one man be in their clutches, although Christ knows you'd have a job of it getting clear. Cast your mind to a prize crew while I'm gone. I'll be giving her to you to command."

"Aye, aye, sir." Howe smiled lightly. "Sorry, sir."

"No matter." Mainwaring stood cautiously, and waited for the boat to lift to the top of a swell. With only a momentary spasm of uncertainty he leaped for the battens, clutching at the splintery wood for a moment until sure he had a footing. Then he took a deep breath and began to climb steadily towards the entry port in the rail high above.

A few moments later he emerged on *Neptune*'s deck, and he made a deliberate effort to keep his expression set in stone as he saw the crowd of dark, hostile faces awaiting him. The order of *Pallas'* decks was not to be found here: men in the dress of seamen or in the grey and blue of the *Troupes de la Marine* stood in haphazard groups about the deck, as if pausing in aimless activity. The seamen held axes and gun tools, and the marines were hefting their muskets and glaring at Mainwaring with thin, sallow faces. Here and there officers in blue and scarlet stood with them, swords drawn, regarding Mainwaring with anger in their waiting, watchful eyes. Smoke drifted across the deck, swirling round the figures, who seemed frozen as if in an artistic *tableau*. The deck was cluttered with debris: bits of shattered gear, shards of wood from a splintered section of rail, dark and sinister stains suggesting that torn, wounded or dead men had lain there moments before. Aloft, the canvas rumpled and thumped in its bonds. To Mainwaring it seemed that the ship had simply paused in its fighting rather than given up. There was no lack of fighting spirit in those furious stares directed his way. What on earth was the French captain doing?

As Mainwaring stepped fully out on deck, straightening his hat, a French officer came forward from a knot of men and made a curt if correct bow, his expression wooden.

"*Vous êtes le capitaine de vaisseau anglais?*"

"Captain Edward Mainwaring. Commanding His Britannic Majesty's Ship *Pallas*," began Mainwaring.

"*Par ici, m'sieu'.*" The French officer had turned away with a gesture and walked to the after companionway.

Keeping his own expression studiedly neutral, Mainwaring followed, conscious of the watching cold stares. As he paused at the companionway, he caught a glimpse of *Pallas* over the rail, at once so distant and so reassuring. His heels thocked on the ladder as he went down, and he became aware of an odd odour, which in a moment he recognised as the characteristic smell of a French warship below decks: tar, garlic, bread, tobacco and urine, and another faint but sickening tang that made him wonder if

40

Neptune's bilges had been the recipient of the bizarre French practice of burying their dead in the ballast. It did not bear thinking about.

Ahead in the darkened passageway that led aft to what Mainwaring imagined to be the ship's great cabin, the French officer led on, the buttons at the small of his blue coat-back glinting in the half-light. He halted abruptly, and Mainwaring could see that they were before a cabin door, flanked by a diminutive *Troupes de la Marine* sentry who looked out evilly at Mainwaring from under a gilt-edged cocked hat that appeared far too large, and cradled a three-banded *fusil-grenadier* that seemed equally oversized. Now the French officer opened the door, and motioned Mainwaring in, stepping to one side.

As Mainwaring entered, his eyes were momentarily dazzled by the brilliant light flooding in through the stern lights of the cabin. He heard a voice speaking in breathy but virtually accentless English.

"So. You are the English captain?"

"I am." Mainwaring was about to speak again when his eyes adjusted to the scene before him.

The great cabin was large, considerably deeper than that in *Pallas*, but roughly the same width. Before the great slanting windows of the stern lights, through which the sun glittered with such blinding intensity off the face of the Indian Ocean, stood a settee similar to that in Mainwaring's cabin. But in contrast to Mainwaring's stark and spare furniture, which reflected the precarious state of his purse, this cabin was furnished with an elegance that bordered on sumptuousness. Over the canvas deck covering was spread a magnificent Persian rug, and the desk and chairs, and even the posted bed – a far cry from Mainwaring's rope-slung box bunk – were of an ornate *chinoiserie*. Bookshelves, wine-decanter racks, framed portraits of distinguished-looking individuals – and one startling nude nymph – added to the elegant clutter that revealed a commanding officer of independent means.

41

But it was the astonishing scene in the centre of the cabin which drew Mainwaring's eyes.

On a chair placed before the desk and turned to face the cabin door, a woman sat rigidly. She was slim, with delicate features and small, graceful hands that were twisting a handkerchief in her lap. Her hair was golden with a reddish tinge, and instead of being tightly dressed and powdered it was gathered on top of her head in a mass of curls, one long line of ringlets hanging to her right shoulder. Her gown was of pale green, the style indicating clearly her rank as that of a gentlewoman, and its brocaded stomacher created a disturbing fullness to the white skin of her bosom. There was a refinement to her features that suggested again a patrician breeding, but her eyes were the most arresting aspect about her: wide and a pale sea-green, they had the urgency of a frightened animal, and were fixed on Mainwaring with a mixture of warning, fear and anger. The cause of the look was obvious: the long, silver-barrelled Boutet flintlock pistol which was levelled a few inches from her temple by a corpulent French naval officer in the lace-hung uniform of a *capitaine de vaisseau*, who was regarding Mainwaring with a triumphant leer.

"What in hell –?" began Mainwaring.

"Please, sir, I beg of you –" The woman spoke in a soft English voice.

"She is my prisoner, m'sieu'," broke in the fat French officer. He was hatless, and wore a full-bottomed and pow-dered *perruque à circonstance*, from under which beads of sweat were running down his cheeks. "An English lady of breed-ing who will die instantly if you do not do exactly as I say!"

Mainwaring felt a cold knot of anger rising in his throat to replace the astonishment.

"Who are you, madam?" he asked, his eyes on hers.

"I am Caroline Grenville," she said, her chin lifting almost imperceptibly. Her lips were softly shaped, and there was something immensely moving in the self-control the woman was displaying.

Memory clicked into place in Mainwaring's mind. "Are you related to Captain Lord Thomas Grenville who now sails with Admiral Anson?"

"Yes. How do you –?" Surprise and relief sounded in her voice.

The fat French officer stepped forward, his face darkening. "*Silence!*" The muzzle of the pistol wavered on Caroline Grenville's temple. "You need ask no further questions, rosbif. And I warn you not to treat lightly what I say!"

Mainwaring became aware of two other French officers in the cabin. One, a tall and smallpox-scarred *Troupes de la Marine* officer in blue and grey, was eyeing him impassively. The second, more youthful and in the uniform of a naval lieutenant, was standing by the desk, his expression pale and troubled, and displaying, Mainwaring thought, not a little shame.

"I am Captain Edward Mainwaring, of His Britannic Majesty's Ship *Pallas*. You have struck your colours to me," said Mainwaring, his eyes like steel points. "Honourable behaviour on your part will be met by honourable behaviour on mine. But my ship rides off your larboard quarter now, and my people will open fire and destroy you and this ship the instant they become aware of this situation!"

"Pah! Not with you aboard."

"Most certainly with me aboard. I have already given the orders to the officer who will assume command of my ship upon my death. You are dealing with the Royal Navy, not –" he glanced at Caroline Grenville, "– victimised gentlewomen."

The fat French officer pulled a handkerchief from his waistcoat and mopped his face, the pistol still hovering off the Englishwoman's brow. "Listen to me, rosbif," he wheezed. "I am not going to lose my ship to you just because the fools and incompetents I have to man her have betrayed me! They struck the colours against my express orders, *hein*? Well, a kind Providence made this woman a

43

guest of my cabin when we took her vessel on its passage to Madras. She will now serve me by saving my vessel for me, *compris?*"

"What is your name, *Capitaine?*" Mainwaring's tone was icy. "I should like to know what officer of His Most Christian Majesty sees fit to cower behind a woman's skirts. Or are you afraid to give me your name as well as fight me honourably?"

The little porcine eyes narrowed for an instant, and then the man laughed in short gasps, his round belly shaking under his scarlet waistcoat.

"Do not try to provoke me, rosbif! You will listen to exactly what I have to say. And you will carry it out, if you wish this woman to live! Clear?"

Mainwaring looked at Caroline Grenville, and saw her mouth take a firm line and her head shake, even as tears formed in her green eyes. He felt a surge of respect for the bravery she was showing now. But then he looked back at the fat officer and asked slowly, "What is it you demand?"

"*Bon!*" exulted the fat man. "I am glad you see reason. It is quite simple. You will order your ship to stand away from us, until she is hull-down. At that point we will release the lady and yourself in a boat. Your ship can then recover you."

"And if I refuse?"

"You will have to live with your choice, m'sieu'. You will have this ship as a prize. But I shall have put a ball through this charming creature's head. *D'une certitude!*"

Mainwaring nodded slowly. "I see. Clearly I have no choice. But do I have your word as an officer and gentleman –" and here Caroline Grenville's eyes flickered as she caught the hint of mockery in Mainwaring's voice, "– that the lady will be released? So that she may safely be taken aboard my ship?"

"But of course, *Capitaine.*" The fat figure was drawn up to its full height. "You have the word of a French officer, *hein?*"

"I trust that in fact this is the case."

The fat man waved the pistol muzzle towards the cabin door. "Please be about sending your ship away. We have no time to wait about unnecessarily. And remember that one false or treacherous move and this delightful woman is a corpse. I hope that is clear?"

"Quite clear." Mainwaring's eyes found Caroline Grenville's and he was startled again by the intensity of their wide, sea-green beauty. "Please do not concern yourself, ma'am. I will return in a moment."

"You mustn't –" she began, only to bite off the words at something she saw in Mainwaring's expression.

The pistol had returned to the woman's temple.

"You are trying my patience, *Capitaine*," wheezed the fat man.

"Be calm, m'sieu'. I am doing as you wish."

"Then be quick about it, damn you!"

A moment later Mainwaring was at the rail of the French vessel, a glowering throng of French seamen and marines surrounding him as he looked down at an astonished James Howe.

"You're to do *what*, sir?" gasped the first lieutenant, incredulously.

"You heard me quite clearly, Mr Howe. The French captain has an English gentlewoman as hostage. To prevent the swine from killing her we – you – are to break off this engagement and stand off until we are hull-down. At that point he intends to put us over the side in a boat."

"Of all the cowardly, beastly – sir, surely you don't *trust* his word? Any man who'd even threaten such a thing is –"

"Mr Howe, you are undoubtedly right. But at the moment I have no alternative that comes to mind. The lady is English, in a difficult situation, and is possibly a sister to Earl Temple, if I remember the family name correctly. She requires our help, whatever her station in life, and I must give it. Don't look so concerned, James. I shall likely survive to buy you dinner at the Star and Garter, even if we can't manage White's."

Howe took off his cocked hat and slapped it in frustration against his thigh as he stood balancing precariously in the sternsheets.

"Sir, let me close to killing range. Make him see he can't escape and that if he murders the woman he'll be hung in the bargain. Christ, we'd have him on his knees in a clock's tick, by the look of that lot around you."

"And Caroline Grenville would be dead. No, James. Get back to the ship. Do as I say. But keep a sharp lookout aloft for us when they drop us."

"*If* they drop you, sir," said Howe darkly.

"You really must try to look on the bright side of things, James. Now, off you go."

"But, sir –"

"That is, as I am sure I need not point out to you, Mr Howe, an order."

Howe nodded. "Aye, aye, sir."

The first lieutenant sat down, grasping the tiller in exasperation. "Fend off, for'rard, there!" he barked at Shanahan, and in a moment the little boat was pulling strongly away from *Neptune* while Howe looked back, his expression dark and anxious.

Mainwaring watched them with a cold feeling in his stomach. The reassuring, splendid shape of *Pallas*, pitching slowly as she waited for the boat's return, seemed suddenly distant and inaccessible.

He felt a cold pressure in the small of his back, and heard the metallic double click of a pistol being drawn back to full cock.

"You will now come with me, m'sieu'," said a smooth voice. Mainwaring turned to see the sallow-faced officer from the great cabin centring a heavy Miquelet pistol on Mainwaring's stomach. "A lady awaits your presence, *hein*?"

Several minutes later the louvred door of one of the

officers' cabins which lined the passageway aft to the great cabin slammed shut behind Mainwaring as he was pushed into the gloomy interior. The deckhead in *Neptune* was lower than that in *Pallas*, and Mainwaring struck his head on a beam with painful force as he went in. His cocked hat fell at his feet, and he gave vent to an expressive curse.

"My feelings precisely, Captain," said a soft voice in some amusement, and as Mainwaring's eyes adjusted to the gloom he could see the pale figure of Caroline Grenville sitting on the edge of the narrow box bunk which took up most of the cabin's space. There was a small desk, a ladderback chair, and a sea chest held shut with a heavy black padlock, but little else. No light filtered in other than through the louvres of the door, and the air was close and stale.

"I beg your pardon, ma'am," said Mainwaring, in some embarrassment. He picked up his hat and rubbed his brow awkwardly.

"Please. I really would prefer you to call me Caroline. It's entirely too matronly to receive such deference, and we are prisoners together, although I appreciate your good manners." Her voice was warm, and Mainwaring felt the hair at the back of his neck tingle slightly.

"Of course. Thank you, Caroline."

"And you've hit your head."

"Ah, yes. Forgot that ships do have beams one can crack a head on. Not very impressive, was it, for an entry?"

She laughed. "You're doing quite well. I fell flat on my face when that obese fellow pushed me in here."

Mainwaring could not resist grinning at her in the dark. Then his expression sobered. "I hope they haven't mistreated you in any way?"

"No, not at all. After what took place during the capture of our ship, I was prepared for anything." She shuddered. "Thankfully the officers displayed some honourable behaviour, the young one in the cabin most particularly."

"I noticed. The one who looked quite ashamed."

"Yes, he was very kind. The fat one was rather horrible to everyone."

Mainwaring glanced at the door. Through the louvres he could see the grey cloth and brass buttons of the coat of a *Troupes de la Marine* sentry, facing the door in readiness. There would be no easy escape there.

"Your name is Edward?" she asked.

"Yes, ma – er, Caroline. Edward Mainwaring."

"Edward it is. And by your accent, from the Americas." It was a statement, not a question.

"Yes," said Mainwaring. "Massachusetts. Actually, an island you've not heard of: Martha's Vineyard."

"You're right, I haven't. But that is likely inexcusable ignorance on my part. Forgive me."

Mainwaring looked at her in the gloom, aware again of the admiration he had felt for her in the great cabin, marvelling now at her composure.

"Not at all. But, please," and Mainwaring sensed more than saw the sea-green eyes watching him gravely, "can you tell me how you came to be in the grip of these people? As a beginning, may I ask what ship you were in?"

"The *Hotspur*. An East Indiaman, I believe you'd call it. The captain was a lovely man." She looked down, and Mainwaring could see her hands gathering the cloth of her skirts into tightening fists. "We were six days out from the Cape when they – this ship – fell upon us."

"Were there many other passengers?"

"There was an army officer. He joined Captain Fitzwalter when they tried to defend the ship. They were both killed in the boarding, after the French had fired their guns at us for an intolerable time. I was sent below, but I made my way to where the ship's surgeon was dealing with the injured and tried to help him." She took a deep, shaking breath. "It was quite dreadful, really."

Mainwaring nodded slowly. He had all too clear an idea of what the woman had experienced.

"Were you bound for Madras?" he asked after a moment.

"Yes. My husband-to-be is deputy commander of the garrison regiment at Fort St George. I was coming out to be with him."

"A difficult voyage. You're very brave, I think."

She smiled at him, wistful and appealing in the dim light. "Bravery had very little to do with it, Captain. I had heard nothing from him for far too long and determined to come out to join him. Not with the particular approval of my family, I might add. But I had to find out what had become of him. The Company either could not, or would not tell me."

"You were travelling *alone*?"

She looked down. "My maid, Charlotte, was killed by the first shot from the French, as we were going down to where we were meant to shelter. There was no one else."

For a moment Mainwaring could think of nothing to say. Inwardly he felt enormous sympathy for this loyal and courageous woman, whose effort to be with the man she obviously loved had brought her to this pass.

"What happened when the French boarded? Can you tell me?"

"There was a great deal of thumping and banging, and I assume the French simply overwhelmed our people. Several French sailors finally burst in on us, and I felt sure that I was going to suffer a nightmarish fate. But a French officer – the young one, in fact – came in and stopped them. They brought me to this ship after it was all over." Her voice faded slightly. "They shot many of our wounded and threw them over the side. There were sharks. It was horrible."

After a moment she shook back her hair and went on. "I had no idea men could be quite so foul in their treatment of one another, and for no apparent end other than to be cruel."

"It's the way with bloody wars," said Mainwaring.

"I'm sorry?"

"War. It's not the men as such, Caroline, although there are always some who enjoy inflicting pain and death, the

49

ones who get too much enjoyment from bear-baiting or from some poor wretch choking out his life on a gibbet. War lets those swine loose, and makes brutal other men who might normally be quite decent."

"You seem to have given this some thought."

"A man who means a great deal to me pointed it all out when at one point in my career I was unsure of myself and of what I had done. Humanity is humanity, with all its capacity for good or evil. It's war one must loathe."

"But if that is –" she began.

Outside in the passageway, heels rang on the deck and with a clink of metal the sentry moved, a musket butt thumping down as he assumed a formal position. A shadow fell over the louvres of the door, a key rattled briefly in a padlock and the door swung open abruptly to reveal the fat officer blocking the narrow doorway with his blue and scarlet bulk.

"*Eh bien*," he wheezed. "You are more closely acquainted, I trust?"

"We've been below long enough for my ship to have sunk her t'gallants," said Mainwaring, his eyes fixed on the Frenchman's. "Time for you to honour your end of the bargain, I should think."

"Bargain?" The fat man laughed, an odd whistling sound that shook his body in a ludicrous jiggling. "You think I am that great a fool, do you?"

"What do you mean?" Mainwaring demanded, turning cold.

"As long as I have you and the lady, m'sieu', I am safe from your vessel until I anchor under the guns of Port Louis. I have no wish to risk the loss of my ship, nor deprive myself of the prize money from this lady's ship, which I have sent on ahead." He sniffed, the little porcine eyes glinting in amusement.

"You'll be my guests for some time, *hein*? And while I am sure you will prove to be a delightful captive ornament to M'sieu' La Bourdonnais' *salon*, madame, your com-

50

panion here should equally grace the interior of one of the King's most repulsive prisons. Its fame has spread far beyond Mauritius, I'm told." He laughed again. "What a fine-looking felon you'll make, after the *forçats* have finished with you!"

2

Edward Mainwaring opened his eyes. For a moment they saw nothing but an inky gloom, and he was unsure of where he was. Then it came to him that he was lying face down on a gritty stone floor, and as he tried to move a searing pain coursed through him from his back, as if a fire had suddenly been lit upon it. He tasted blood on his lips. With enormous effort he put his hands underneath him and levered up on to his hands and knees. The pain from his lacerated back was like a knife and he waited for it to pass, panting as if from exertion.

The gloom was a little less impenetrable now, and he could see that a shaft of starlight from a small window high in one wall was painting a pale square in the far corner of the cell. As Mainwaring watched, a thin brown rat appeared in the square of light, sat up on its haunches and regarded him with steady, glittering eyes.

"And why are you here, rat?" croaked Mainwaring. "Theft of His Most Christian Majesty's cheese?"

The rat twitched its whiskers dismissively and vanished into the shadows.

Mainwaring looked round: to one side was a low wooden shelf – a bed, bereft of any covering or pillow – and he crawled to it, pulling himself up on it into a sitting position. He locked his hands on his knees until the flaming pain of the movement ceased.

"If you can hear me, rat," he croaked again, "don't try to make a dash for it unless you've got a clear path. The gentlemen running this inn are somewhat unforgiving."

He scrubbed his face with one hand, feeling the stubble and grime, the cut and swelling lip. He was ragingly thirsty, and clutched at a battered tin cup which was on the bed. It was half-full of tepid water which he drank greedily.

Setting down the cup he looked up at the dim square of light high on the opposite wall. The cell was no more than six feet by twelve, and the window would have to be ten feet high above the floor. He could see nothing but a few stars, cold and impersonal, and he shuddered as he felt the recurrent cold clutch of claustrophobia closing in on him. With an effort of will he forced himself to retrace the events that had brought him here, in dirty and now ragged small clothes, barefoot, and with his back lacerated by a convicts' lash.

Even as he had stared in furious anger at the fat officer in the small cabin aboard *Neptune*, a thunder of feet had suddenly sounded in the passageway, and several villainous-looking seamen had burst in and seized Mainwaring. They had bundled him roughly out of the cabin and off forward, their curses drowning Caroline Grenville's cry of alarm and protest as he was carried off. With a hail of punches and kicks Mainwaring had been hauled to the hatchway leading to the cable tier. His hat had been flung off, his boots pulled from his feet, and his coat torn from his shoulders before his hands had been bound behind him. Then the hatch had been lifted open, and he had been thrown down into the darkness, impacting against the stinking, slime-covered coils of anchor cable with a force that left him senseless. There he had lain for hours, perhaps days, in a growing torment of discomfort and thirst until abruptly he had been dragged out once more, many hands pushing him out of the cable tier, until he stood in the passageway above. A hood had been pulled over his head and he was pushed and kicked in shin-banging roughness up on deck. The sea air had roused him, even through the black folds of the hood, and the sounds of the ship, clearly shortening sail. Then land smells, rich and tropical, were in his nostrils, and he heard the hubbub and clop of a harbourfront and the woosh of collapsing and furling sails over the rattle of blocks.

The thump and scrape of a gangway being pushed into place were followed in a few moments by the sharp stab of a musket butt that sent him stumbling and falling down the slanting, battened planking, cursing the hood and the unthinking swine whose blows propelled him onward. Then he was sprawling, his knees banging in pain on rough cobble stones, only to be picked up and thrust into a splintery-sided cart that set off on a jerky, clip-clop journey through a seemingly endless soundscape of narrow streets echoing to the animal's hooves, the squeal and rumble of the cart wheels, and the jabber and call of the voices to either side in an oddly patois French.

Hands had held his wrists at one point as the cart clattered and rocked along, and his bonds had been cut away; a flagon of beer had been thrust into his grip and the hood partially lifted, and he had gulped down the brackish liquid in a rush. The smells of the air had pressed at him, laden with the same smells that Mainwaring remembered from the Caribbean: coconut oil and palm; flowers and uncounted spices; salt, sweat and human waste; sugar-cane and fish.

Then the cart had clattered through some form of archway, jerked to a halt, and Mainwaring had been dragged from it, to be marched between men with a muscular grip into the cool and mouldy-smelling interior of a building where he was pulled up short and the hood wrenched from his head. He was in a dark, torchlit passageway in front of a small, heavy door with a low, barred aperture. The men holding him were in the grey and blue of the *Troupes de la Marine*, but before he could study them the door of the cell, as it soon proved to be, was kicked open, and he was thrown bodily in, sprawling painfully on the gritty flagstone floor. The door had banged shut with a clank behind him, and an echoing coarse laugh.

He sat up, flexing his back with slow care. He had tried

to escape, of course. After some hours, perhaps a night, of darkness in the foul little cell, he had been pulled out again by two burly men of the *Troupes* and let into a narrow, dusty courtyard with high masonry walls to either side. At the far end was a lower wall which clearly sat perhaps ten feet above an open expanse of blue water that glittered out to where half a dozen ships lay at anchor. An inexplicable impulse had seized him, and without looking about him he had bolted suddenly for the low wall, his feet crunching painfully over the pebbles of the courtyard. But before he had covered more than a few paces, a whistling sounded in his ears, and his ankles were clamped together in mid-run by what felt like a coil of steel. He fell with a gasp, hard and painfully, only to hear shoe leather scuff on the flagstones, and then hands were clutching at him, hauling him to his feet, and a blur of figures in the familiar grey and blue were throwing him hard against one wall, his arms pinioned out to the side while the shirt was ripped from his back.

"*Eh bien, m'sieu' rosbif,*" a deep voice had said, almost in a sigh. Then the first blow of the lash had struck him, unbelievable in its pain and force. Mainwaring's breath was dashed from his body as if by a fist to the small of his back, and he could not hold back the cry. But his mouth merely opened in a soundless rictus of agony, for which he was oddly grateful through the white intensity of the pain. Several more blows had fallen, the gunshot crack of the snaking leather echoing in the narrow yard as the pain convulsed him. An incredible pressure seemed to be building within him, as if in the next instant his face would burst from his head with the unspeakable agony. Then consciousness had slipped away, the hands releasing their grip, the hard, dirty stone coming up to meet his face, and the laughter, mocking and scornful, etching deep into him.

Damn them. Damn my stupidity for falling into their bloody trap! said his mind. The image of *Pallas* somewhere at sea, splendid and reassuring, sprang into his mind, and he felt a catch in the back of his throat.

"I'll see you again, my girl," he said out loud, the ship still clear in his mind. "And when I do, these bastards will know of it. By God, they shall!"

A hard light came into his eyes. He felt along the wood for the tin cup, and looked up at the narrow window high above, thinking rapidly. Then, with deliberate care, he began twisting and pressing the tin of the battered cup into the first rough form of a tool.

His Britannic Majesty's Ship *Pallas* pitched slowly ahead over the grey early-morning swells, under topsails, head-sails, and spanker. An uncharacteristic fog was slowly dissipating, and as *Pallas* moved in quiet dignity through its curling folds, she bore a huge, gently-drifting white Bourbon ensign at her stern staff.

Aloft in the foretopgallant crosstrees, James Howe swallowed to counter the tightness in his throat that his lofty perch produced, and shifted a vice-like grip on the royal shrouds to look down at the blond locks of Stephen Pellowe, monkeying with annoying agility up the topgallant ratlines, the leatherbound tube of the great quarterdeck telescope clamped under one arm.

"Careful with that bring-'em-near, Stephen," said Howe. "The damned thing'd knife through to the keelson if you dropped it from here."

Pellowe looked up, a broad grin spreading. He had left his cocked hat on deck, and his wind-tousled locks gave him the look of a ship's boy rather than *Pallas*' second lieutenant.

"Aye, sir, no fear. Here you are, sir." Locking his legs around the narrowing shrouds, Pellowe extended the long glass up to Howe.

"Thank you. Damme, are you not even a touch giddy up here? I would – oh, dear – part with my lunch easily if the old girl rolls like that again."

Pellowe laughed. "No, sir. Spent too much time chasing about the tops of my first ship. Hard to lose the skill."

"Really? Damned commendable on your part. I shouldn't like to do this more than once a cruise. Now, for the bloody glass." With a good deal of writhing round to keep his grip and hold himself steady, Howe pulled open the long glass and raised it to look to the south-east, over *Pallas'* slowly pitching jib-boom end.

"See anything, sir?" asked Pellowe.

"No. Damned fog's still – wait, now. Yes, it's lifting. What's that bloody north cape called?"

"Er, Cap Malheureux, sir."

"Right you are. Got that clear, at least." Howe passed the glass slowly to the right along the grey mass of the humped, distant land. "Now for that sharp peak that's supposed to lie behind Port Louis. What the devil was it called?"

"Dutch name, sir. That'd be Pieter Both. Should lie to the left of another one, Le Pouce."

"You're very annoying at times, Stephen, but I'm glad one of us studied the damned chart. Yes, there they are. And Port Louis should be – just – below." He paused. "Got it. Clutch of rooftops. Church spire. That'd be the Saint Louis, what?"

Pellowe grinned. "Right, sir. Your memory's fine."

"Flattery works wonders, I know, Stephen, but I'm far too cynical to be moved by it." Howe tried to picture the shape of Ile de France, or Mauritius, as the Dutch called it. Like a pear, with the narrowing top of the fruit the north cape, Cap Malheureux. Then, half-way down the widening western side of the pear, three bays: Baie de l'Arsenal to the north; Baie du Tombeau farther south; and then the larger bay, at the shoulder of the fruit, where Port Louis, the island's major port, lay. *Pallas* was standing in under a gentle north-westerly, and if the apparent angles Howe had been calculating by eye were accurate between the bearing of Cap Malheureux and the sharp knife-edge of Pieter

Both, *Pallas* would be no more than three leagues off Port Louis.

Hence the damned Bourbon rag, for insurance, Howe thought. He took a slow, panning look up and down the coast and then pushed the long glass shut with a snap.

"We're about three leagues off the place, Stephen. If they haven't seen us by now they soon will. We'll stay at Quarters, and double the lookouts as we stand in. Hard to tell what that white ensign will buy for us in terms of time."

Pallas rolled and Howe clutched at the topgallant mast as the wind whistled in his ears.

"Anything, of course, to be able to get down from *here*," he said, through gritted teeth.

"What do you plan to do, sir?" asked Pellowe, mindless of the expanse of sea that now yawned below his perch.

"The captain *has* to be in there, Stephen," said Howe. "We saw the Frenchman put in, and he hasn't left. And nothing's been on the face of the sea except those odd, Arab-looking little fishermen, which suggests the French have their ships in there, readying 'em."

"D'ye think he's in a ship, sir, or prison?"

"Either, or they might play the gentleman and keep him as a guest at the governor's house, giving parole, and all that sort of thing. Somehow I doubt it. They were a villainous-looking lot.

"What I propose we do, Stephen," said Howe after a long, thoughtful moment, "is go in and get him."

"With the *ship*, sir? Wouldn't their batteries get us, before we even got a party ashore? And where would we look? There's also likely garrison troops o' some kind –"

"Of course, Stephen, of course. What I have in mind is the sort of thing the captain would do." A firm light came into his eyes. "We're going to stand away, flying a fever flag. They'll be glad enough to see us stand off for a bit, but when dark falls, we'll send in a boat."

"But to look *where*, sir?"

Howe shook his head. "I have no idea, Stephen, no idea. But by God, I intend to try!"

Edward Mainwaring held his breath and froze as the heels of the guard in the passageway slowed by his cell door. He knew the cell would appear inky-black from the lanternlit passageway, but where he clung, part way up the cell wall, he would be fully visible to anyone looking in through the narrow iron grill of the door. The heels slowed, paused for a moment, and then went on.

Twenty minutes, or thereabouts, thought Mainwaring. *Almost predictable.*

He let his breath out slowly, feeling again the trembling weakness in his fingers and knees. He was almost to the small, barred window and his toes and the fingers of his left hand clung to the crumbling edges of the indentations he had dug precariously with the bent spoon until the crumbling, gravelly plaster gave way. He had pressed himself like a spider against the dusty, chalky wall each time the sentry had passed, clinging in heart-pounding immobility to his bat's perch. How many times had the man passed? Six times? Twenty?

But now he neared his goal. Agonisingly he scraped away at what he hoped would be the last shallow handhold, clenched the battered spoon in his teeth, and forced his fingers into the narrow cleft. With slow, sweating care he eased himself upward, flattening his belly against the rough plaster until he felt the toes of his left foot touch the next hold. He jammed his toes into it, feeling a shaking fatigue threatening to overcome him, and stretched his free hand upward, straining, until suddenly his fingers were at the lip of the window opening.

Dear God, his mind cried, *thank you! Only let the bars be loose!*

With the same painful caution he reached with his other hand, and the rough, knobbled feel of rusted iron bar was against his palm. For a moment the bar resisted his steady pull, and then abruptly came away towards him in a shower

59

of plaster dust and pebbles. Mainwaring choked back an involuntary cry of fear as his balance wavered with the bar's release; desperately he dug his fingers and toes into the crevices, the sweat pouring from him in rivulets. The moment of peril passed, and he still clung there, high above the stony floor that would smash him if his grip faltered.

His mind spoke again. *Keep moving. Keep going. Do it!*

It was difficult to make out what was left of the window barring, as, beyond, there were no stars. The sky was overcast, and the night like tar. He laid the bar down carefully to one side of the sill and reached out until he found the outer lip. With his fingers hooked to it like a grapnel, he wormed his way up and over the edge of the sill. As he moved, Mainwaring realised that with the one bar gone, an opening had been created which was almost as wide as his shoulders.

Free! he exulted silently. But he was lying awkwardly half-in, half-out of an opening no more than eighteen inches wide, with his legs still dangling over a bone-breaking fall back into the cell, while before him almost nothing was visible.

"Dear Christ!" he muttered out loud. "I could be thirty feet above a stone courtyard!" He wriggled forward again, and now his head came level with the edge of the outer wall, and he was abruptly staring down into a narrow, beaten-earth street some sixty to seventy feet below. It was lined with odd-looking, low houses with what appeared in the gloom to be mixed thatch and tile roofing. The street itself was deserted, and beyond the roof line Mainwaring could see off to one side the wink of ships' riding lights. Below, the street and the faces of the houses were lit fitfully by a few lanterns hung on their irons beside several doorways, the low orange light glinting on a rivulet of sewage that trickled along the middle of the street. A thin dog, trotting in the over-the-shoulder watchfulness of the true cur, passed along the street, its tail between its legs.

Mainwaring's heart sank. At this height a leap would

either kill or cripple him. The only other option was to slither back into the caged despair of the cell and await Christ only knew what.

Then he felt his heart skip a beat.

Looking directly down the face of the prison wall, he could see a tree, not very tall but bushy, growing close against the building. It was difficult to judge its height, but it might be as much as ten feet or more from the leafy crown to the dirt street.

Mainwaring made up his mind in a matter of seconds, even as another voice inside him was shrieking, *You fool: you'll be killed!* He wriggled over the edge of the outside sill, working round so that he hung at last by his fingertips, his bare feet dangling over empty space.

My dear Anne, he thought unexpectedly as the face of Anne Brixham came into his mind. *How I love you.* Then he let go.

James Howe moved in the darkness to the rail of *Pallas*, looking off for a moment to the western horizon where all that was left of the sun was a thin band of deep red along the black line of the sea. For all that it was in the near-tropics, the wind off the sea now was cool, and Howe shivered inside his plain brown seaman's jacket. He shifted the light flintlock fusil he carried from one hand to the other, put his free hand on the rail and peered over.

"Mr Hooke, are all your men in the boat?" he called.

"Aye, aye, zur," came Isaiah Hooke's growl from below, over the slap-lap of the sea against the ship's side and the rustle of the boat's brailed sails. He was standing in the sternsheets of *Pallas*' double-lugsailed longboat, which was hooked on at the larboard forechains, the brails gathering the dark sails against their yards, and the thwarts bearing a clutch of sombrely-clad, cross-belted men who steadied muskets between their knees and looked up at Howe high above. "Oi've Slade, Sawyer, Jackman an' Winton, zur. An' wiv Serjeant Fell, there's Wallis, Pasco, Delvin an'

'Arris. Ten all told, mustered to rights, an' wiv breadbags an' ball cartridge, zur.''

"Very good. Each man's firelock is in good order? It'll be no bloody time for misfires.''

"Aye, zur. The lads sprung an' sparked afore strikin' into th' boat.'' The sailing master spat off into the darkness. "Oi drew 'em plain jackets, out o' slops, as you ordered, zur.''

"So I see. Sombre and shadowy lot indeed. Well done. How much ball cartridge?''

"Sixty rounds a man, zur. Mr Davies had 'em fresh rolled.''

"Very good. Stand by.'' Howe turned to where a white-faced Stephen Pellowe, ever-boyish even in the graceful dignity of full-skirted coat and cocked hat, watched him with a hard set to his jaw. "We'll be off, then, Stephen. The ship is yours. Mind that land breeze. Aback like this she's vulnerable to any cat's paw. Let Jewett play the role of sailing master.''

"Sir. Damned if I think you should be going, sir, if you'll pardon the liberty.''

"I know, Stephen. We've been through this. There simply is no other way. I don't think either of us could abide the prospect of sitting out here while our Ned – the lads do call him that, don't they? – sits in there barely a league or two away, as far as we know. And be damned to any catch-as-you-may French squadron.''

"Yes, sir. We don't want to lose you as well as Edwa – as Captain Mainwaring, sir.''

Howe managed a small smile. "With a bit of luck and incompetence on the part of the Frogs, likely you shan't, Stephen. Now, you're quite clear as to your duties?''

"Aye, aye, sir. I'm to cruise between Cap Malheureux and Tamarin for four days, under French colours and flying the fever flag. If after that time you don't appear, I'm to sail for the Coromandel and seek out Commodore Peyton.''

"Precisely. I shall hold you to that, Stephen, as the captain would.''

"Sir. Hooke has a small chest of navigating instruments and Baker penned a copy of part of the Indian Ocean chart. One never knows, sir. The boat's victualled and watered: biscuit for ten days, water for ten, and I've struck in a small butt of neat rum, sir. Hooke has it under his feet."

"Thoughtful indeed, Stephen." Howe sighed and crammed his cocked hat down over his brow. "Now to get on with it."

Pellowe looked shoreward. "Will you be able to see well enough, sir?"

"If the stars stay out, I should think so. The moon would be better, but then it would reveal us as well to any guardboats or sentinels. It doesn't rise until later, and before then I'm going to try to get us in to the harbour mouth there at Port Louis. Those notes in the *Neptune Oriental* say it's circular with a battery at each side of the mouth. On the left-hand one – that'd be the north – there's a long spit with a beach, and a lagoon behind, the Mer –"

"The Mer Rouge, sir. Like a kind of flooded tidal flat."

Howe raised an eyebrow. "Been poking about in the captain's books, have you?"

"Well, actually, sir, I –" began Pellowe uncomfortably.

Howe laughed. "As well you should. At any rate, I intend to bear in for there, away from the busier shore. We'll hide the boat as best we can, leave a guard on it, and push in for the town." He sighed again. "Bloody forlorn hope, to a degree, Stephen. Where the captain will be, I haven't a clue. But we've no choice. We both would do anything in our power to find him, wouldn't we?"

"Indeed, sir." Pellowe's voice was hoarse.

"Then I'd best be off," said Howe. He slung his fusil and went out through the entry port, scrabbling his way down the battens until in a moment he was sitting in the crowded sternsheets of the boat.

He nodded to Hooke beside him. "Unhook and bear off. Ease the brails and steer us for that shoreline, yonder."

"Zur," growled Hooke. "Let go for'rard. Slade, shake

out th' fore. Sawyer, the main. Clear away those sheets, lively, now. Winnie, you be a-castin' off o' them turns." And within a minute or two, the heavily-laden longboat turned away from *Pallas* and was punching over the swells, the double dark lugsails driving it off towards the humped and shadowed mass of the distant island.

Anne Brixham was grinning at Edward Mainwaring as he lay in sprawled comfort on the cool sand of the beach. His head was in her lap, and her strong, sunbrowned hands were gently kneading his scalp in a wondrously relaxing way.

"Really," she said, "I've never seen anyone look quite so smug." She tweaked the end of his nose.

"Smug? Sink me, not this lad. What you're seeing, m'love, is the bliss of contentment. The evening sun sets in the west, I've not a single damned responsibility, I have my head in the lap of the woman I love. Need I go on?"

The circle of dark curls round her face danced as she laughed silently, her full breasts shaking against the rough cloth of the simple seaman's shirt she was wearing.

"And I suppose you're about to tell me," she said, "that you're off to sea again. More bloody letters from afar every six months." Her voice was low and musical, and the smile was still there, though a little less wide.

"If Their Lordships –" he began.

"Oh, bugger Their Lordships! I see too little of you, *Captain* Mainwaring!" She bent and kissed him, warmly and quickly. "My father is expecting us to marry this spring. *I* expect us to marry this spring. I won't hear of your being hauled off to sea again!" She bit him gently on the nose. "Admiralty or no."

Mainwaring grinned up at her. Then he frowned. She was holding a large cloth that looked wet, and her hair was lighter-coloured now, almost red, her lips pouting in concentration as she leaned forward, bringing the cloth towards Mainwaring's face.

He awoke as the cloth touched his forehead, dabbing gently. He gasped at the pain in his head, aware that he was lying on some kind of low daybed. His vision was still blurred, and in a kind of panic he began to struggle upright.

"Stay quiet, there's a good lad, else ye'll bleed loike a stuck pig, ye will!" purred a soft female voice with a strong Irish accent.

"What the devil –" Mainwaring began, trying to sit up. Then he felt the lacerations on his back, opened again and, by the wet feel, bleeding again. The pain was appalling, and he fell back, biting his lip to keep from crying out.

"Sure, an' it's fearsome brave y'are, sorr, an' I'd no choice but to lay you on yer back, t' do yer head. But that's bleedin' no more, so I'll trouble yew t' turn over, gently now."

The cloth was covering Mainwaring's eyes, and he raised a hand to pull it away when another small, soft hand caught his wrist.

"No, sir, try an' keep that pressin' against yer poor head, even after ye've turned. Else it'll bleed again, sartin."

Mainwaring felt other hands on him, pushing him gently to roll over. As he did so, the searing pain from his back was joined by the aches and stings from a multitude of welts and bruises over his body.

"Good Christ, what happened to me? And who are you? That bloody tree –"

"That bloody tree, sorr, is what saved ye, and Oi'm after t'inkin' ye're a lucky one indeed, t'live. Didn't we find ye on th' roadway, more dead than alive?"

Mainwaring winced as the hands pulled gently at his shirt, lifting it away from the bloody cuts on his back. Cool ointment suddenly touched his skin and was carefully spread over his torn flesh.

"You found me on the roadway, below the tree against the prison's wall?"

"Sure, an' we did. Leastwise, our man did, and he's our sworn trusty, never you fear, sorr."

"But who are you?"

Low giggles sounded from several points in the room, and Mainwaring heard the rustle of fabric. He lifted his head, pulling away the cloth, and found himself staring at the figure of a young woman sitting at the head of the small daybed on which he lay. The woman was pretty in a hard sort of way, with powdered curls pinned with bodkins atop her head, and startling white make-up against which a star-shaped patch stood out high on one cheek. She was regarding Mainwaring with a mixture of concern and amusement, all the more startling for the fact that, other than a pair of white hose which rose to her mid-thighs and were held by pink garters, the girl was naked.

"Good Lord," muttered Mainwaring, looking somewhat wild-eyed around the room. A small but firm hand at the back of his head pushed it to the pillow, tucking the cloth in place, but not before Mainwaring had seen that he was surrounded by several other girls, also either partially or fully disrobed, their softly rounded bodies glowing like a work by Boucher or Titian in the light of the candle sconces. The room itself was some kind of lady's closet or dressing-room, hung about with shifts and chemises, billows of gowns thrown across chairs, bonnets on hooks, and large propped-open chests with bright-coloured fabrics spilling out of them. A scent of flowers and perfumes and of freshly-boiled linen pervaded the room. And the warm, musky odour of a woman's skin touched with a sheen of perspiration. After the harsh masculinity of *Pallas'* gun decks this totally female world struck Mainwaring almost like a blow.

"Sink me," he murmured wonderingly as he felt the expertise of the little fingers working on his back. "I take a header from a prison window, and wake up in, er –"

"A home for temporarily inconvenienced young ladies, I'd be after putting it, sorr," said the Irish voice, evidently belonging to the owner of the skilled fingers.

"But you're *Irish*," said Mainwaring. "What –"

"What is a good Catholic girl from Connemara doin' bein' on th' account, loike, wiv th' French gentlemen, an' on a French island?" Her voice paused for a moment. "An affair of the heart, to be sure, an' me followin' me own Patrick Conolly to France, thinkin' he'd make a good woman of me. An' him bein' faithless, an' Mary Riley, who I am, needin' t' live, an' eat, same as any poor craiture o' God's creation."

Mainwaring lay still, feeling Mary Riley's sure and gentle touch on his tortured back. He could think only of what might have brought the girl to this. Made pregnant by a local lout in a tiny, lost Irish village; following the father in footloose and penniless wanderings to France, to be spurned by him; and then entering into the 'employ' of the whore-mongers, who gathered the abandoned, frightened or desolate girls from the streets of port towns and shipped them to the outposts of colony, the ships' masters getting their share for safe delivery, the cribs waiting in the godforsaken backwaters of Cayenne or Port Louis, or even fog-shrouded Louisbourg. There the girls would 'work', servicing the hard, lonely and sometimes vicious men of the ships and the garrisons, until they lost their looks and were thrown into the streets to die, or contracted the pox and died sooner, but in equal solitude and abandonment. It was a horrifying fate.

"Where are we, then, Mary Riley?" Mainwaring asked as gently as he could. "What is this place?"

"The best house on the rue Dauphine, an' to be sure, it'd be the Coq d'Or." There was an appreciative giggle from the other warm shapes around Mainwaring.

"Are we near the harbour?"

"We've only a short walk to the cathedral if ye turn right, out th' door, an' th' same to the Place d'Armes if ye turn left. The harbour'd be beyond that, barely a pace or two to th' sea wall, yer honour."

"Good. Please, that's enough." Mainwaring rolled over and sat up, to stare into a pair of wide-set, intelligent blue

67

eyes below red tousled curls. Like the others, Mary Riley was virtually naked, save that round her white throat was a green ribbon that carried a delicate white cameo. Her breasts were full and rounded, and Mainwaring's eyes dropped of their own accord to their soft, pink nipples. They shook when she laughed, and she made no move to cover herself.

"So, now, the pain isn't after maskin' the plaisures o' bein' a man," she said, with a little laugh.

Mainwaring flushed, and forced himself to look into her watchful, amused blue eyes.

"Mary, thank you for what you've done for me, you and your friends. But I must get to the harbour. Can you show me the way?"

The girl reached for a Chinese silk robe and stood, pulling it on with deliberate slowness. She stood so close to Mainwaring that he could feel the heat from her rounded hip. She smiled impishly at him.

"Oi'll set ye out th' right door, me wall-climbin' Englishman. But once out, sure, an' ye'll have t' find yer own way t' the sea. The gennulmen of th' house would be sartin unkind to us for stirrin' a foot beyond the door, d'ye get my meanin'?" There was a hint of sad bitterness in the girl's voice, and Mainwaring's eyes softened as he saw what was in the pale blue gaze.

"Yes, Mary, I do get your meaning. Please, now, show me."

The girl moved noiselessly to the door. "Come. We'll have to pass through one of the – one of th' visitin' rooms, so t' speak. Ye'll have to tread quietly and y'are to pay no mind to what's happenin'."

Mainwaring nodded, rolling gingerly off the daybed. The carpet was smooth under his bare feet, and the searing pain in his back had eased greatly. Only an ache in his shoulders and neck, and a hundred little cuts and welts, reminded him of the fall into the tree. He knew he was lucky to be alive.

The girl lifted the latch, opened the door without a sound, peered round the edge, and motioned him to follow. Mainwaring padded after her through the doorway. He was several paces into the dimly-lit room, following the girl's round, gliding shape along the wall towards another door at the far side, before he risked a look sideways at the contents of the candlelit chamber. With a spasm of effort he kept himself from stumbling.

An elaborate canopied bed hung about with florid drapery occupied the centre of the room. The bed's covers were thrown back in a welter, and a naked couple writhed in energetic coupling. The woman still wore stockings gartered above the knee, and her legs were locked round the body of the swarthy, heavy-set man who was atop her, grunting in a repellent, animal way.

Mainwaring was noting that the man had a remarkably long and greasy rattail queue down his back, when he was astonished to see the woman's eyes peer at him over the man's shoulder, their quick and meaningful flick from Mainwaring to the door towards which Mary Riley glided carrying a clear message.

Mainwaring recovered himself and sprang noiselessly after the Irish girl, catching up to her just as she reached the door. Timing her pull of the latch to coincide with the rhythmic creaking of the bed, she opened the door and slipped swiftly through, Mainwaring at her heels. Then they were in a dim, small foyer where another door waited.

Mary Riley shut the inner door in quick silence, just as a bleat of satisfaction signalled that the Frenchman had achieved that for which he had paid his few coins. Her face impassive, she looked steadily at Mainwaring and indicated the outer door.

"If ye slip out o' there, an' turn to your left, sorr, keepin' on past the cathedral, ye'll find yer harbour, sure enough."

"How much do they pay you, Mary?" Mainwaring asked, seeing the humiliation and pain in the blue eyes.

"I've been known to be worth a louis or two, to be sure."

Mainwaring reached for the door latch, and slid back the heavy bolt. "You're worth far more than bloody money. Thank you for what you did for me."

Her eyes glistened with tears. "Ye needn't think we like this line o' work, sorr. Ye can believe that a kitchen, an' a good thatch o'erhead, and a little one or two around the knees, would be what I'd want, what all of us would want. But God made us whores, sorr," she said bitterly, "and isn't it likely a whore I'll die." She palmed away a tear. "And who'll pray for me poor soul then, I'm after askin'. In the name o' sweet Mary, will ye not go!"

Mainwaring nodded. The bolt was back, and he lifted the latch, pulling the thick door open. With a last look at the miserable girl, he slipped out into the darkness, crouching in the gloom as the door thumped shut behind him. He heard the bolt slide home, and for a moment thought he caught the faintest of sobs.

He was in a narrow, shallow entranceway that allowed him to inch forward in shadow before peering into the street. The night air was humid and heavy with the molasses smell of crushed sugar-cane. The street was no more than a dirty mud lane, with the same trickle of sewage down the middle. It was lined with single-storey shuttered houses, steep-roofed in a strange cobble of Dutch and French styles, leading off in either direction. Another thin dog trotted by with a sidelong glance at Mainwaring, its eyes showing white in the gloom. To the left, Mainwaring could see that the street ended at a broad, shadowy square, and he stepped out of the entranceway and padded along swiftly, grimacing at the thought of what his feet were squelching through.

At one point he pressed himself into a doorway and kept still as two soldiers, their arms linked over their shoulders and swigging on bottles, staggered by, their linen coats stained with grime and filth from the street, their cocked hats perched on the backs of their heads. They were half-singing, half-muttering a song he had heard in the old Hôtel de la Marine in faraway, fog-shrouded Louisbourg, and he felt a sudden yearning for the distant, cold world of the North Atlantic shore. Then the soldiers were gone, thumping noisily through the same doorway out of which Mary Riley had sent him, banging and clamouring for entry. Mainwaring shuddered and pressed on, more swiftly now.

In the next minute he had arrived at a corner of the street that opened out on the deserted, shadowy square, very likely the Place d'Armes. Crouching behind a cluster of barrels that stood below a very Dutch-looking cargo davit projecting from the eaves above, he scanned the scene carefully.

The Place d'Armes was ringed by low, shuttered houses, and several streets ran off it in odd directions. Through a gap in the chimney pots and steep rooftops in the line of houses opposite him, Mainwaring could see the topgallant masts and yards of several ships, dark against the starlit sky. The harbour!

Your next landfall, Edward, my lad, he thought to himself. Then he sank into the shadows as a door banged open in a house to one side that bore a swinging innkeeper's sign, and the windows of which glowed with lantern light. From within came the jabber and clink of tavern noise, and a knot of soldiery abruptly lurched through the door, roughly pushed by a huge man with a grenadier's moustache and wearing an apron, who swore at the sprawling men in a deep *basso profundo* before clanging the door shut. The soldiers rose unsteadily from the mud, pushing at one another and cackling in drunken glee, before setting off unsteadily down a side lane which appeared to lead towards those topgallant masts.

They reeled amiably along the narrow, shadowed lane towards their harbourfront quarters, bellowing out a bawdy *chanson* at full volume. They did not notice the ragged figure that flitted quickly across the rough cobble of the Place d'Armes and which attached itself to their inebriated little party, trudging along like a *fusilier* who had forgotten his

71

coat and shoes somewhere, and taken the worst of a tavern brawl, but who was shambling along drunkenly a few feet behind the main clutch of men. To all appearances the addition was another grubby colonial musketman of the *Troupes de la Marine* making his way back to the verminous straw of his bed in the *casernes*, but the eyes were watchful and alert within the shadows of his smudged and darkened face.

Five minutes later the band of revellers emerged almost at jettyside, the towering, dark shape of a lantern-hung East Indiaman looming suddenly above them like a wall. The roistering figures lurched away down the line of darkened ships, gingerly avoiding the thick cobwebbing of the lines that kept the ships to the jetty, and watched for the most part good-naturedly by the solitary deckwatchmen of the sleeping ships.

But one figure remained, ducking unseen behind a vast coil of anchor hawser, and waiting there in the shadows until the soldiery had vanished noisily through the entry arch of a long, low building farther along the jetty, presumably the *casernes*, and the watchmen had resumed their lonely pacing.

Mainwaring raised his head carefully, looking along the jetty and then at the dark hulk of the East Indiaman above him. He knew what he wanted: a small boat, ideally a lug-rigged little *chaloupe* that might look like a fisherman, small enough to handle, but large enough to get out to the open sea and survive there until he somehow found *Pallas*. For a moment it struck him that he was assuming the ship would be waiting for him; and he shivered at the brief thought that *Pallas* might not be there at all.

He narrowed his eyes. The East Indiaman and the ships tied up alongside the jetty fore and aft of her were too close to allow boats to be alongside them on any but the outboard side; that would mean the necessity of crossing one of the ships, and that was a tactic to be resorted to only as a last resort. Beyond the next ship in line, an odd-looking *tartane* with a raked foremast, there was an indentation in the jetty wall; marking a basin from which a clutch of masts protruded, the dark sails brailed against masts or yards. There would be the sort of boat he wanted, most likely, snugged in for the night like ducks on a lee shore. But it was hard to tell what was actually there, in the play of moonlight against the backdrop of ships and buildings. Closer to the edge of the basin was an ox cart, resting on its long tongue, and sitting before a stack of half a dozen or more heavy tumbrils: a cargo awaiting its lading bill.

And shelter for me, thought Mainwaring. In the next instant he was up and running, the night air whistling in his ears, his feet noiseless over the dirt and planking of the jetty surface.

3

The tall officer in the uniform of a *capitaine de vaisseau* stood braced against the weather quarterdeck rail of His Most Christian Majesty's seventy-gun ship *Achille*, his eyes on the dark headland that lay off the ship's slowly plunging larboard bow. It was cold in the dim, pre-dawn light, and the officer blew on his hands and rubbed them together, watching as a squat lieutenant made his way up the quarterdeck ladder. The lieutenant doffed a cocked hat edged with an overabundance of egret feathers and pointed towards the headland.

"Cap Malheureux on the bows, m'sieu'. And the foretop lookout reports the English vessel is still under reduced sail, barely round out of sight. He's not seen us, I'm certain, m'sieu'!"

"For your sake, Dionne, you'd better be right. If the rosbifs see us before we spring at them, I'll have you roasted on a spit." The tall officer's voice was edged with steel. "Are the men fully at Quarters?"

"*Oui, m'sieu'!*" Dionne sweated visibly. "As you can see. Gun crews closed up, *fusiliers* in the tops, the *maître* on the helm. *Achille* is ready to strike, m'sieu'!"

"Very well." The *capitaine de vaisseau* turned to look at the dark shore, his eyes on the white flicker of surf that marked the cape's meeting with the sea. "You're quite sure they've not seen us?"

"Quite, m'sieu'! Since we first saw his topgallants at dusk last night and put in behind the cape, I've been careful to keep us well hidden. I've not set a topgallant, and only the lookouts are high enough aloft to see him. We raised him at the first light, standing in on a slow tack towards the headland." The lieutenant drew a long handkerchief from his cuff and mopped his brow, in spite of the morning cool. "I've called the people to Quarters at first light, as is customary, m'sieu', but with no drum or pipes. The Englishman doesn't suspect a thing."

"Perhaps. But I wish nothing to go wrong. You'll go forward and see to the readiness of the boarding parties, *hein*? If our gunnery doesn't destroy the fellow, then we'll take him by the sword."

Dionne looked a little pale. "It isn't an easy matter, boarding an Englishman, m'sieu'. They fight like the very devil."

The tall officer's dark gaze transfixed Dionne, like a snake with a rabbit.

"Do I detect *fear*, Dionne?"

The handkerchief flew again. "No, no, m'sieu'. Of a certainty. It is simply the fact of the matter –"

Dionne trailed away, wilting back against the rail as the tall officer stepped close.

"Listen to me, you slack-bellied rodent," he hissed. "You will display for me and for these people a courageous certitude that taking the Englishman will be an easy matter. Because if you do not, I shall replace you as the *seconde* of this vessel. And enjoy cutting your throat in the bargain. Do you follow?"

Miserably Dionne nodded.

"M'sieu' le Comte de la Bourdonnais," went on the tall man, "will be pleased when we put in to Port Louis and inform him that this English vessel, about which he has undoubtedly been concerned, has been destroyed by *Achille*'s guns. And he will have little argument with my demand to be given a certain role in the squadron he has assembled for the descent on the Coromandel and that English fool, Peyton. All of this must come to pass, Dionne, or you will most certainly have to die, even if only to alleviate my anger a touch. Can I make things any clearer, in truth?"

Dionne shook his head, looking sick and pale in the growing light.

"Very well. Now get to your battery. Unless I'm mistaken, we'll have the cape abeam in a moment, and the rosbif will see us. With the windward gauge as we have, we should be on him before the turn of the glass."

"*Oui m'sieu'!*" The lieutenant put on his cocked hat and groped wretchedly down the waistdeck ladder.

"One other thing, Dionne."

"M'sieu'?"

"You'll hoist the red flag at our foretruck. And see that all hands hear the order for no quarter. I want every Englishman killed even if we have to do it like shooting rats in a tub. All of them!"

Dionne stared, aghast. "M'sieu', the rules of war do not –"

"I make my own rules, Dionne!" The tall officer's voice was like velvet-sheathed steel. "They are to die. And if you fail to execute that order, so shall you, of course."

The lieutenant nodded numbly, and went off along the waistdeck to a clutch of officers and warrant men who were waiting at the mainmast foot. As he began to speak to them, their faces turned up to the dark figure on the quarterdeck in shock and disbelief.

But their expressions were lost on the tall officer, who paced to the weather rail, ignoring the white-eyed crew of a six-pounder who crouched ready at their weapon nearby. He peered at the distant headland, thinking he could see the slim black pencil line of a masthead moving behind it.

"Come along, now. Come along and meet your destiny, Englishman!" murmured the Chevalier Rigaud de la Roche-Bourbon.

Achille was a heavily-armed ship, her seventy guns making her capable of 'lying in the line' of battle. On her upper, or weather decks, she carried six-pounders on the quarterdeck and long twelves in the waist. Below on her gun decks, she was armed with long eighteen-pounders, which gave her a full broadside of almost half a ton of flying cast iron. As she prepared to pounce on her unwary prey, those guns were being served by almost three hundred men, while others stood ready for the sailhandling orders the battle would bring.

Roche-Bourbon watched the headland intently. He could clearly see a break in the humped, tree-clad shape. A mast-head, with a tiny, faint flutter of colour. The foremast Jack. Now another, the mainmast, with a thin, snaking tendril of a commissioning pennant. Then a bowsprit and jib-boom, and suddenly the ship itself, a graceful forty-gunner, still and toylike over the grey water, ghosting along under head-sails and topsails. And there was the pathetic ruse of the Bourbon ensign, floating at the ensign staff.

"What a fool you are, Englishman!" Roche-Bourbon muttered to himself, with a smile. He cupped his hands to cry for the loosing of the topgallants, and in the bows a portfire arced down, and a pink flash and thump marked the firing of one of *Achille*'s long eighteen-pounder bow chasers.

Roche-Bourbon smirked in satisfaction as he saw the English vessel's foretopsail shiver, a neat black hole appearing in its grey surface.

"Up helm!" Roche-Bourbon cried, exulting. "Steer for him! Braces, Dionne, damn your fat hide! And the gun captain that misses his mark will feel the lash, I promise you all!"

And with new canvas rumpling out aloft, *Achille* surged down the wind towards her smaller prey.

Edward Mainwaring crouched in the shadows of the ox cart, waiting while a deckwatchman in a Portuguese stocking cap padded around the deck of the nearby *tartane*, spat over the ship's side, and went below. Mainwaring rose and, looking round to see that he was not readily visible in the mixture of moonlight and shadow, padded over to the edge of the basin and sank down behind a large tub which was speckled with gleaming fish scales and reeked of offal. Ignoring the ghastly stench, he quickly scanned the small sailing craft that lay tied there.

Several were ship's boats of the jolly boat variety, likely belonging to the vessels he could glimpse between the dark jettyside hulks, riding at anchor out in the silver-dappled harbour. There were two twenty-foot *chaloupes*, pudgy, lateen-rigged fishing boats with square-coaminged catch boxes amidships, and a grubby, fish-scaled look of hard work. One of these would do. The lateen yard, if he could hoist the thing alone, would give good speed, and would almost be self-tending, if he –

There was a sudden flash of movement inshore, along the facing walls of the houses and sheds that lined the dock road. Swiftly running figures ducked from shadow to shadow along the rutted road, perhaps half a dozen men in seamen's dress, with firelocks and cutlasses, and an oddly familiar look to them.

"No, this isn't possible!" breathed Mainwaring.

Now more men were appearing, pressing in single file like the seamen along the edge of the buildings, the firelocks ready at the Recover, a steady regularity to their progress.

At the head of them all, a slim officer in sombre clothes moved with lithe grace from doorway to doorway, a light hanger flashing in his hand. Beside him, the blade of a cutlass gleaming dully in his grip, was a thickset, burly man of muscular solidity.

Mainwaring's heart leaped. "Isaiah! And James! How in the name of God –"

At that point a doorway in the low guardhouse that flanked the *casernes*, where Mainwaring's drunken escort had vanished, banged open. A sentry, lit by the doorlight and clad in the white gaiters and linen summer uniform of the *Troupes de la Marine*, stepped briskly out on to the *pavé* and levelled his musket at the party as they froze motionless in the shadows.

"Alte, là! Qui vive?"

There was no answer or movement from the crouching figures, and the sentry advanced a few quick paces, the musket still levelled. He challenged again, his voice rising, a thud of shoes sounding in the guardroom behind him.

"At him, lads!"

It was James Howe's voice, clear in the still night air, and instantly there was a rush of running men, the scuff and clink of leather and metal, and the sentry went down with a muffled cry under a knot of figures. A knife blade gleamed in the moonlight, plunging down.

But now a dozen soldiers, several only partially dressed but all with bayonet-fixed muskets at the ready, were tumbling out of the guardhouse. As Mainwaring watched, they formed a ragged line, levelled their muskets, and fired in response to a shrieked command, the volley thunderous and uneven, the pink flames of firearms bright against the gloom. As the musket smoke swirled round the scene, a cry from the shadowed street indicated at least one of the Pallases had been hit.

Mainwaring was up and running, ignoring the sudden tumult and shouting on the dark decks of the ships behind him. He sprinted over the dirt and *pavé* of the jetty towards the line of *fusiliers*, seeing several of them fire again, a flash of answering flame here and there from the shadowy positions of the Pallases. As he ran, Mainwaring's mind was soundlessly willing them to fire back. Then it struck him that Howe or Hooke, sensible men both, would probably have kept the men from priming and loading their firelocks to avoid an unplanned discharge. The orders would have been to use cold steel, in silence: the dreaded trademark of a British night attack. Now they were likely scrabbling furiously at their cartridge boxes as the French prepared to fire again.

Now Mainwaring was there, the backs of the French ghostly white before him, one in the gold-laced coat of a *sergent* responding to a sudden sense, and turning in wide-eyed astonishment to see a barefoot, ragged figure sprinting with lowered shoulders and launching himself through the air at knee-height at the back of the line of musketmen.

Mainwaring's body cannoned into two men with grunting force, and with a curse and a squeal they went down, slamming hard to the ground in a welter of cartridge-box belts and flying coattails. Mainwaring felt one man land hard on his back, and he forced himself to keep rolling, kicking upward to push the man off. From somewhere he heard an English voice bellowing, and a storm of flying fists, thudding kicks, and the curse and scuffle of desperately struggling men surrounded him. A musket blast beside his right ear rocked him, the flash blinding in the night, and in the next half-second a musket butt thudded into his stomach as he struggled to his feet. Nausea washed over him, and he clutched at the weapon as he fell back, hard and painfully, to the ground. The weapon came away from its owner's grip as Mainwaring twisted it with a gasp of effort, and with some reserve of energy rolled over to his knees and then to his feet in a crouch, a struggling mass of men surrounding him, steel clashing against steel, and now a gurgling shriek proving a blade had found its mark.

Mainwaring was thrusting the bayonet before him when suddenly a French musketman was there, staring at him wild-eyed and hatless for an instant before throwing his own musket to the shoulder and firing point-blank at Mainwaring's face. As Mainwaring saw the flash in the pan he turned his head, and as the thunderous blast of the weapon enveloped him, he felt a lancet of pain across the top of his shoulder. Then he was lunging forward with the bayonet into the reek of smoke. The blade struck home, sunk to the socket in the Frenchman's stomach, and the man dropped his own weapon with a clatter, staggering back with his hands clutched round Mainwaring's musket barrel, a thin, high scream issuing from the horrified mask of the man's face. Still staring at Mainwaring, the Frenchman sat down heavily as a bloody froth burst from his lips, and then sagged to one side, limp in death.

A new wave of nausea overcame Mainwaring, and he staggered back, releasing his grip on the blood-sticky weapon to put his hands on his knees and be wretchedly sick on the sodden ground. The retching passed, and as he straightened he was aware that the fighting was over, and that only in the distance were voices still shouting in alarm, and feet pounding on ships' decks or on laneway *pavé*.

"Christ, we're for it now, zur!" an English voice was saying. "Th'alarm's up, sartin!"

But the figures were gathered around Mainwaring and one of them was James Howe, staring in wonder.

"*Captain?* Is it *you*, sir?"

Mainwaring managed a thin laugh, wiping the back of his mouth with his hand. He wished the terrible trembling in his body would stop.

"I may look somewhat ropey, James, but it is me, all right. What the devil are you doing here?"

His words were lost in a rush of affectionate and relieved laughter as the men crowded round him in a knot, ignoring the twisted corpses at their feet and the tumult sounding in the ships and in the darkened buildings. James Howe, reticence and reserve gone for the moment, was embracing Mainwaring in a hug of surprising strength, soon joined by the vicelike grip of Isaiah Hooke's brawny arms.

"Gentlemen, we can't go on meeting like this or you'll have to make an honest woman of me!" Mainwaring gasped.

With a burst of embarrassed laughter, both men released him. All around, Mainwaring could see the warm, exultant grins, and there was a tightening in his own throat so that for a moment he could not speak.

"Lor' lummee, zur, but you be a soight!" growled Isaiah Hooke, huge in the moonlight. "You look as if you've been sojerin' about in a cable tier. Beggin' yer pardon, zur."

"Close enough, Isaiah. I was in a damned prison, in

81

fact. But I think we'd best save our explanations for later!" Mainwaring peered round. "Who've you got here, Mr Howe?"

"Besides Mr Hooke and myself, nine men, sir. Seven here, and two back at the boat."

Mainwaring nodded. "No one hurt in that fight? I thought –"

"That was me, sir," said a voice that Mainwaring recognised as Winton's. "Bugger shot me earrin' off, is all. Gave vent t' me feelin's, so t' speak, sir."

Mainwaring grinned. Then he spun to look at the *casernes*. There was the thunder of running feet within now, and a drum was thumping urgently.

"James, we've got to get out of here. Where is the boat?"

"Just round the harbour mouth, sir, past a brackish pond, on a spit o' beach, hidden in a few low bushes."

Mainwaring bent and picked up a French musket. Grimacing, he wrestled a cartridge box from one of the corpses and slung it over his shoulder.

"Right, then, we'd best get to it, and on the run. Go!"

With Howe in the lead, the little knot of men moved off at a hunched, watchful run along the shadowed street, leaving the sprawled and bloody bodies of the French lying where they had fallen in the cold moonlight.

The smoke of *Achille*'s guns still poured up the open companionways and swirled aft over the French vessel's quarterdeck, to where the Chevalier Rigaud de la Roche-Bourbon stood in the centre of a group of officers. Above them, the white ensign of the Bourbons curled in pale majesty over the men clearing away the gun tools of the quarter-deck battery.

Roche-Bourbon flexed the steel of his sword blade in two hands and looked with satisfaction off to leeward where the battered and smoking hulk of His Britannic Majesty's Ship *Pallas* sank lower and lower in the water, surrounded by floating wreckage and the still forms of dead men.

On *Achille*'s crowded decks, her gun crews gleefully thumped one another on the shoulders and jabbered excitedly, until the entire ship was a scene of hooting and celebration. A few hands were tugging at sheets and braces, and *Achille* began to foot ahead slowly with the breeze that was returning after dying at the first blasts of the gunnery, when *Achille* had begun her swift and brutal destruction of her English prey.

Roche-Bourbon smiled. The English had never managed to fight back with their usual cohesion or power. *Achille* had rushed down on the frigate almost as soon as she had cleared the headland, and it was obvious that the English vessel had not been at Quarters, for its drums had begun to beat only moments before *Achille*'s first broadside had roared out. Roche-Bourbon had given the hapless *Pallas* the larboard battery, then worn *Achille* about and finished the English vessel with a devastating, short-range salvo from the starboard battery. Holed below the waterline and sinking within five minutes of *Achille*'s first fire, *Pallas* had been abandoned by her company. Those who had reached the French ship's side had been hauled aboard and thrust into a sitting group in the waist. But the *Troupes de la Marine* musketmen were only now ending their deliberate sniping at the struggling Englishmen still clinging to wreckage, one by one putting an end to their cries.

Roche-Bourbon beamed in pleasure as *Pallas* heeled slowly to one side, lifted her jib-boom like a lance to the sky, and then with a deep rumbling hiss of escaping air, slid backwards into the deep. In a moment, there was only a swirling eddy on the face of the sea littered with the bits of wreckage and floating bodies of dead men. Already, gulls were beginning to circle, their cries plaintive and expectant.

Dionne approached the quarterdeck ladder, lifting his hat as he looked up at Roche-Bourbon.

"These prisoners, m'sieu'," he said, looking over his shoulder at the twenty-odd men who sat huddled in the waist, guarded by several of the *Troupes*. "What are your orders? Shall I have them out below until –"

"*Below?* Why, Dionne?"

"To secure them until we return to harbour, m'sieu'."

"Dionne, did I not tell you to give no quarter? Surely your way is clear, *hein?*"

The lieutenant stared. "I don't understand, m'sieu'."

"Don't you?" Roche-Bourbon's voice was smooth. "Your musketmen require some practice shooting at marks. You've done a bit already. Over the side with the lot of them, and we'll stay hove to until all the 'marks' are satisfactorily dealt with. Clear?"

"M'sieu', have we not killed enough? These men –"

"These men will be put to death in the manner I have ordered, Dionne," said Roche-Bourbon in a steely voice, "or I shall see *you* at a yardarm. Now, had you best not get on with it?"

The lieutenant's face was like pale stone. He turned and gave several clipped orders, and in a moment the English were being thrust out of the entry port, voices raised in anger and pleading. As they struck the water, splashing in frantic despair, the bark of the muskets began, the musketmen jostling one another at the rail for the clearest shot.

Dionne stood at the rail, listening to the steady firing and hearing the screams and splashing below, his face expressionless. But a tear coursed from one eye down his cheek, and his hands gripped the rail with such force that his fingers turned white.

It seemed to Mainwaring that they had been running for hours. Behind him, Isaiah Hooke was gasping with all the effort of a surfacing whale, and as they approached the end of the narrow street, Mainwaring barked out a call to halt.

"Over here, lads! In the shelter of this tree!"

With a rush of feet and the slap and clink of their accoutrements, the men followed Mainwaring into the shadows of an enormous, umbrella-like tree, the dark ground below dappled with moonlight. They crouched in a circle round him, wiping their foreheads with their sleeves and spitting off to one side, their eyes white in the gloom.

"What time do you make it, James?" asked Mainwaring.

"Almost first light, sir. You can see it warming a touch, to the east, there."

"You've a boat? I presume that's how you got here."

Howe grinned. "Aye, sir. Ahead, there, past that cluster of low huts, the cart track angles off round the harbour on its right shore. There's a point o' land, and one o' the two harbour-mouth forts. The spit runs off to the north from it, enclosing a tidal pond. The boat's hidden in some bracken there. Two of Fell's men are with it."

"How far?"

"Half a mile, sir, no more."

Mainwaring peered back along the road. "There were lanterns moving about the harbour and it'll only be a matter of moments before a pursuit party comes after us. Pray God they're not mounted. We've got to move quickly, and I need to know if any man can't keep up. What about you, Mr Hooke?"

Isaiah Hooke ran fingers through his shaggy hair. "Do me best, is all, zur. I be no buggerin' dune dodger."

Mainwaring grinned. Then he froze, listening intently. Faintly over the night air, from back in the harbour area whence they had come, the sound of a cavalry bugle was carrying, with shouts and calls of many men.

"Christ!" Mainwaring spat. "Horsemen, more'n likely. Listen carefully, lads. Who've we got here?"

James Howe was pointing. "With myself and Mr Hooke, we've Slade, Sawyer, Jackman and Winton, sir. Of the marines, Sergeant Fell has Willis and Pasco."

"Oi've put Delvin an' 'Arris as guards on th' boat, sir, beggin' yer pardon," said the burly sea-regiment sergeant.

"All right. We'll move out now, in two files, one to either side of the cart track. If I make this signal," and here Mainwaring made a sideways motion with his arm, everyone moves immediately to cover off the cart track. No one crosses it. Clear?"

The men nodded.

"Good. Mr Howe, you'll take the starboard file. I'll take the larboard. Sergeant Fell and the marines, with Mr Howe. Mr Hooke and the others, with me. Now, where's Slade and Sawyer?"

"Here, sir." The two small and wiry men were so similar they could have been brothers, yet sprang from the opposite sides of the Atlantic.

"Good. Sink me, you're like peas in a pod. Slade, you'll put yourself twenty yards ahead of us, but on one side or the other. Get back to me, silently, if you see ought that's amiss. Sawyer, you'll fall in astern of us, likewise. Watch our wake for the pursuit. Clear to all?"

Again there was a general nodding of heads, and the men rose from their haunches as if on signal.

"Good." Mainwaring glanced at the sky, which was becoming a pinkish grey. He could almost distinguish the men's features. "We've no time to lose if we want to get to the boat before full sunrise. Fall in on the track, and quickly!"

As they trotted out on to the road, Mainwaring took James Howe's free arm. "James, what of *Pallas*?" he asked in an undertone.

"I left Stephen in command, sir. She's cruising between a point off this harbour and Cap Malheureux, with orders to watch for us, or for a signal of some kind. If we can sail or pull out without the Frogs cutting us off, he should see us, sir. Why?"

Mainwaring shook his head. "I don't know, James. Just an odd, troubled feeling about the ship." He hefted the French musket in his free hand. "No matter, we'll soon see." He raised his voice. "Right, lads. Let's find the bloody boat!"

The retreat to the boat soon became an endurance test for the men, muscularly strong but unused to the demands of a long march after months at sea. Howe and Mainwaring kept up a good pace, Mainwaring for his part cursing and limping as the rough road cut into his bare feet. They were determined to avoid being run down by the pursuit they all sensed was building behind them. Ahead, Slade's small form flitted in and out of the shadows from the overhanging trees, the light becoming greyer all the while, his cartridge box's shiny flap gleaming dully at his hip. Howe kept his file staggered back from Mainwaring's along the cart track's edge, and the men were wide-eyed and watchful as they dog-shuffled along, muskets held cradled outward in their arms, their eyes peering into each dark doorway and narrow lane as they swept past. The cart track remained deserted save for themselves, and the two files of men trotted and stumbled on, the only sounds the kick and scuff of their feet, the slap of leather and accoutrement, and the heavy breathing as each man strove to keep up. Their clothing was sombre and dark, the seamen in the dark slop jackets that Howe had issued, and the sea-regiment men in the brick-red sleeved waistcoats that turned an innocuous grey in the dim light. Fell's men wore odd little cut-down felt caps rather than their unwieldy mitres, and to any watchful eye only the crossed buff belting of the marines made any mark to aim by on the quickly moving party.

Sawyer came pelting up from behind, his bare feet slapping on the hard clay of the cartway.

"Cap'n!" he panted. "Dragoons, sir, a goddamned packet of 'em, comin' up astern, all sheets to th' knot!"

"Halt, lads!" At Mainwaring's bark the two files stopped, crouching where they stood. Howe trotted to Mainwaring as the latter peered down the cart track, swearing softly.

Sawyer was pointing. "There, sir! See 'em?"

At the far visible end of the narrow road, in the small space between the low and shuttered houses, Mainwaring could see a dark mass of horsemen, the dim light gleaming off breastplates and heavy, straight-bladed swords carried high. Pressed together in the confines of the track, the horse-men were at virtually full gallop, two and perhaps three abreast, a cloud of dust boiling up behind their black shapes, the thunder of their hooves carrying clear on the air.

Glancing quickly around, Mainwaring saw to the right a narrow lane that ended at a wall and, to the other side, a shallow courtyard of a barred and shuttered single-storey house. Ahead and behind were still more buildings. It was a good two hundred yards to the nearest lane off to one side, or to the end of the row of houses, behind which lay the bracken and open, sandy soil of the harbourside point of land.

"But they'd cut us to pieces in the open!" Mainwaring muttered. Then he raised his voice in sharp command. "Sergeant Fell! You and your lads, with Slade and Sawyer, form a kneeling line across the road, evenly spaced! Quickly!"

"Sir, what –?" began Howe, as beside him the wide-eyed Slade came panting in from his leading post.

"Not *now*, James! Prime and load, Fell! James, fall in beside 'em on the right flank, by the wall! On your right knee, lads! Loaded? Good! Move quickly, now!"

Sensing what Mainwaring wanted, the sea-regiment men and the two little topmen sprang into a rough line, the road so narrow that Fell on one side and Howe on the other almost touched the rough-plastered house walls with their elbows. They dropped to one knee, hurriedly checking their priming or frantically tearing at cartridges with their teeth, their faces pale and set. The moving black and silver mass of the horsemen were no more than five hundred yards away, thundering at them at full gallop, jostling and clink-ing against one another in the narrow cartway.

"Mr Hooke and the rest! A *standing* rank now, behind the first! Lock up, so your musket muzzle projects ahead of your shipmate below you! Primed and loaded? Good! Hold at the Recover, ready t' fire on my order! *And only on my order*, d'ye hear? Winton, you've lost your priming. Keep your pan tightly shut! Steady, now, steady."

The horsemen were two hundred yards away, coming on at a frightening rate, huge in the morning light. They were big men, in dull, silvery breastplates and blue uniform, with broad cocked hats alight with white Bourbon plumes, long dragoon swords angled ahead towards Mainwaring and his men, the horses' heads lifting and plunging, eyes wild and nostrils flaring, a thunder of hooves and jangling tack filling the narrow cartway, the horsemen so huge suddenly and rushing at them so quickly it seemed impossible for them to do anything but trample and crush Mainwaring's men like so many insects. On they came, the horses black and lathered, brushing against the house walls, shouldering into one another, their hooves a deep, sonorous drumbeat. The sword blades gleamed, the men's faces split in a high, keening, killing cry that sent a chill down Mainwaring's spine.

"Christ, sir!" cried Jackman, at his elbow. "Let us fire, sir!"

"*No!* Wait for my order, damn you!" Mainwaring quickly checked the priming of his own musket, hefted it to the Recover, and spat into the dirt behind him. His knees were trembling uncontrollably.

Now the horsemen were barely a hundred yards away along the cartway. Now fifty. The thunder of their rush filled the narrow space and the ground shook underfoot. In a moment it would be all over. The huge, powerful horses and their steel-clad riders would strike like an avalanche at the pathetic double line of waiting Englishmen, smashing them down like clay dolls and crushing them as they died, screaming in dust-caked agony under the pounding, steel-shod hooves, and the terrible, glittering long swords.

"Front rank!" Mainwaring cried. "At the horses! Make ready! Present! *Fire!*"

The muskets fired almost as one, a thunderclap of sound in the narrow space, the muzzle flashes and pink pan 'huff' brilliant in the gloom, a sudden wall of smoke obliterating the nightmarish dark mass of the horsemen. There was a hideous scream from somewhere ahead, and two horses were tumbling, rolling, hooves kicking skyward, other beasts beside them leaping high to clear them, only to trip and crash to the ground in earth-shuddering impacts. The breastplated men astride the huge beasts went crashing to the dirt in a welter of coattails and flying cocked hats, their curses and shrieks loud in the cartway.

"Rear rank! Make ready! Present! *Fire!*" shrieked Mainwaring. His own musket came level. Ahead in the smoke he saw an enormous black horse towering above him, struggling to extricate itself from the kicking mass of fallen men and horses underfoot, its rider hatless and bellowing, his tall dragoon boots gleaming with polish. At his own command Mainwaring pulled the trigger, and with the others his own weapon fired with a terrific bang, the weapon bucking hard against his shoulder, the pan flash singeing his cheek, a wall of reeking smoke before him.

He was scrabbling at his cartridge box, hands trembling, unable to see in the inky stench of the smoke, his ears deafened with a horrid cacophony of horses' screams, the curse and bellow of men, a wild thumping and jangling of struggling animal and man. His own voice was shrieking out again, even as he moved with frantic effort through the motions of loading the firelock.

"Front rank! Make ready! P'sent! *Fire!*"

Again the muskets fired, and before him Mainwaring sensed rather than saw the kneeling row of Howe's men, their weapons spitting out the pink lancets of flame, the smoke so acrid and thick that Mainwaring was coughing uncontrollably. The din from the struggling horses and riders, a dark, surging mass beyond the smoke, was unspeakable. Again his voice sounded, cracking now with strain.

"Rear rank! Make ready! P'sent! *Fire*, damn you!"

The volley banged out, Mainwaring's musket punching hard at his shoulder. Then an enormous dark shape appeared before him, looming up in a strange slowed motion, resolving into the shape of a dark horse and hatless, sword-whirling rider, the horse's hooves drawn up as it leaped, a dark shadow through the smoke, vaulting up and over the two lines of Englishmen. Mainwaring ducked low, feeling the great hooves brush past his scalp. Then the horse struck, already mortally wounded, its forelegs giving way, the vast, round-bellied body crashing in a tremendous tumble to the earth, all flailing hooves and jangling tack, the wretched animal screaming in an ear-splitting steady shriek, bright arterial blood pulsing in arcs from a ghastly crater in its neck.

The rider was suddenly there, thrown clear and rising to his feet, emerging back at a run through the smoke. A tall man, taller than Mainwaring, his enormous dragoon boots and the gleaming breastplate made him huge in the gloom. He was hatless, his unqueued hair swinging about his shoulders, his dark face full of fury as he lunged towards Mainwaring's head, aiming a swinging, two-handed cut of the long dragoon sword that would have split the American to the groin.

At the last second Mainwaring reacted, throwing his musket up over his head in a guard position, the blade of the sword gonging like a bell as it struck, so powerfully that Mainwaring's arms gave way, and his own musket hit him painfully on the crown of his head. He fell with a grunt to one knee, and the Frenchman was recovering, the great blade glinting and then whirling in from the side, aimed to lift Mainwaring's head from his shoulders. With a gasp Mainwaring crouched beneath the blow, hearing the blade hum like a bird's wing as it passed over his head, and then drove the reversed butt of his musket into the man's groin in a lifting, uppercut blow. The Frenchman's eyes clouded, and he staggered back in a half-crouch, the dragoon sword clattering to the ground. Mainwaring's hands joined at the muzzle of his musket, and with all his strength he swung the butt end in a roundhouse, clubbing blow to the man's head. The sickening crunch of the impact snapped the musket cleanly at the small of the butt, and the dragoon spun like a hunched, hideous top before his knees gave way and he collapsed, bloody froth pouring from his nose and mouth.

Mainwaring threw down the ruined musket and spun. The lane was thick with smoke, and the dark shapes of several fallen horses struggled and heaved, shrieking and whinnying. Howe and the others, Mainwaring realised, had fired again by ranks on their own, and were feverishly reloading.

"Front rank, *stand*!" Mainwaring croaked. "Together, now! Primed and loaded? Very well!" He coughed, willing back a retch and the shaking weakness in his legs. "Make ready! Present! And *fire*!"

All nine muskets fired as one, the report deafening, the muzzle and pan flash painfully bright, but muted now in the thick smoke that choked the scene and obliterated whatever carnage was taking place.

"This way, lads!" Mainwaring cried, his voice cracking. "Come on!" He stooped to grab the dead dragoon's sword, stepped awkwardly over the twitching legs of the dying horse, and staggered off, almost losing his balance as he slithered in an enormous, steaming pool of the horse's blood. Stumbling on, he could hear the others behind him, cursing and coughing as they ran, with the voices of Hooke and Howe urging them on.

For several minutes they forced themselves on, until they had cleared the last of the closely-set houses and the grey morning light showed the harbour waters with the anchored dark hulks of ships off to the left and they were moving forward under overhanging palmetto on a deserted, sandy beach track. Mainwaring pointed to a broad tree whose branches hung almost to the ground, affording a kind of shelter.

"In here, lads, rest for a bit," he gasped, and turned in, slumping to the ground. In a minute the others had sunk down beside him, gasping with exhaustion and strain, their faces and hands black with powder, their clothes soaked with sweat and streaked with sprays of dried blood.

"Mr Howe," Mainwaring called, forcing himself up on to his knees. "Casualties. Anyone?"

Howe was sitting with his head in his hands. One sleeve was torn away, revealing a deep, purplish wound from which blood was slowly oozing.

"Pasco, sir. Pistol ball, I think. Left him there. No one else."

"Your arm, James. Can you –"

"I'm all right, sir."

"I'll see to it, sir." It was Winton, rising to his knees and tearing off a strip of his own shirttail. "Always said I'd give the shirt off me back to proper officers."

Howe grinned weakly. "Don't expect favours, Winton. I'm on to your games."

Winton was deftly binding the wound. "Not me, sir. Just you belay talkin' a spell while I lashes you up, sir. Beggin' yer pardon."

Mainwaring looked round the slumped men. "Anyone carrying a canteen or gourd? Good, Sergeant Fell. Share it out, will you? Mouthful or two per man, only. And chew some biscuit if you've got any." He ignored the aching hunger very evident in his own innards, rose, and padded over to Hooke.

"Isaiah," he said, quietly. "How far is the boat? We may have delayed the pursuit by half an hour or so with that bloody business, but no more. And with the men as worn as they are –" He did not finish.

Hooke sat up, pushing back a shock of his grey-shot blond hair. He was pointing.

"That way, zur. Over that line o' dunes. Get round some o' that palm an' you can spy th' 'arbour-mouth fort, zur. If we keep down in th' dunes, in th' 'ollows so's the gunners don't see, it's no more'n a couple o' cables away. Do it in minutes, zur."

Mainwaring spotted Slade, the wiry little Cockney, who

was kneeling half-hidden in a palmetto clump on the far side of the track, still carrying out his picket's role.

"Slade? What d'ye mark?" he called in a low voice.

"Nought, sir," came the whispered reply. "I c'n see some o' th' townsfolk out, looking at th' dead sowjers, sir."

"No more pursuit?"

"Not a bleedin' fing, sir."

Mainwaring nodded, his lips a tight line. It was clear that they had earned a breathing space with the bloody repulse of the dragoons. The French would know, however, that they were dealing with an armed party rather than a group of bandits or shipwrecked buccaneers. That meant the next force sent after them, by road or by boat, would be adequate to do the job.

"It'll be horsemen again," Mainwaring muttered to himself. "Horsemen. If they are clever enough to deduce we have a boat on the shore, and send horsemen to get *between* us and the boat –"

"Sorry, sir?" It was Howe, arriving at his elbow.

"Nothing, James. We've got to get moving. They'll be on to us again in minutes, if I know the French." Mainwaring rose, and pushed his cartridge box back on his hip. He looked at the long, brutal blade of the dragoon's sword and shuddered at its efficient killing design. But for luck they might all have been dead back there, hacked to death with these terrible weapons. He spat and shook the thought from his mind.

"Anyone else hurt?" he asked quietly, walking round the slumped and panting men. "Can ye walk or run, as needs be? Good. On your feet, then, lads. We've a boat to get to."

As the men struggled to their feet, their kit clinking about them, Mainwaring stepped out through the palmetto fronds and squinted both ways along the cart track.

"Still nought, zur," said the half-hidden Slade.

"Very good. Fall in ahead of us. Come on, lads, form your two files. How's that arm, James?"

Howe winced as he slung his musket over one shoulder.

"Damned painful, sir, but Winton lashed it up well enough. I'll do."

"Good. Now, lads, keep your firelocks primed and loaded and don't sling 'em unless you have to. Muzzles outboard, same formation as before, and eyes and ears open. Not a word, mind. To the front, march!"

They shuffled off into the dunes, following Slade as he picked a ducking and weaving path through the sand hills and sharp grass that kept them hidden from the boats and ships in the harbour, from the watchful eyes that presumably were there on the low ramparts of the harbour-mouth fort, after the din of the little battle. They were angling away from the harbour towards the shores of the shallow tidal pond that Howe told Mainwaring was called the Mer Rouge. *Pallas'* longboat was hidden on the long spit that cut the Mer Rouge off from the sea; hopefully it was still there, along with Fell's men. As Mainwaring trudged quickly along, he looked towards the brightening pink and orange of the dawn sky to the east, trying not to think of what might happen if the boat were not there. A last stand in the dunes, being overwhelmed by a superior force of grim French anxious to avenge their dead was not an appealing thought.

In a few moments they were splashing along in the warm, sandy shallows of the Mer Rouge, a great heron flapping slowly away in long-legged dignity as the two files of stumbling men pushed out of the waist-high grass. To the left, the play of palmetto-cloaked dunes hid them well. The seaward rise of the sand spit loomed in front of them and a moment later they were toiling up its ankle-deep, maddening sand slope, glancing anxiously over their shoulders as they gasped and puffed their way up. Now they were on the crest of the spit and could look back at the town and harbour, but they knew only too well that they were silhouetted clearly against the horizon.

Howe panted up to Mainwaring, pointing. "There, sir, the second thicket, past the log."

As Mainwaring peered, a figure in a brick-red sleeved waistcoat emerged cautiously from the cover of the low vegetation, and then waved them on.

"Harris. Good show!" breathed Howe. "We're all right, sir."

"We can but hope. Come on, lads, down off the skyline and to the boat, smartly!"

As the group straggled in through the sand to the thicket, the two sea-regiment men were grinning at them, and then stared in astonishment at Mainwaring.

"Report, lads," said Mainwaring, amused at their expressions. "And, yes, it is me. Did ought occur?"

The thin, red-haired man called Harris nodded under his odd round cut-down cap. "Riders, sir. There was nought durin' the night, then about first light there was a bit o' musketry in towards th' town, an' riders 'ave been out on th' dunes ever since. Three of 'em, dragoons by the look, cantered by 'ere scarce ten minutes or so ago, sir."

"Christ!" muttered Mainwaring. "Our luck's getting a fraction thin."

"A pure wonderment they didn't see you, sir," said the man.

"Indeed." Mainwaring turned to Howe. "They'll be back, any moment, once they realise we've come this way and not gone round the inshore track. Get the boat into the water, James, and quickly!"

"Sir!" Howe was suddenly all vigorous movement, the arm and its bloody bandage momentarily forgotten. "Set to, lads! Get that brush cleared away! Slade and Sawyer, find us some driftwood to use as a roller, to push 'er off! Lively now!"

It took several minutes of feverish work to clear away the carefully-created screen of palmetto branches that had hidden the longboat. Soon all hands were lined along the gunwales of the craft – which Mainwaring saw unveiled with a burst of inner emotion so strong that he hid it with difficulty – and with a gruff "Two t' six, 'eave!" from Hooke, the heavy boat rumbled over the few logs that Slade and his mate had found, and then was sliding over the dark, wet sand at water's edge until with a final shove she rode clear in the shallows. While a few men held the boat, the remainder waded out and wrestled themselves over the gunwales, dripping and awkward, until they were all in. The last to board was Slade, and as Mainwaring nodded to Hooke he hauled the little man bodily in over the quarter.

"Out oars, Mr Hooke, and pull to seaward, smart as you can! Set that tiller bar in place, Slade. My, but aren't you a wet dog come in out of the rain! Mr Howe?"

"Sir?" Howe was across from Mainwaring in the stern-sheets, wrestling off his musket with his good arm.

"Can you step her masts for sailing?"

"Aye, aye, sir!" said Howe, the musket clattering on the floorboards. "Come on, there, Winton, pitch in with that foremast. Jackman and you two, on the main. Loft 'em up. Lively, now, all!"

Hooke poured forth a stream of imaginative curses and oath-laced orders until he had the marines gathered at the boat's oars, and they had wrestled them awkwardly but willingly on to their thole-pins and begun to pull the heavy craft forward. The sea was calm with an offshore breeze, and the creak-thump of the oars steadied into a creditable rhythm as they worked the boat away from the broad sandy beach. In a welter of confusion, the men struggling to step the masts and clear away the lugsails for hoisting clambered around and over the marines as they pulled. Each man knew that they were still dreadfully exposed to view, particularly from the grim little harbour-mouth fort off to their left, but were now almost beyond musket shot of the beach.

"Riders, sir!" burst out Fell, who was stroke oar. "More o' them buggerin' dragoons, likely!"

Mainwaring spun in the sternsheets. Half a dozen horsemen with the same blue and steel appearance of the dragoons they had fought in the streets of Port Louis, were thundering and splashing along the water's edge from the direction of the fort. They reined in to a stamping, whirling halt where the longboat had slid into the water, voices raised in frustration and anger. Suddenly a ripple of white puffs appeared and several little geysers of water spat upward half-way to shore as the pop of the pistols reached the boat.

"Too bloody late, mongsewer!" breathed Fell, with an extra strong tug at his oar.

"There'll be more after us than dragoons on a beach," said Mainwaring, his expression hard. "The masts, Mr Howe!"

"Raising now, sir. Mind yourselves, there. Jackman, slide over a foot or so. Winton, the larboard shroud there is fouled on the bow's thole-pin. Handsomely with it, now. We can't afford to have anything carry away."

Several more minutes of sweating effort saw both masts stepped, the oars brought aboard with much thumping and cursing as they were lain fore and aft along the thwarts, and the sheets cleared away to run.

"Halyards, Mr Hooke. I'd be obliged if you and Sawyer would hoist the main. Jackman and Winton, the fore." Howe was holding his wounded arm and looked pale. "Haul away, now, together!"

The dark sails rumpled and thumped as the yards creaked up, and soon the sheets were being hauled in as the halyards were belayed round their pins. Mainwaring settled himself at the tiller, content to let Howe see to the hoist and set of the sails, although looking at him with a worried expression. Soon even Howe was beaming, the colour returning to his cheeks as the boat lay over gently and began to foot along before the offshore breeze.

"I'm going to stand out till we're beyond gun range, and then work nor'rard along the shore, James," said Mainwaring. "If *Pallas* is there, we should see her in a matter of hours, I'd think?"

"Yes, sir. I'm surprised she's not visible now. A Frenchman may have caused Stephen to stand off for a bit. If we can hold one good alongshore beat we could be off Cap Malheureux before nightfall, sir. Bound to see her then."

"I bloody well hope so, James. Damned inconvenient if he's off dodging some Froggy frigate while we sit out here at the mercy of the elements and any other Frenchman who comes along." Mainwaring realised with a start that he was ravenously hungry. "What did ye strike into the boat as stores, James?"

Howe grinned. "Thought you'd never ask, sir. Butt o' water, for'rard of the main, as usual. An extra breadbag. And a small cask o' rum, which I'm glad to see Harris and his mate left well enough alone."

"Thank Christ! Then break out bread and water for all, if you please, James," said Mainwaring. "And I want to take another look at that arm of yours. In honour of that, I'll trouble you to serve out a double tot, all round. 'Nancy Dawson' sounds like a good tune to hear just now, but we lack a fiddler!"

There was a cheer from the men crowded in the boat, and Mainwaring saw with a start how dirty and tired they looked. But they were grinning at one another, and Mainwaring realised how desperately proud of them he was.

"Your thoughts, James?" he asked quietly, as he saw Howe looking at him darkly.

"I'm bloody worried, sir," Howe replied in a voice only Mainwaring was meant to hear. "We should have seen *Pallas* by now. There was no weather to drive her offshore and I can't think Stephen would have let himself be driven off hull-down by a Frenchman, so as to lose sight of us. I don't like it."

"You're quite certain Stephen knew what he was meant to do?"

"Yes, sir. She should be out here, sir. But she isn't."

Mainwaring pursed his lips. "All right, James. Not a word of our concerns to the men, yet. We'll stand along to the cape and hope for the best. If she's gone –" He shook his head. "If she's gone, we'll have to think very carefully what next to do."

He spat thoughtfully over the side, and squinted up at the sails again.

"*Very* carefully, indeed!"

His Most Christian Majesty's Ship *Achille* swung slowly to her newly-dropped anchor in the small harbour of Mahébourg on the south-east shore of the Ile de France. The Chevalier Rigaud de la Roche-Bourbon smiled with satisfaction as he watched the canvas aloft being furled with great care and exactness. The thoroughness with which he had seen to the killing of the crew of the defeated English frigate seemed to have brought about a change in the spirit of *Achille*'s people. Now each order was carried out with fearful alacrity and that pleased Roche-Bourbon, who had a marked distaste for tasks done untidily.

Now he looked shoreward, where the somewhat smaller *Neptune*, pierced for fifty guns or so but only, he remembered, carrying some thirty-four, rode at anchor. Roche-Bourbon knew that *Neptune* had come around from Port Louis earlier the previous day, and although the *Neptune*'s captain was a fat fool who deserved little respect, the governor himself had come round in the ship to see the vessels anchored at Mahébourg, and now, it would appear, to visit *Achille*.

Roche-Bourbon shot a cuff. He had his instructions and papers in order, of course, and the governor would find little to quibble about.

"Deck, there!" came a call from the deckwatchman Roche-Bourbon had sent aloft. "Boat approaching, m'sieu'! It carries the governor's pennant!"

Roche-Bourbon looked into the waist where Dionne was hastily assembling a side party at the entry port. The Chevalier looked away, stifling a yawn: Dionne could worry about such inconsequential details. But there would be no avoiding the governor, he thought, as the latter's boat came alongside *Achille*, her oars tossed smartly as she hooked on.

A few moments later Bernard François Mahé, Comte de la Bourdonnais, governor of Ile de France and Ile de Bourbon, after whom the harbour in which the ships rode had recently been named, was standing on *Achille*'s quarterdeck, staring in astonishment at an elegantly bowing Roche-Bourbon.

"You did *what*?" burst out La Bourdonnais, who was a short, wiry man of dark intensity.

"It saved Your Excellency the necessity of keeping and hanging prisoners, or housing them, of course. Surely you would agree with such a measure of economy?"

"Did no one survive?" asked the governor, his face ashen.

"To the best of my ability, I trust not," Roche-Bourbon replied languidly.

The governor stared at him. "Do you realise what you've done, Rigaud? That wasn't war, that was murder!" La Bourdonnais' face was clouded with anger and disbelief. "You are burdened with the responsibilities both of command of a king's ship and the conduct of a gentleman. Which of these, may I ask, encompasses the slaughter of a surrendered English ship's company?"

"The reality of war, m'sieu'."

La Bourdonnais' eyes narrowed in cold fury. "The reality I am aware of provides for desperate struggle when the occasion demands but clemency and humanity when possible, never the butchery of a helpless opponent."

"Then, with respect, m'sieu', we share a differing view of war's reality."

La Bourdonnais' face turned to stone. "Were I not forced to rely upon both you and this ship to form the core of my squadron for the attack on Peyton on the Coromandel, Rigaud, I should relieve you of your command. Your lack of ethical sense disgusts me." His eyes glittered. "But I need you. In future I will expect you to behave with the civility I require from each and every officer under my command!"

Roche-Bourbon removed his egret-edged cocked hat in a small bow that barely stopped short of mockery.

"As you wish, of course, m'sieu'," he said lightly.

"Very well. I will see your orders presently. You have been, I trust, instructed in formal terms to be part of my squadron against the English in India?"

"Indeed."

"*Bon.* I have the *Neptune*, for which I have managed to cobble together but thirty-four guns. The *Bourbon*, thirty-six, and the *Duc d'Orléans*, twenty-six, are also carrying less than they are pierced for, more's the pity. The others, *Phénix*, *Saint-Louis*, *Lys* and *Insulaire*, all carry some thirty guns, although all were built as forty-fours or thereabouts. It is the best I have been able to do, by impressing every poor East Indiaman I can arrest. Yours is the only ship of the line I have. You will be the centrepiece of my attacking force!"

"I am honoured, of course."

"As well you might be. Defeat the English under Peyton, Rigaud, and we all go home wealthy men. You will ensure that takes place by obeying my orders to the letter. I trust that is absolutely clear."

"*D'une certitude, m'sieu',*" said Roche-Bourbon.

La Bourdonnais' expression softened, but the suspicion still lurked behind his eyes.

"Very well. You will only be able to water, wood and provision here briefly. I require that you work round the island to Port Louis, where I have assembled the other ships and where I will see that you are properly provisioned. As soon as the squadron is ready for sea, I intend we sail to attack Peyton before the onset of the north-east monsoon. You should sail for Port Louis as soon as the wind is fair."

"As you wish, m'sieu'."

La Bourdonnais made to return to his boat, but then turned back to Roche-Bourbon.

"There is one other task I will require of you, Rigaud. A young English noblewoman, Lady Caroline Grenville, was taken by the *Neptune* in an English prize some time ago. She was travelling with admirable courage to be with her husband-to-be at Madras. I have given her my word that I will see her safe to India, regardless of the state of war which exists." He paused. "When we sail, she will go with us. The safest place for her will be in *Achille*. I will therefore require you to accept her on board within the hour, and for her to be suitably accommodated."

The governor fixed Roche-Bourbon with a steely look.

"This woman is a gentlewoman, Rigaud. And I shall expect from you as her host the most meticulous of gentlemanly behaviour until we manage somehow to give her to the English. Do I make myself clear?"

Rigaud de la Roche-Bourbon's dark eyes glittered in a way that made La Bourdonnais shiver slightly, in spite of himself, but the man's reply was smooth and casually given.

"You may rest assured, m'sieu'. I shall give her every possible personal attention and expend every effort to ensure her comfort and security." He smiled slowly. "*Every* effort."

The sun was setting towards the west behind a cloudscape of purple Gothic spires and fantastic towers, as *Pallas'* long-boat pushed along ahead of the steady south-east wind. Cap Malheureux lay broad on the starboard bow, the humped green mass of the island rising behind it and off to the south.

In the boat, the men looked sombrely round the horizon. Mainwaring had the tiller, easing the boat along on a broad reach with Hooke and Howe beside him, their eyes scanning the sea face.

"She's not here, gentlemen," said Mainwaring finally. "She's –"

"Sir!" It was Winton, ahead in the bows as look-out. "Wreckage ahead, sir. See it every time a swell lifts us!"

"Give me a hand bearing for it," said Mainwaring. "Ease

the sheets, there, a touch. Belay. Are we bearing on it, Winton?"

"Aye, sir! Terrible litter o' stuff, sir!"

Within a few minutes, the longboat had entered a broad expanse of floating rubbish, lifting and falling on the face of the swells: bits of timber that thumped against the longboat and then slid past; snarls of rigging and cordage from smashed sections of spar, some with sailcloth still bent on; boat oars, barrel staves, crates, unidentifiable fragments of ship joinery; pitiful scraps of torn clothing.

"Dear God!" breathed Howe. "Sir, is this –"

Mainwaring's face was grim. "I can't say, James, but I don't like the looks of it."

The men sat in silence, watching the rubbish slide past.

Then ahead, Winton was pointing, his voice cracking in excitement.

"Sir! Someone in the water! Clingin' to that bit o' gratin'! Luff up, sir!"

"Keep your eyes on him, Winton!" barked Mainwaring. "Ease the sheets, there! To the knot, lads! We're rounding up!" He craned to see forward. "Can you get him, Winton?"

"Aye, sir! Come on, you lot, lend a hand!"

The boat's twin lugsails thumped and shook as Mainwaring put the helm down, and the craft rounded up into the swells, lifting and plunging as it met wind and sea bows-on. Winton was leaning over the bows with Jackman beside him, while behind them Sawyer grasped a fistful of each jacket to keep them aboard. Then they were hauling a limp and dripping figure over the bows.

"It's Mr Pellowe, sir!" Winton blurted.

"Dear God!" breathed Mainwaring. Beside him, Howe stared horrified at the wreckage. He could see now other floating shapes: the figures of dead men, their hair drifting in the lifting swells, wavelets lapping over their sightless eyes.

"This is *Pallas*, sir," Howe murmured.

"Sir?" It was Winton.

"Is he alive?" demanded Mainwaring.

"Barely, sir. He's breathin', is all. 'E's got a bloody awful ball wound in th' back, sir."

"In the *back*? How serious?"

"Can't say, sir. Bled a lot, looks like."

Mainwaring swore. "Isaiah! get for'rard. You're the best to look at a wound without a surgeon about."

"Zur," growled Hooke, clambering heavily off forward.

"Stand by the sheets, there!" barked Mainwaring. "Pay attention, damn you! We'll harden up to a starboard tack and make for shore. How far off are we, James?"

Howe did not answer, but kept gazing in mute horror at the wreckage and bodies.

"*Mr Howe!*"

"What? Sorry, sir. You asked –"

"Get command of yourself, Mr Howe!" said Mainwaring in a low, hard voice. "I need your estimate. You've seen the chart of this shore. Where are we, and how far off are we? Can you answer that?"

Howe shook himself like a man waking from a foul dream. "Aye, sir," he said. "That's Baie de l'Arsenal, there, sir, about twenty points abaft the headland. We're about a league and a half off, sir. There's no protecting reef, and the shore is uninhabited hereabouts."

"So we could shelter there?"

"Likely so, sir, unless we're seen putting in."

Mainwaring shifted his grip on the tiller, his eyes on Stephen Pellowe's ashen face cradled in Winton's lap.

"A chance we'll have to take. We must get Stephen, and all of us, to shelter before nightfall. And I can bear to look at this graveyard no longer." He spat over the side. "Haul in your sheets, there! Down in the boat! Jackman, your weight to starboard, if you please. God *damn* the French!"

And with the lugsails trimmed taut to the steady wind, *Pallas*' longboat stood in towards the land.

* * *

Caroline Grenville sat in stiff silence in the great cabin of *Achille*, her eyes fixed on the tall figure in scarlet velvet behind the cabin's desk.

"You are welcome aboard my ship, Lady Caroline," said Rigaud de la Roche-Bourbon in smooth and accentless English. "I trust you will find my quarters comfortable. I shall be moving to my first officer's cabin."

Caroline nodded faintly, her gaze never leaving the dark, intense eyes across the desk. "It is an improvement over my quarters in *Neptune*." She took a deep breath, feeling the same sense of foreboding she had experienced upon first boarding *Achille*. "And is M'sieu' le Comte not sailing with us?"

Roche-Bourbon rose from the desk and paced to the stern lights, his well-shone boots gleaming as they thocked across the painted canvas. His cocked hat was thrown to one side on the settee, and Caroline noted that his glossy black hair was dressed back with meticulous care into a silk-wrapped queue. As with everything she had seen about this strangely ominous Frenchman, no detail was out of place, no blemish showed, to the point where something in her was repulsed and frightened by the unflawed perfection of his appearance. That Roche-Bourbon was a striking figure of a man was not lost on her, but something in the darkly handsome face called forth more apprehension than admiration. She shivered involuntarily.

"No," Roche-Bourbon was saying. "M'sieu' La Bourdonnais prefers to carry his broad pendant in *Neptune*, rather than *Achille*. She is a handy vessel, there is no doubt."

"I found him to be a gracious gentleman."

"Really? Perhaps he has no knowledge of what to do with a beautiful woman."

Caroline Grenville's eyes flashed, and her chin came up. "I beg your pardon?"

Roche-Bourbon paced slowly towards her chair, his eyes never leaving her. "There is a delightful irony, if I may call it that, in your being taken captive by that fool in *Neptune*, and then placed in the hands of Bernard Mahé. A woman like yourself, virtually a fruit at the choicest moment of plucking, first in the charge of an incompetent, and then in that of a pedantic moralist. Such a waste."

Caroline shuddered as the tall figure passed behind her chair "You sound rather like a bad novel, m'sieu', and in neither case was I subjected to anything worthy of rebuke. The governor was a gentleman."

With a swift move, Roche-Bourbon was beside her, his fingers lacing into her blonde curls, pulling her head back with painful force until his mouth was inches from hers, his other arm locked like a steel band around her.

"Stop! You're hurting me!" Caroline struggled against his grip, feeling it tighten, and seeing the dark eyes burn with pleasure. "How dare you!"

Her words were cut off as Roche-Bourbon's mouth came down, hard and cruel, on hers. His hand in her hair forced her against him, while his free hand came to the top of her gown, gathered the cloth in his fist, and tore it open to her waist. Her breasts were full, with softly pointed pink nipples, and his hand was on them like a claw, crushing them painfully.

"Ah, God!" Caroline tore her mouth free for an instant, fighting him with desperate strength, pulling away the hand that tortured her breasts, and then beating with her free hand at his face. But the brutal kiss found her lips again, and with an animal growl of fury in her throat, her teeth bit down hard on his lip.

With a curse, Roche-Bourbon snapped his head away, thrusting her from him with such force that she fell heavily from the chair, clutching at the torn front of her gown, a sob of anger and fury choking in her throat as she struggled to her feet. For a moment Roche-Bourbon fell back against the edge of the desk, staring at the blood on the back of his hand as a rivulet of scarlet ran down his chin. Then his eyes seemed to light with cold flame and he lurched towards her, his face thunderous as she shrank against the far bulkhead of the cabin, her hair dishevelled and tumbling over her cheeks, her eyes looking from side to side like a trapped animal seeking escape.

Suddenly a sharp pounding rattled the cabin door, and Dionne put his head in.

"I regret the intrusion, m'sieu', but –"

"What is it, you fool?" snarled Roche-Bourbon.

Dionne looked at the blood on Roche-Bourbon's hand, and then stared wide-eyed at Caroline Grenville as she turned away, tugging at the torn material of her gown.

"I am sorry, m'sieu', but *Neptune* has slipped and will pass close aboard us. The governor is signalling that he wants to speak with you as she passes." The lieutenant's face was like pale stone.

"Very well. I shall come on deck immediately. Be off with you!"

"M'sieu'!" He threw a last look at Caroline Grenville and then closed the door.

Roche-Bourbon pulled a handkerchief from his sleeve and dabbed at his chin, his eyes fixed on Caroline Grenville.

"We will continue this conversation at a later time, madame," he said, his voice like velvet.

"You bastard!" breathed the woman, turning on him. "How dare you assault me like this!"

"I dare many things, madame. What I want, I take. And I have a fancy to take you, *hein*?"

Caroline's eyes widened with fresh anger. "Not bloody likely!" she said, through gritted teeth.

Roche-Bourbon paced over to her and she could not keep herself from flinching further against the bulkhead. But her furious gaze met his evenly.

"You do not seem to understand your position, madame. We have a long voyage to India before us and I shall be your host for that voyage. I shall leave it to you to decide how you will accede to my wishes, willingly or otherwise."

"You and your 'wishes' disgust me, m'sieu'."

The dark eyes glittered. "I would caution you against

108

irritating me too greatly, madame. The consequences could be most unpleasant for you."

Roche-Bourbon moved to the cabin door and put his hand on the latch.

"Think on this. Either you will grant me all that I wish willingly, or you will grant me the same favours as a means of avoiding the pain I would take great delight in inflicting upon you. I have found, to my surprise, that the screams of a woman in agony are as pleasurable to me as the cries of a woman in passion. It will be for you to choose."

"You swine. You filthy animal," breathed Caroline Grenville. "I'd sooner cut my own throat!"

"Indeed? Choose well, madame," said Roche-Bourbon smoothly, and went quickly out of the door.

Behind him, Caroline Grenville after a moment gave vent to the storm of sobs that burst from her.

4

The beach was semi-circular, a wave-lapped, sheltered shore of the lushly forested Baie de l'Arsenal, on the island's north-west coast. The heavy palmetto growth overhung the water's edge but left enough room below for a man to walk crouched over. It was here that the longboat was hauled up into the shadows, its white transom masked with a few fronds and branches. The surviving men of *Pallas* sat or lay nearby, watching Edward Mainwaring and Isaiah Hooke finish the bandaging of a revived Stephen Pellowe.

"Now, Stephen," said Mainwaring, "sit well upright, and take half a breath."

"Er, half, sir?"

"Oi needs to lash down this 'ere bandage, so's you c'n still breathe, zur," rumbled Hooke.

Pellowe complied, wincing as Hooke briskly tied off the knot of torn shirt linen.

"You're damned lucky, Stephen. The ball went clean through the fleshy part of your back. Took a sizeable chunk of you with it. How do you feel?"

"It's painful, sir, but bearable. And it wasn't what put me out of things, sir. It was the Frenchman's first broadside." The youth's eyes had an agonised look in them. "Sir, are there no other survivors? None at all?"

Mainwaring's face was grim. "I'm sorry, Stephen. We were lucky to have found you. The others we could see were dead."

Pellowe put his head in his hands. "Dear God," he moaned. "All of them. I killed them all. Oh, Christ."

"Stephen, look at me."

Pellowe looked up, the tears clearly but a moment away.

"I need you to be in full control of yourself, for the men's sake as well as our own. Tell me precisely what happened, in a calm manner, if you please."

Pellowe took a deep, shaking breath. "Aye, sir. It was at first light. As per Mr Howe's orders, we were cruising between Port Louis and Cap Malheureux under French colours, waiting for the boat to come out to us, or a signal ashore. I had just given the word to Jewett to call the hands to Quarters, it being dawn, when the Frenchman came at us from windward."

"Where had he been? Was he not visible to you?"

"Kept the headland between us, sir. Watching our topmasts. Somehow we didn't see his. He ran down on us from behind the cape, under all sail, clawing up at the last minute. It was a big ship, sir, a line vessel. Seventy-gunner, I'd think."

Mainwaring narrowed his eyes. "Could you not have stood away from him?"

"Not soon enough, sir. I ordered the helm up, and hands aloft to set more canvas. We were under topsails and headsails. He overhauled us before we could set enough."

"Go on."

"He swung broadside to us while a half-cable away, sir. We were turning to bring our guns to bear when he fired. It was a tremendous broadside. The flash and report. After it I remember nothing –"

"Yes? Except what, Stephen?" asked the American.

Pellowe shook his head. "It's hard to recall, sir. I was in the water and the other lads were there, too. They were crying out to the French to throw them a line. Some of 'em were pleading for mercy, sir."

"*Mercy?*" Mainwaring stared.

"The French were shooting 'em in the water, sir, as they swam. They kept firing, and firing. I don't remember anything else until I woke up on the beach here, with you."

Hooke stared at Mainwaring, his face darkening. "Christ, zur, the Frogs murdered them!"

111

Mainwaring took a deep breath. "Are you sure of what you recall, Stephen?" he asked in a low, stricken voice.

"Yes, sir. It did happen, sir."

"Very well. Get your head down now. Mr Howe? See that the lads get out a bit of bread and a cup of water. And serve out a spoonful of rum to Mr Pellowe."

"Sir," said Howe, beckoning to Winton and Jackman, his face the colour of pale stone from what he had heard.

Mainwaring rose and walked into the warm shallows, feeling the white sand trickle between his toes. He stared out at the waters where *Pallas* and her company had died, as Hooke sloshed over beside him.

"Bloody grim news, zur," offered Hooke.

"All those men, Isaiah. Lieutenant Beresford. Mr Stewart. Aubrey, Davies, Evans. Shanahan. And Jewett. Killed for no reason. Shot like swine as they begged for help. Christ save me, Isaiah, where do these butchers come from?" The anguish in Mainwaring's voice was painful to the grizzled sailing master to hear.

"Dunno, zur. The Frenchies c'n be Christian people, enough. An' then there's the sort, loike uv which we met at Toulon, zur, as tortured an' murdered th' fisherfolk, and them their countrymen."

"Yes. At the hands of that one particularly black bastard. Roche-Bourbon!"

Hooke's eyebrows rose. "'Im? Y're not thinkin' that off 'ere in the buggerin' Indian Ocean, 'alf ways round th' world, it'd be the same bastard we run up against in Toulon, an' Panama afore that?" He spat into the sea. "Tain't 'ardly possible, zur."

Mainwaring's eyes narrowed. "I know. It couldn't be the same man. But I have this peculiar feeling in my guts, Isaiah, a feeling that says there is something familiar, in a ghastly way, about that kind of butchery. It takes a foul mind to bring it about, a particularly foul one."

Hooke put his hands on his hips. "Wot d'ee plan next for us, zur?"

Mainwaring turned back to look at the small circle of men hunched under the trees beside the half-hidden boat, Howe making a last adjustment to Pellowe's bandage, the others watching him with a dismayed, lost look in their eyes.

"It's time to tell them. Come on."

He splashed out of the water until he stood where all the men could see him. At the look on his face James Howe rose from beside Pellowe, and moved to stand with him.

"Listen to me, if ye will, lads," said Mainwaring, in a low, steady voice. "By law, ye've no need to take my commands now. The ship is gone, and with it my authority over you. But before you consider what best to do, hear me out." He paused, looking again for a moment at the open water where *Pallas* had died. "Out there, we lost our ship to the damned French. To begin with, they used a foul trick to get me away from you and gave themselves safe passage, hiding behind an English gentlewoman's skirts. It meant that you had to risk sending a boat in ashore after me, and thank God, we found one another. But we've lost the ship and our shipmates through no fault of Mr Pellowe." He paused. "We're at the bitter end, lads. Our choices are few. We could attempt to make Madagascar to the west, but I've no sextant or charts and our rations are too low. India's too damned far away, to the north, to attempt joining Commodore Peyton's squadron. That leaves one option."

"Raise hell with the Frogs, zur?" asked Hooke.

"Exactly. What d'ye say, lads? We've nought to lose. I put it to you that we work back along the coast, keeping out o' sight as best we can. After our brush with the dragoons, I'd think the place is alive with troops on the lookout after us. We know their main anchorage is in Port Louis and it's from there that the French will sail against Peyton."

"Wot d'ye propose, zur? We've nought but a boat an' a few muskets, zur, beggin' yer pardon." It was Winton, leaning on his musket.

"We go back as close to the harbour as we can – damn

113

me, *into* it, if we dare – and raise, as Mr Hooke put it, hell with the Frogs! See what we can do to put fire to some of their ships, scuttle boats, whatever opportunity allows. Remember what we did in Toulon? We can do the same here." His expression sobered. "There's one difference. This time we have no escape, no waiting ships to take us aboard. This will be a passage with very little likelihood of return. You'd best all be aware of that. We may be able to take a small vessel but there's no guarantee of that, or even that we'll keep our lives."

Winton spat into the sand. "Damn me, lads, it's die here or die takin' a few of the murderin' bastards wiv me. I know which pin my line's belayed to!"

Sawyer, the whippet-thin Martha's Vineyarder, rose. "You be sayin' that we ain't got much chance, other than what ye say, sir? Speakin' plain?"

"That's right, Sawyer. Speaking plain."

Sawyer thought a moment, then he grinned. "I followed ye this fur, sir. Can't run from th' colours now, nohow."

"Me, neither, sir." "Aye, sir." A chorus of voices echoed Sawyer's. "You be capting, zur!"

Mainwaring nodded, looking round at the faces, feeling the old emotions rise within him.

"Very well. Thank you. Thank you, all of you." He coughed. "Mr Howe, set a sentry. The rest of you, get your heads down. At nightfall, we begin working back along towards Port Louis, under oars, if we have to. And this time, we give no quarter, by God!"

The moon had risen, low behind the dark, humped shape of Montagne Longue. The rainforest was silent around the still waters of the Baie de l'Arsenal, and the stars in the night sky glimmered like lost pearls in the water of the sea. Other than the occasional call of a hunting predator, no sound marred the stillness of the night.

A figure arose from the shadows beneath the palm and ebony trees and now another, and soon almost a dozen were moving. They clustered round the low shape of a boat that gleamed dull white as masking branches were pulled away, and they talked quietly, readying the boat.

"Right. Everyone's gear in the boat?" demanded Mainwaring in a low voice. "Mr Hooke, I'll trust you struck in that fruit?"

"Aye, zur. Lot o' damned monkey grub, t' my mind, is all."

"You'll soon be fond of it. Stand to, lads, on the gunwales. Take a grip. Two t' six, *heave!*"

With muscular tugs, the men forced the heavy boat over the damp sand and into the shallows, sloshing out with it until finally it floated free and they were wading in thigh-deep water.

"Got the bowline, Jackman? Good. Right, then, into the boat with you. Winton, help Mr Pellowe, will you?"

Within a few moments the men were in the longboat and at a word from Mainwaring they began wrestling the fourteen-foot oars into place.

"Carry on, Mr Hooke, if you please," said Mainwaring. "Have 'em pull easily but steadily. And steer us close inshore as you can, southbound."

"Aye, zur," growled Hooke. "Steady up, you lot. Prepare t' give way. Gently, Pasco, there's a good marine. Sawyer needs t' keep 'is 'ead, don't 'e. Ready all? Give way, together! Take yer stroke from Winnie. 'Andsomely, now, 'andsomely."

The oars creaked and thumped rhythmically and the boat began to make way. Hooke put the tiller over, and steered for the dark snout of the next headland, back along the coast they had sailed off that morning.

"D'ye think we'll be seen, sir?" asked Howe who was sharing the sternsheets with Mainwaring, Hooke and Pellowe.

"Not from seaward, James, while we're pulling. It'll be eyes on the shore that'll twig to us first. If we pull along the shore at night and shelter in some cove by day, we should avoid notice for a bit." He scratched his stubbled chin. "We'll be seen eventually, James, but I hope we sell ourselves dearly by that point."

"Aye, aye, sir. Thank you."

Mainwaring looked at Pellowe, who was asleep against Howe's shoulder, his blond locks gleaming in the pale moonlight and accentuating again his youth. "How is he, James?" he asked quietly.

"Sleeping well enough, sir, but his skin is hot. I hope there's no putrescence in the wound."

"We'll change his dressing often as we can. Not that any of us has much of a shirttail to spare. A fairly ragamuffin lot we've become."

Howe managed a grin. The seamen were barefoot, their caps and hats mostly gone, the jackets tossed on the floorboards. The sea-regiment men still wore their brick-red sleeved waistcoats, but most had lost their queer little caps and were either bareheaded or wearing bandanas in the seamen's manner. Of the officers, only Hooke still wore shoes, and all were bareheaded and rough-looking, with Mainwaring virtually in rags. Given that none of them had shaved for days, the boat's occupants looked desperate indeed.

"A king's hard bargain, might be the expression, sir," suggested Howe.

"Aye. Now look there, James, that dark headland. Ye say it's another deep bay, just beyond?"

"Sir. No more'n a quarter league, now. Baie du Tombeau. No settlement shown on the chart, or in the *Neptune Orientale*."

Mainwaring peered ahead at the approaching shoulder of the headland. No white breakers gleamed there, and at the good pulling rate the men were setting, the longboat was cutting swiftly across the placid waters of the Baie de l'Arsenal and would move round the headland in a matter of minutes. There seemed to be little longshore current, and so he would have Hooke steer close for the point, to be as close inshore as possible when rounding it, and thus keep to a minimum the time when the boat was most visible.

"The *Neptune Orientale* you refer to, James, is that the little tome you bought for three shillings in Cape Town?"

"Yes, sir. It's a new translation of a pilot written by a Frenchman. Odd thing about it is that he wrote it because he felt it improper for French ships to have to use Dutch or English pilots when they came out here."

"I see. So here we are, English using a French pilot written because the French didn't like using our pilot, which presumably was better than theirs in the first place."

"Yes, sir. And now his is better – than ours, sir."

"Damned inefficient of us, don't you think?"

"Bloody silly, sir." Howe grinned.

"Like everything in this damned war," said Mainwaring. "Mr Hooke, take the helm. We'll be round that headland in a moment. Watch for breakers. Steady stroke, now, lads."

The longboat pushed slowly on through the night, the men pulling well, enjoying the release from anxiety that came with concentrating their efforts on keeping the loom of the oars moving away at waist height, pulling back to them at shoulder height, using their backs instead of their arms, the steady creak-thunk, creak-thunk that was both lulling and soothing.

"Look 'ee, zur, in the bay! A brig, or I'm damned!" burst out Hooke.

Mainwaring's head snapped up as Hooke growled at the men to keep the stroke. The longboat was nosing past the headland, a sloping shore hung with palmetto and ferns, with a gentle, wave-washed beach of pale water ending at white sand. The longboat was no more than twenty feet off and glided over its own moonlit shadow on the silvery seabed below, the oar shapes moving like insect legs.

Ahead, the dark curve of the shoreline was opening in. The bay's broad surface was ruffled by the breeze and in the middle lay a ship lit only by the glow of a single lantern at its stern. It was a brig, its canvas gathered up against its yards in haphazard fashion, the great fore-and-aft main only partially brailed in against the mainmast below its standing gaff.

"D'ye see any colours on her?" whispered Mainwaring.

"None, sir!" said Howe. "Nought but the stern lantern, and there's some kind of glow for'rard, from one of the gunports, like it's only partially shut and there's light within."

"No boats, zur," said Hooke. "Not unless they've got 'em alongside on th' other side."

"Wait, now." Mainwaring's ears were tingling. "Oars! Lay on 'em for a moment, lads!" The hands stopped pulling, holding the blades clear of the water, staring back at Mainwaring with suddenly bright and watchful eyes.

"D'ye hear that?" he asked.

Howe cocked his head to one side. "Voices, sir! Singing, and none too sober by the sound of it." All in the boat could hear now the drink-thickened voices, the faint tinkle and crash of glass, harsh laughter ringing out over the song, a muffled thumping and clumping.

"They'd be 'avin' a right jolly time of it, I'd say, zur," said Hooke. "Three sheets t' th' wind, by th' sound of it."

Mainwaring nodded. "Aye. The question is, have they posted a deck watch?" He looked at Hooke. "Is she French?"

Hooke squinted. After a moment he nodded. "Aye, she's a Frog, by rights. Steeve o' th' jib-boom, same size topmasts. An' that canvas is too bloody white t' be a Dutchman or whatnot."

"Very well. Steer for her, Mr Hooke."

"What d'ye plan to do, sir?" murmured Howe.

Even in the darkness the glint in Mainwaring's eye was evident.

"Do? Sink me, James, I'd say we're in the market for a ship. Wouldn't you agree?"

Howe stared at him, and as the grins and muffled oaths

of pleasure rippled through the men at the oars, he smiled too.

"Ah, er, of course, sir," he managed.

"Right. Now listen carefully, lads. Mr Hooke, you'll steer us for her counter. Let's see if she's left any lines adrift. We'll row with four oars only, stroke, second stroke, midships and second bows. That means, Slade, you get your oar in *now*. Keep a steady, quiet stroke, Winton. The rest of you, prime and load your firelocks, but for God's sake, take care. One premature discharge and we might die like rats right here in the boat. Turn to it, all!"

With Winton setting a determined, slow pace, the boat crept silently towards the brig, the splash and dip of the oar blades almost the only sound other than a faint clump as the men not on the oars fumbled for their weapons and pulled open cartridge boxes. Their eyes white in the darkness, they looked anxiously from Mainwaring to the brig and back again.

James Howe rested his heavy firelock on the gunwale and opened the pan, looking to see that it was still filled level with powder. He turned to Mainwaring.

"What about you, sir? You've only that bloody great dragoon sword."

"Which will do quite well, James," said Mainwaring, looking down at the long, basket-hilted weapon that gleamed at his feet. "Can't tear cartridge and bark abuse at you lot at the same time."

"Aye, sir," grinned Howe.

Hooke was steering them for the brig's stern, and now they could see clearly the stern lights, the slanting windows across the ship's transom structure. They were dark, with no hint of light. The sailing master pointed.

"Look 'ee, thar, zur, trailin' from the transom rail. A line, likely bein' streamed t' straighten it, an' forgotten when they came t'anchor, belike."

"Right. That's perhaps our gangway aboard, Isaiah. Steer for it. Handsomely, now, lads!"

"An' not a squeak from any of ye!" rumbled Hooke.

The brig loomed over them unexpectedly quickly, dark and huge, the water lapping gently under the shadowed overhang of the counter. As the boat crept closer, Mainwaring scanned the rail, watching for any hint of movement that would reveal a watchman, but there was none.

They were almost directly under the overhang of the brig's narrow gallery. The line hung slackly from the transom rail and several hands clutched at it, passing it aft.

"Hold water, there!" hissed Hooke. "Fend off, Jacko. Butt end o' th' hook. Quietly!"

Mainwaring took hold of the line, tugging at it, testing its bristly strength. It felt secure and firm, a thick enough line to hold a man's weight if it was belayed aloft properly. The risk would have to be taken.

"Listen carefully, lads," he whispered. "Mr Howe, I'm going up this line. You and Mr Hooke are to pull round to the larboard side. Mr Hooke, you'll leave one man in the boat, watching to landward. Take a party with you on to the main channel, but first let Mr Howe off at the forechains with those who aren't with you. Both of you, go over the rail at the same instant. Mr Howe, you'll secure the foredeck, Mr Hooke the waist, after ensuring the boat is at the battens. Slade, you'll come with me. The quarterdeck will be our responsibility, and I may need your knife. Clear?"

Hooke and Howe exchanged a glance and nodded. Slade was clambering aft over the thwarts, his musket already slung. As he arrived, he pulled a thin, vicious-looking little knife from the neck of his shirt. He grinned like a ferret at Mainwaring and clenched the knife between his teeth.

"How very piratical, Slade," murmured Mainwaring. Then he stood up, thrust the dragoon sword into the back of his belt, and reached up the line for a grip.

"Good luck!" he hissed.

With a heave he pulled himself free of the boat, hearing the line pop and groan, wondering wildly if it were snugly tied on above him, feeling its splintery rigidity. He monkeyed up several feet, the line trembling as Slade began his climb.

"Give way, together!" came Hooke's hiss, and Mainwaring sensed, rather than saw, the boat pull away from below him. He was breathing heavily, and his next surge up the bar-taut rope brought him level with the stern gallery windows. He had a horrifying thought of a gaping pistol muzzle being levelled at him from the inky darkness behind the glass, but shook it off, willing himself to move upward. Now the line was virtually touching the broad surface of the transom below the rail, and then Mainwaring was reaching up with one hand, the fingers finding the lip of the rail, and with careful effort he muscled himself up until his eyes came level with a view of the quarterdeck and the expanse of the dark deck beyond.

"Sink me!" he murmured. "Not a soul!"

Below him the line trembled, and Slade's hand touched Mainwaring's foot. It was time to move on.

Mainwaring pulled himself up until his scrabbling feet found a toe hold, and then vaulted lightly over the rail. As he landed on the slanting deck, eyes wide and watchful, the point of the heavy sword thrust into the back of his belt thumped hard into the deck, and he swore luridly as he wrenched the weapon free and wrestled it out of his belt.

Behind him Slade was slithering noiselessly over the rail to crouch beside Mainwaring. He took the knife from his teeth and hefted it, and looked inquiringly at Mainwaring.

"The main companionway," whispered Mainwaring. "Get to it and watch for anyone coming up from below!"

"Sir!" The little man was off in quick weasel moves, soon hunching himself beside the lip of the dark companionway at the foot of the quarterdeck ladder. The slim blade of his knife gleamed dully in the dim light.

On silent feet Mainwaring padded to the waistdeck rail, peering forward past Slade's crouching form along the ship. There was no movement or trace of human presence, and now no sound from below.

Where the devil are the people? thought Mainwaring.

A sudden flurry of movement occurred along the larboard side, and as if at a stage director's cue, two rows of heads appeared over the rail at the fore and main shrouds, looking quickly fore and aft. Then Hooke and Howe appeared, rolling over the rail to the deck, their men behind them, the dim light glinting off the barrels of their firelocks.

Mainwaring leapt down the waistdeck ladder and moved to them, seeing their eyes flash whitely as they turned. They were ready to fight, and it struck Mainwaring how frightening they looked, and how evident the purpose in their dark, shadowed faces and the posture of their bodies.

"Where the deuce be they?" growled Hooke.

"A damned good question, Isaiah," breathed Mainwaring. "Sergeant Fell?"

"Sir?"

"Post one man at the for'rard companionway, another at the after one to relieve Slade, and a sentry each on the foredeck and quarterdeck. Watch for movement of any kind, shoreward or seaward," said Mainwaring in a low, tight voice.

"Aye, sir," responded the dark-faced Fell. "Wallis, you tyke th'fore companion. Pasco, th'aft. Lively, now!"

Mainwaring moved to Howe, motioning Hooke over to join them.

"Where's Stephen?" he asked.

"In the boat, sir," replied Howe. "He's awake, but feverish. I'm worried about him, sir."

"I know, as am I. We'll do what we can for him, as soon as we get him aboard. James, take a man and go down the for'rard companionway. Isaiah, you take the aft. Leave me Slade and Winton on deck. Report what you find immediately. If they're down there, don't risk yourselves, but get back on deck. We'll pen 'em below if we have to."

"Aye, aye, sir," said Howe briskly. "Come on, Sawyer. Jackman, you're with Mr Hooke." The four men moved quickly off, their bare feet silent on the decking, and van-

122

ished down the companionways as the sentries peered watchfully after them.

"Slade?" Mainwaring turned to the Cockney, who had come up. "Leave your firelock here. I want you to get up into the maintop. Put a sharp eye round all points o' the compass to see if there's a boat ashore, a fire, movement, virtually anything. Clear?"

"Aye, sir!" The little man put down his long firelock by the mainmast timber bitts and was up on the rail, out round the deadeyes and lanyards and on to the ratlines, where he began scampering up the shaking rigging to the top.

Mainwaring turned to Winton, who was eyeing him expectantly. "Winton, if we're to get this vessel to sea, you'll have to be our boatswain. Do it well and I'll see you get your warrant."

"*Sea*, sir?" Winton stared. "You're keepin' 'er, sir?"

"If she's worth it. Get for'rard and see how she's anchored. Is she on one or two anchors, is the cable nipped up to a traveller or belayed round the bitts? Then have a look at her canvas and running rigging. Tell me what we're dealing with, and lively!"

"Aye, aye, sir!" said Winton, thumping down his firelock beside Slade's. "If she's ridin' t' one killick, only –"

"Deck, there! Deck!" It was Slade's voice from high aloft in the top. "Shoreward, sir! Boats!"

Mainwaring sprang to the rail, Winton beside him, and both men peered intently towards the dark mass of the shore.

"There, sir!" Winton pointed.

Following the gesture, Mainwaring's eyes found a darker indentation in the bay's shore that might have marked a hidden inlet. Emerging from the shadows there, torches flickering with dim orange flame at their bows, three white-hulled boats were pulling towards the brig, their oar blades lifting and falling unevenly. The boats were crowded with figures, and over the dark waters and the shimmering ribbons of light cast by the torches, the sounds of voices reached the Englishmen's ears: men's voices, guttural and raucous, thick with drink, and women's voices, high-pitched and raised, though whether in laughter or alarm was uncertain.

"They was ashore, sir. Assemblin' a packet o' doxies fer jollity afloat, beloike!" whispered Winton.

Mainwaring nodded. "Aye. Women or no, there's still a lot of them!" He spat over the side. "Get below, Winnie. Find Mr Howe and Mr Hooke, and get 'em on deck here as quickly as you can!" He felt the cold steel of the dragoon sword's blade. "If we're to keep this ship, we're going to have to meet them with a very warm welcome!"

The hanging lanterns in the great cabin of His Most Christian Majesty's Ship *Achille*, at anchor in the harbour of Port Louis, cast a dim light over the interior of the cabin and showed the rivulets of sweat escaping from beneath the Comte de la Bourdonnais' shoulder-length *perruque à circonstance*, running down his cheeks and vanishing in the gathered lace at his throat.

The governor, however, was ignoring the sweat as he paced irritably up and down the painted black and white squares on the canvas deck covering, his red heels flashing and the full skirts of his uniform coat swinging about him as he turned. He stopped and once again eyed the languid figure of Rigaud de la Roche-Bourbon, sitting relaxed behind the cabin's desk.

"I don't think, Rigaud, you fully grasp the gravity of our situation, and how perilous conditions have become for the success of our enterprise against the English."

"Perhaps not, m'sieu'," replied Roche-Bourbon smoothly. "I would be grateful if any failings could be enumerated."

La Bourdonnais' eyes narrowed. "Don't play me for a fool, Rigaud. I know you too well for that. Kindly display some damned commitment to a resolution of these issues, if you please!"

Roche-Bourbon tossed a thin knife on the desk and spread his hands. "You have but to direct me."

"Very well. Why were you so tardy in putting round from the anchorage at Mahébourg? The wind has been fair for this place for three days!"

"I was, ah, readying my ship, m'sieu'. The difficulties of the voyage out, you will understand."

"I understand only that because of your delay I have not yet seen to getting *Insulaire* alongside the hulk to step a new bowsprit, and *Saint-Louis* and *Lys* still want the greater part of their powder and shot, not to mention their victualling!" The governor took off his egret-feathered cocked hat and slapped it against one velveted thigh in frustration. "We simply do not have time to delay in this manner! The north-east monsoon grows closer every damned day, and if we do not get out to sea within three weeks at the very latest, we will face foul winds and worse, and be fortunate to shelter at Réunion, let alone attempt to sweep Peyton from the Coromandel coast! Do you not see this, in the name of God?"

"Of course, Bernard. I –"

"M'sieu' will do," said La Bourdonnais icily. "You have made no effort to begin the watering and victualling of your ship. The arsenal has received no requisitions for powder and shot. You indicate that you have rigging problems and an insufficiency of a host of other stores. I am required by the *amirauté* to attend to *Achille*'s needs first, inasmuch as this is, reputedly, a king's ship and the rest of this puny squadron are impressed East Indiamen. But I cannot do so, *chevalier*, until you as well choose to *act*!"

Roche-Bourbon's handsome features remained placid. "What would you have me do, m'sieu'?"

"Do? In the name of Christ, man, you know what is required! We must sail before the north-east monsoon makes it impossible. *Achille* is the key to our success. You must act *now* to ready her for sea, and without any further infuriating delay!"

Roche-Bourbon nodded. "Of course, m'sieu'. I apologise for perhaps misunderstanding the urgency of the situation. I shall meet with my officers within the hour."

"Very well." La Bourdonnais nodded warily. "And we are beset with other problems, which have not arrived at the most propitious hour. A party of brigands or banditti of some kind – one rumour has it they are a mob of disaffected *métayers* – has got loose in the town, shot some of the *Troupes de la Marine* and then, if you can believe, actually beat off a patrol of colonial dragoons before getting away in a boat to seaward. They also might have been, of course, the damned Arabs."

Roche-Bourbon raised an eyebrow. "*Arabs?* A little too southerly for them, isn't it?"

La Bourdonnais resumed his worried pacing. "I would have thought. The slavers stay inshore along the African coast. They literally infest the Mozambique Channel, along with God knows what refuse of pirates and other filth. But a creole cutting ebony on the slopes of Le Pouce told one of the garrison captains that he saw a big lateener, a galley or a dhow, off to seaward in the sunset." He crammed his hat back on his head. "That would be the finish, the absolute finish. To be late getting to sea for the Coromandel, be driven into shelter from the damned monsoon over half the Indian Ocean and have the place beset by wild-eyed Mahometan pirates – sweet Mother of God, spare me!" He paused. "One other thing bothers me, Rigaud. One of the dragoons said he was sure this party of banditti were speaking English."

Roche-Bourbon sat up. "Is he certain of that?"

La Bourdonnais nodded. "As certain as an ignorant trooper can be about what he sees and hears. And the banditti fought as if they were line infantry, hardly the stuff of throat-slitting riffraff." The governor paused as he passed the desk. "You did say, Rigaud, that you killed all the English in that ship?"

Roche-Bourbon's eyes glittered. "To a man."

La Bourdonnais turned to go. "It may be, Rigaud," he said cuttingly, "that you missed some of them in your slaughtering. Perhaps a boat's crew of them, in fact. I can hardly think of anything more irritating at this moment than to have to add *them* to the equation with which I must deal. And, of course, there is the vexing matter of the English captain lured into *Neptune* by the use of the Englishwoman as a hostage to escape their guns. You say the vessel you destroyed was a forty-four? A frigate?"

"Yes, m'sieu'."

"Precisely, I should think, the vessel *Neptune* encountered. I wonder, Rigaud, if it were not indeed that same vessel you destroyed. All to the good, of course. Prevents him from getting back to Peyton, if that were his aim. In any event, I had the Englishman safely put away in prison until the *salaud* escaped over the walls – the same night, incidentally, that the dragoons ran into that lot on the Mer Rouge cartway."

Roche-Bourbon picked up the slim knife again and began idly turning it in his fingers. "Perhaps I was not, in fact, thorough enough, m'sieu'. Perhaps a surviving boat of the English, which we somehow missed, were ashore, trying to find their captain. It is the sort of audacious but unexpected attempt the English would make." He sat forward. "Even if it is true, what chance do they have, *hein*? With no ship they'll be run to ground, picked up by the *milice* or a guardboat at some point. Or they may die at sea, or be cut to pieces by the damned Arabs, if indeed they are about." He shrugged. "One way or another, they are insignificant."

La Bourdonnais pursed his lips as he paced. "Perhaps, but I cannot afford to treat them so dismissively. I am sending two companies of the *milice créole* along the Baie de l'Arsenal cartway, and instituting patrols elsewhere by the dragoons. It is certainly not what I wished to be dealing with at this point." He moved abruptly to the door. "I must go. For God's sake, Rigaud, get on with things!"

Roche-Bourbon rose. "Of course. But may I ask –"

"Yes?"

"Two things, m'sieu'. To begin with, I lack sufficient coin to pay my ship's company, and I find the use of scrip unpalatable. I should like – "

"The East India Company has arranged to let me forward their assets by the first available ship to l'Orient, as I have commandeered their ships. In the meantime I have had their chests and strong boxes moved to a safe location ashore. I should be able to advance you sufficient credit against the East India funds if you need coin to keep your people in whoring and drinking money. Simply tell me the amount."

"With due respect, m'sieu', is it wise to allow their holdings to sit ashore, in a vulnerable casemate or wherever?"

"I assure you it is not vulnerable."

"Of course. Forgive me. But would you not prefer to have it under your own eyes, even if you sail against Peyton, m'sieu'?"

"I don't follow you," said La Bourdonnais, turning back.

"It really is quite simple, m'sieu'. The Company, and indeed His Majesty, will be concerned about the safety of such a vast amount of negotiable assets."

"It is not that significant a hoard, Rigaud."

"With respect, I should say that three hundred thousand louis in plate, bullion, coin, and other things, is indeed a significant hoard, m'sieu'."

La Bourdonnais paled. "*Sacristi!* How did you – "

"I have my sources, as I believe the saying goes. Three hundred thousand louis, left behind without significant protection while you, charged with that very protection, are off serving the greater interest of the Company by destroying Peyton's squadron. A noble task which will have little import if this enormous sum falls victim to some vagrant Englishman, or inconvenient Arabs, or – "

"What is your point, Rigaud?" La Bourdonnais asked coldly.

"The point, m'sieu', is for you to bring the East India

Company assets with you when you sail, where you may know precisely what is happening to it. Regardless of the outcome of this expedition to the Coromandel, you can then send it off to l'Orient as and when you deem it safest, and in the safest vessel. You spare yourself the anxiety of wondering if it is being plundered in Port Louis while you – while *we* – are engaged five hundred leagues away."

"You're suggesting I load it into *Neptune*?"

Roche-Bourbon smiled, thinly and precisely. "No, m'sieu'. Only one vessel is of sufficient size and strength, fully armed and manned, and seaworthy enough to make the voyage to l'Orient regardless of monsoons or Peyton's luck in war."

La Bourdonnais' own smile was cynical and without humour. "I see. Of course. *Achilles*, I presume."

"Indeed, m'sieu'. I guarantee its safety, and its safe return to l'Orient as and when you direct. *Achille* will, after all, be part of your squadron – dare I say the most powerful part? – under your orders and surveillance at all times."

La Bourdonnais' eyes narrowed in thought, his discomfiture evident.

Then Roche-Bourbon played his trump card.

"It is regrettable that your need for *Achille* to serve as the strongest vessel of your gallant squadron has led you to be distressed over the unavoidable delays we have experienced. Naturally, to be charged with the responsibility of the safekeeping of the East India assets would provide a needed, in fact, essential, spur to readying her."

La Bourdonnais' lips turned white. After a moment he said quietly, "Are you threatening me?"

Roche-Bourbon rose from his chair and inclined himself in a graceful bow.

"On the contrary, I assure you, I am merely advising you as to how your responsibilities may be resolved in the most expeditious manner possible." Roche-Bourbon's eyes were fixed on La Bourdonnais with a steady intensity. "You, of course, must decide."

La Bourdonnais took a single quick step towards Roche-Bourbon, his mouth opened to give vent to a surge of temper. Then he paused and his eyes took on a glacial coldness.

"The *capitaine de la ronde* tonight will see that longboats will come alongside *Achille* half an hour before midnight, bearing the East India assets. There will be a bill of lading which I will expect you to sign, so that it may be returned to me," he said in an expressionless monotone. "I will expect *Achille* to be ready for sea in the most expeditious time possible thereafter, Roche-Bourbon, and a meticulous attention to every order I issue thereupon."

Roche-Bourbon bowed again. "You have my word, m'sieu'."

"*Your word?*" snorted La Bourdonnais. "Fail in this, Roche-Bourbon, and nothing will protect you, least of all from me. Is that clear?"

"I would expect nothing less from you, *Bernard*."

La Bourdonnais' lips tightened. "You clever bastard, for your sake I hope so!" he said hoarsely, and spun on his heel. In the next moment he was gone, the cabin door banging shut behind him.

Rigaud de la Roche-Bourbon smiled thinly, listening as La Bourdonnais' heels sounded up the after companionway. There was a rush of feet on deck as his boat was called away.

"You may come in now, Dionne," said Roche-Bourbon in a conversational tone.

The first lieutenant of *Achille*, his hat in both hands, entered from where he had been hidden on Roche-Bourbon's private quarter-gallery.

"You heard everything, I trust?" said Roche-Bourbon.

"Y – yes, m'sieu'." The man's dark features were fixed on Roche-Bourbon with an expression that mixed fear and a kind of awe.

"Particularly what he had to say about the East India Company assets, Dionne?"

"M'sieu'."

"Then listen carefully, Dionne. I want you to select ten trusted men, the sort who if they smell the chance for gold would slit their mother's throat to get it. I want no pious milksops. You'll bring them to me in the beginning of the first watch, and I will tell them all that is necessary. No other member of this ship's company is to know what is being brought on board tonight on pain of death, and I guarantee it will be an excruciating death in screaming agony. Do I make myself clear, Dionne?" Roche-Bourbon's voice was velvet smooth.

"Very clear, m'sieu'."

"*Bon*. And another thing, Dionne. Select the men well, for if any of them betray us, I will draw a knife across your own worthless throat as a matter of course."

Dionne's face was like white marble. "I understand perfectly, m'sieu'."

"Splendid." He paused. "One more thing, Dionne. Tell the sentry at the door I am not to be disturbed under *any* circumstances. Is that clear as well?"

Dionne nodded. He put on his hat with trembling hands, remembered at the last minute to touch it in salute, and was gone, the door clicking shut behind him.

Roche-Bourbon waited until the footsteps had died away, and then he moved slowly to the closed door of his sleeping cabin, opening it with a thrust of his wrist.

With a gasp, Caroline Grenville turned and backed against the box bunk, her hands behind her. She was in the torn gown, its bodice roughly pinned together. Her hair was unbound and one long wisp lay across her forehead and down her cheek.

"I hope you enjoyed the dinner I had sent in, madame," said Roche-Bourbon. "Sea fare, of course, but we must all partake of that."

"What do you want?" Her voice was low and her eyes like those of a trapped animal.

Roche-Bourbon's eyes drifted down her body and a slight smile came to his lips.

131

"Why, merely to begin enjoying your beauty, my dear. And such beauty in the bargain." He moved closer and she shrank further against the bunk. Her breathing was quick and shallow, and her breasts moved against the torn cloth in a way that held Roche-Bourbon's glittering gaze.

"I have thought, for example, how ready I am to sample again a true kiss from those soft lips!" In sudden quickness he reached out and seized her shoulders. His head lowered, and his mouth was suddenly against hers, harsh and cruel, his tongue thrusting into her throat.

In the next instant he was reeling back, spitting out a foul oath, his hand coming up to the dark, oozing slash that had appeared on his cheek. Caroline Grenville stared at him in hot-eyed defiance, her hands gripping a thin, bloody-bladed dagger that she had reversed and now held with its point pressing into the soft flesh between her breasts.

"You –" Roche-Bourbon swore and lurched towards her, but her cry and the wild flash in her eyes stopped him.

"Touch me and I'll thrust this home! I'd sooner die than let myself be fouled by you!"

Roche-Bourbon's eyes were like firelit black glass. "Where did you find that?" he hissed.

"It's the pair of your desk toy. You left me alone a touch too long. Don't touch me, or I'll do as I say!"

Roche-Bourbon pulled an immaculate handkerchief from one cuff and held it to his bleeding cheek, his eyes riveted on her with cobralike intensity.

"I should have let the fo'c'sle dogs have you. *Sacristi*, I'll –"

"You'll leave me alone, or you'll have to tell your governor that you murdered the Englishwoman, won't you?" Her eyes flamed with anger. "By God, how I hate swine like you! Cruel, manipulating bastards who use women like some kind of animal, to whip and to cudgel and use, and then throw into the gutter when you've finished! Well, not me! D'ye hear? *Not bloody me!*" The blade's point pressed into the white flesh until a drop of ruby blood welled out round its tip.

Roche-Bourbon stepped back, dabbing again at his cheek. "I will wait for awhile, madame," he said in a voice full of chill menace, "while I devise what means I shall use to provide you with the most appropriate agony. You will tire in time and then I shall come for you."

Caroline Grenville looked as steadily as she could into the glittering black eyes.

"You may go to hell and be damned. There is nothing in you that suggests a man to me, only a disgusting monstrosity. Is that your problem, then? Not too successful as a man? You must give pain because you aren't good enough to give a woman pleasure?"

For an instant the woman thought the tall figure would leap forward at her in a rage, but then Roche-Bourbon turned and put his free hand to the door latch.

"You will regret that remark, madame. In a hundred screaming moments, when you beg me for release from your pain, you will regret that remark, I assure you." And in a swirl of velvet coat skirts he was gone.

Behind him, Caroline Grenville stood motionless, hearing the heels thock away and out into the passageway, the outer door slamming shut. Then she sank down, falling across the box bunk, pressing her face into the hard pillow, finally letting a desperate, miserable sobbing take control of her as she lay still clutching the vicious little knife to her breasts.

Twice, said her mind. *Twice, now. But the third time . . .*

5

Edward Mainwaring crouched by the brig's rail, his fingers alternately tightening and loosening their grip on the heavy dragoon sword. He was peering through the gloom at the three approaching boats, trying to make a rough count of the men in them. The flailing oars and flickering torchlight made it almost impossible to determine.

There'll at least be more than us, he thought. Then Slade, who had monkeyed silently down the off-side shrouds, was scuttling in a breathless crouch across the deck and dropping to his knee beside Mainwaring.

"How many of them are there, Slade?" asked Mainwaring. "I can't make out a damned thing from here. Could you see from aloft?"

The little Cockney shook his head. "Not a chance, sir. Too full o' torchlight, an' too 'ard t' tell if they was women or not, sir."

Mainwaring nodded. "Three boats. At least four oars a boat, and a coxswain. That'd make at least fifteen men, perhaps more." He spat over the rail. "Where the devil is Mr Howe and –"

A slap and thump of running feet sounded behind him, and he spun to see Winton emerge out of the forward companionway past the crouched, watchful form of Wallis, the latter's musket barrel gleaming in the pale light as he hefted it. Following Winton was Howe, and Hooke's burly shape was close behind. In a scuffling rush all three men crossed the intervening deck space and squatted, panting, at Mainwaring's side.

"Well, James? Is she –"

Howe's expression was one of astonishment. "You're not

going to believe this, sir. She's an *English* ship, a prize taken by the French. The *Hotspur*."

Mainwaring stared at Howe, the image of Caroline Grenville suddenly before his eyes.

"English?"

"There's more, sir. A good dozen lads of the *Hotspur*'s people are in irons below! The French must have been intending to offload 'em at Port Louis. They had only two guards, and those half-drunk!"

"What have you done with the guards?"

Hooke grunted. "'Tweren't difficult, zur. Sawyer did fer 'em wiv 'is knife, silent an' sweet like, zur."

Mainwaring took a deep breath. "All right. The prisoners. What kind of state are they in? Are they wounded or hurt?"

"Dunno, zur. We could 'ear 'em movin' about a bit an' groanin' behind th' bulkhead. They're penned up in th'orlop, zur. Jackman's workin' on th' padlock. Couldn't find a key on the buggers."

Mainwaring glanced again at the approaching boats which were perhaps five hundred yards off and coming on rapidly. "Isaiah, get back below and keep Jackman with you. Get those lads free, however you can, and report to me on their condition. Send Sawyer back to me. Quickly, now!"

Hooke nodded. "Zur!" In the next instant he was shambling off in a low run for the companionway.

Mainwaring cupped his hands. "Sergeant Fell! Bring Pasco and Wallis to me here, at once! Slade, recover your firelock and take up a position beside me. James, beside him. Lively, lads!" As the sea-regiment men arrived, Mainwaring was pointing. "To the other side of the entry port, Sergeant! See to your priming, and then take up a firing position at the rail towards those boats. But for God's sake keep low, and do not fire until I command you!"

"Sir!" barked Fell, gesturing to the two men as they came up. They were quickly kneeling at the rail, readying the

135

priming of the long firelocks and eyeing the approaching boats, gauging the distance.

"Me, too, sir?" asked Winton, reaching for his musket.

"No, Winton. Get for'rard as I originally ordered you. See to how she's anchored, and get back to me. Is she on one hawser, is the messenger line still rigged, the lot! Clear?"

"Aye, aye, sir!" the man said, and loped off forward.

Sawyer burst out of the forward companionway and came pelting over to Mainwaring. He sank to his heels, panting and wiping his forehead with his forearm, his musket cradled in the other arm.

"Jackman's fair near got th' padlock off, sir! You should hear the lads behind, when they heard us a-jabberin' in English!"

"You took care of the guards, I gather."

"Aye, sir. Quick an' silent, Injun fashion. Got 'em stowed by a gunport so's we can heave 'em out when there's time, sir."

"Well done. Get to the rail, there, beside Mr Howe, and wait for my order."

Mainwaring turned again, still crouching. The boats were thrashing noisily along towards the brig, the torches glittering and bright in their bows. Women's voices rose in shrill, piercing laughter over those of the men.

"No captives, those, at least!" muttered Mainwaring. The boats were two hundred yards away, their oars lifting and falling unevenly, the babble and tumult coming from them a clear indication of loose discipline and unchecked drink.

"Make ready!" barked Mainwaring. "We'll fire for the water, ahead of 'em. No sense in putting a ball into a woman. Keep low, now!"

As the boats thrashed closer, figures were rising to their feet unsteadily to peer at the ship; men in rough seamen's garb, and occasionally the grey-blue of the *Troupes de la Marine*. Here and there a woman was clasped in a welter of billowing skirts and feathered bonnets, bottles waving in free hands. At least one voice was beginning to hail the brig, calling out a name and following it with what sounded like inventive abuse.

"Present!" said Mainwaring, in a low, hard voice. Behind him he could hear a sudden noise: the thump of feet along the lower deck beginning to slap on the rungs of the companionway ladder.

The barrels of the muskets came level, their browned metal gleaming dully in the gloom, the men sighting along them, white-eyed and breathless.

"*Fire!*"

With a rippling flash of pink flame, bright in the gloom, the pans of the muskets flared, a split-instant later the muzzles spitting out two-foot lancets of flame towards the approaching boats. The thunderous report of the ragged volley echoed in a rippling series of crump-crumps from the dark shoreline.

But the sounds were lost in the shriek of alarm and curses that rang out from the three boats as they slewed round, their oars flailing suddenly out of control as the half-dozen thin jets of the musket shots' fall jetted up, slim fingers of spray, a few yards ahead of the boats. Pale faces were staring at the brig in open-mouthed incredulity.

"Prime and load!" commanded Mainwaring. "Make ready! P'sent! *Fire*, damn you!"

Again the muskets barked in a spluttering salvo, the pink flame bright, the curling smoke acrid, and more little geysers shot up in front of the boats.

Sawyer was rising from his firing position, ducking a bit to see past the drifting smoke, and pointing shoreward.

"Look, sir!" he marvelled. "They're turnin'!"

Mainwaring stood, coughing as a tendril of smoke reached him and lodged like a burr in his throat. Then the smoke was drifting clear, and he could see the boats, slewing round broadside now, oars flailing and chopping the water into white froth. The figures in the boats were lost in a tumult of thrashing arms, screams, oaths, and cries of rage or alarm.

But they were turning.

"Heading for shore, sir, right enough," James Howe confirmed, standing.

"Indeed," said Mainwaring. "Let's hurry them on their way. Prime and load!"

The cartridge-box flaps slapped and the ramrods clinked as another round was driven home. On Mainwaring's command the long weapons fired again, this time a parade-ground thunderclap worthy of a Guards company.

"That's done it, sir!" exulted Fell, in the swirl of smoke. "Look at 'em run!"

"Yes, and we'd damned well better pray they don't return too soon! Mr Howe? I'll trouble you –"

Mainwaring did not finish, turning instead as a clutch of men surged up the forward companionway, with others now appearing up the after one. Seamen, by the look of them, thought Mainwaring; in rags, some of them, and mostly filthy, a few unsteady from hunger or abuse. But seamen. And at their head, a broadly smiling Jackman and Hooke.

"'Ere they be, zur!" beamed Hook. "All lads from *Hotspur*, zur! Prime 'ands, right enough!"

Mainwaring rose, looking closely at them, seeing the reassuring strength of their bodies, the steady gazes in darkly weathered faces as they grouped before him, nodding and exchanging grins with Sawyer and the others.

"*Hotspur*'s lads," said Mainwaring, wonderingly. "Then they didn't do for you all!" He scanned the rugged faces. "Who's senior here?"

A powerfully-built man in a check shirt and ragged petti-coat breeches, the thick blond hair before his ears twisted into small pigtail copies of the long queue down his back, stepped forward on broad, splayed feet and knuckled his forehead.

"That'd be me, zur. Elusha Rumford, boatswain's mate.

I thank 'ee fer deliverin' us, zur. Them Frogs what took us were proper swine; put shot into half the lads afore givin' over, an' takin' us into irons, zur."

"We know, Rumford." Mainwaring looked over the ready, expectant faces. "How long were you below there? Did they feed you?"

"Some bread, more like chalk dust, an' a butt o' water, zur. Kept the life in us, but nought else."

"We'll see to that, as soon as it's safe to get a galley fire lit." Mainwaring glanced ashore at the boats which were vanishing into a shadowed cove.

"Listen to me, Rumford, all of you," he said, his tone brisk. "I am Captain Edward Mainwaring of the Royal Navy, and until recently I commanded *Pallas*, forty-four guns. But we've lost her, and these are all of us who are left. I have no authority over them or you, unless you choose to grant it. D' ye follow?"

Rumford nodded. "Aye, zur, that'd be clear enough. But your Mr 'Ooke, 'ere, told us a bit about 'ee, zur, beggin' yer pardon." He looked over his shoulder at the other men. "We'll sail under 'ee, zur, you an' yer officers, if ye be meanin' t'ave anuvver go at th' damned Frogs, zur."

Mainwaring grinned. "That I do, Rumford, that I do!"

Rumford nodded, like a yeoman approving the purchase of cattle. "Then we'll sail under ye, zur, an' fight, if ye'll 'ave us."

"Have you?" Mainwaring laughed. "Christ, Rumford, I'll pay you all the bounty out of my own pocket, when I can. Aye, I'll have ye!"

There was a growl of approval from the watching Hotspurs, and Mainwaring felt a pulse of emotion in his chest, a glimmer of hope and possibility, where a moment before there had been little but resignation.

"Now, as to our recent visitors –" Mainwaring turned to look shoreward, where the boats had vanished in the shadows. But now lanterns were beginning to move and bob like firefly specks along the darkened shore.

He turned back, rubbing his hands together briskly. "Listen carefully, now. This is Mr Howe, my first lieutenant. The second lieutenant, Mr Pellowe, is wounded and is in our boat alongside. He'll need help aboard. Mr Hooke's the sailing master, and you've met him. These other lads you'll meet quickly enough. Rumford, I'll begin by rating you boatswain."

"Thank'ee, zur!" the man beamed.

"No thanks needed. I'm sure you'll earn your warrant, and I'll speak for it if you do. Mr Hooke? Winton is for'rard, looking at how she's anchored. Find out what he's discovered. And then," and he spat over the rail as if for emphasis, "I'd be obliged if you lads would get some damned sail on this gallant *Hotspur* of yours!"

"Aye, zur!" puffed Hooke, suddenly all muscular purpose. "Jackman, you git b'low an' fetch Winnie back up 'ere, an' report on that 'awser. She's got two anchors aslung, an' may be on th' bower. Off wiv ye!"

Jackman put down his musket and was off in a run.

"Rumford?" Hooke was jabbing a finger at the man. "Crikey, I'll 'ave t' call 'ee *Mister* Rumford, aye? Set yer lads to forem'st and main. Slade and Sawyer there be topmen. Ye can take one apiece fer aloft. Sing out as ye gits 'em told off."

Rumford nodded and turned to the waiting Hotspurs. "Right, then. Time t' get canvas on 'er, lads! Jones, Macauley, Jewkes, Bennett, Thompson. You'll take th' fore. Anderson, Yeo, Taffy, Stewart, th' main. The rest o' you lot tail on t' th' lee an' weather braces an' sheets, an' listen up fer Mr 'Ooke, 'ere. Jump to it! Lively, now, lively!"

Mainwaring glanced at Howe, watching the *Hotspur* men move to the ratlines, his face clouded with concern.

"D'ye think they've the strength, James?" he asked quietly. "I'd have liked to get a cookfire lit for them."

Howe nodded. "I know, sir. I think they'll do for a bit. They're right on Slade's heels, going aloft. But I'll get someone told off as cook and have a cookfire started as soon as we get clear, sir."

"Good." Mainwaring turned back to the rail. "Sergeant Fell? You and your lads get Mr Pellowe aboard and into the great cabin, directly. James, see that the boat is walked aft and made fast securely. We'll tow her until we're clear."

"Sir," said Howe. Fell had echoed the reply and was already monkeying over the side in seamanlike quickness.

"Mr Hooke?" called Mainwaring. "You'll need topsails and headsails, I'd think. The breeze is slight, but it's off-shore. And there seems to be negligible current."

"Aye, zur. Tops'ls an' 'eads'ls it'll be, zur."

"Mr Howe? You'll take the wheel, James, until we can get a seaman told off once we're under way."

Howe smiled. "Aye, aye, sir. Actually, first time at a wheel since I was a snottie!" He moved quickly to the great double wheel, casting off its lashings.

There was a thumping up the companionway forward, and Winton appeared, grimy and breathless. He loped aft to Mainwaring and knuckled his forelock.

"Yer pardon, sir. The ship's held only on the bower, an' that wiv a spare cable rove off round the windlass an' then to th' forem'st timber-bitts, sir. Ain't on her prime killicks, nor cable. Like she was ready t' slip at a clock's tick, sir."

Mainwaring nodded. "D'ye hear that, Mr Hooke?"

"Aye, zur," said Hooke from the mainmast foot where he had been watching the men scramble aloft. "Freedom's worth a bower anchor, t' my mind, zur."

Mainwaring glanced ashore at the moving lights. The response from the French would not be long in coming.

"To mine as well. Get for'rard again, Winton. Find yourself an axe from Mr Rumford. The moment I give you the word, cut the cable. But on my command, mind!"

"Aye, aye, sir!" In the next moment Winton was off, with a quick word with Rumford who bellowed after him that an axe was secured to a bulkhead at the foot of the fore companionway.

Mainwaring turned on Howe. "Now, James, how does she lie? Head to wind? I can't tell if there's any set to the current or tide here."

"Aye, sir. The wind's nor'easterly, what there is of it. Puts the 'sprit bearing almost on the far headland. Damn my eyes, sir, if we flat out the stays'l and jib to starboard, and put the helm over to larboard a touch, she should fall off and let us reach clear out of the bay, on a starboard tack!"

Mainwaring looked aft and then forward again. "Aye, but that damned lee shore is close. We put her in irons, my friend, and we'll see the inside of that French jail –"

A pink flash lit the night from deep in the shadowed shore where the lantern pinpricks had been dancing. The punching concussion of a heavy gun resounded in Mainwaring's ears even as a sound like ripping linen reached them, and then with a slap and hiss a towering, glittering geyser of spray leaped up ahead of *Hotspur*'s bows, tumbling back in a drifting mist over the ship's deck.

"Oh, Christ!" breathed James Howe.

"More likely the French, James," said Mainwaring drily. "Sink me, I was a fool to think they wouldn't have a battery of some sort covering every anchorage! Mr Hooke! Can ye set canvas?"

"Aye, zur!" came the bellow from forward. "Castin' off th' gaskets, now, zur! Stand by them jib an' stays'l halyards, you two! Off pins, an' haul! Roundly, now! Sheets, there! Flat 'em out t' starboard! *Move* y'selves!"

Mainwaring cupped his hands as he saw two of the Hotspurs hauling like fiends on the headsail halyards, and the pale triangles of the sails began to snake rhythmically up their stays.

"Winton! D'ye hear me? Cut the cable!"

An acknowledging cry came from below in the ship, and axe blows began to sound.

Hooke's roar continued in a torrent of orders and instructions interwoven with ingenious oaths and obscenities that sent the Hotspurs' eyebrows rising even as they scrambled to obey. "Let fall tops'ls! Overhaul that whoreson buntline on the fore, there! Sheets an' braces, now! *Haul*, ye pox-arsed duck! Where'd ye think ye were a sailor? A soft-titted wench'd do better! *Haul!*"

With a whump that shook the deck, the great grey surfaces of the fore and maintopsails fell open simultaneously, the sheet blocks rattling as, sweating with effort, the men at the pinrails stretched the great quadrilaterals out to their full shape, the falls collapsing in snakelike coils round their bare feet.

"Haul in, snug!" barked Hooke. "Now, ease 'em, ease 'em till they fill, full an' round, like the woman ye'll never have!"

On the foredeck, several men had seized the clews of the foretopmast staysail and the jib and were leaning out over the starboard rail, holding the tall sails' feet out to force *Hotspur*'s bow off to seaward.

"She's startin' t' swing, zur!" Hooke bellowed.

Mainwaring felt the breeze on his face, tantalising him, and saw the bows begin to move, the finger of the jib-boom tracking along the dark shore. But soon she would fetch up against the cable as the slack was taken up . . .

There was another pink flash, lightning-bright in the night, from the hidden shore gun, and again the concussion punched at *Hotspur*. The tearing sound was in the air, and then with a jetting hiss, the ball struck mere inches, it seemed, from *Hotspur*'s larboard quarter. The geyser shot up in a gleaming blade of pale water that collapsed back in a drenching downpour over Mainwaring and Howe where they stood on the quarterdeck.

"Too damn close, sir!" spat a suddenly sodden James Howe, cuffing at his face.

"Aye!" Mainwaring shook the water from him like a dog and sprang to the waistdeck rail, watching the vessel's swing slow, seeming to stop. Then the axe blows ceased, there was a cry of exultation from Winton, and the ship began again to swing. But the dark snout of the headland was still not across the bows.

"Come on, come *on*!" murmured Mainwaring.

"Steerageway, sir!" cried Howe in the next instant, even as high overhead the topsails suddenly filled with another deck-shaking thump. Under their feet *Hotspur* heeled, began to move, water gurgling round her forefoot and under her counter. The rigging creaked, a marvellous sound to Mainwaring's ears, and the masts popped against their wedges as the power of the faint but steady breeze began to be transferred down through the ship's rigging.

"Heads'ls, there! Ye've done it! Let go, an' haul!" Hooke bellowed. On the larboard side, the staysail and jib were rippling and then punching out into still curves, while the sheets to leeward were being hauled in with quick, brisk movements, the weather sheets writhing and snaking round the stays.

"Christ save us, she's afoot, zur!" exulted Hooke in the waist.

"Aye, Mr Hooke, and I'll trouble you for the t'gallants and the forecourse, if ye please," Mainwaring boomed back. He spun to Howe. "What's your ship's head, James?"

Howe's eyes flicked to the binnacle. "Nor'west by west . . . nor'west . . ."

"Meet her! Steady on nor'west! Not a bit to windward! Sheet in, there, Mr Hooke! Secure the forecourse tack well for'rard!"

"Nor'west, aye, sir," said Howe, as intent as any barefooted foremast hand on his muscular task, and a far cry from the slim, almost dandyish young man who had hesitantly entered Mainwaring's great cabin several years before.

Hotspur was beginning to sense the high, cool winds off the dark land mass, spilling out over the warm sea, and her speed began to increase noticeably. The reef points started to tap against the still, arched canvas, and the rush and hiss of the sea along her flank sounded above the creak and pop of her rigging. The ship was alive again, and the faces of the men on deck showed exultation; freedom from their emprisonment, freedom as well from the dangers of the land.

Hooke was cupping his hands. "Well 'nough, aloft, there! On deck with ye!" He bounded in ursine glee up the quarterdeck ladder.

"Them Froggies ashore ain't fired again, zur!" he said, peering aft over the transom rail to the shadowed, receding shoreline.

"You could be mistaken any moment, Isaiah!" said Mainwaring, looking aloft at the masthead pennant. "Steady, James. Full and by, now. Does she have a weather helm?"

"A touch, sir. A spoke or two. She –"

There was another flash astern, and as the thump of the gun, more muted now, echoed out over the water, the ball struck a good hundred yards in their wake, the geyser harmless and oddly beautiful in the dim light, like grey silk.

"Bloody awful gunners, zur!" snorted Hooke, and spat over the side.

"More's the luck for us," said Mainwaring quietly. "We'll need a helmsman, Mr Hooke. I'd suggest Winton first to relieve Mr Howe until we can set a watch system. Then get below and see if Mr Pellowe's settled – I saw Fell helping him below. And we'll want that cookfire, and a look at the water casks. James, you'll join me with Stephen in the great cabin as soon as you're relieved. Let's see what we've got to work with!"

Hooke jabbed a thumb at the huge white Bourbon ensign that curled and rippled over their heads.

"Want me t' strike that rag, zur?"

Mainwaring looked up at it for a moment. "No," he said thoughtfully. "No, Mr Hooke, leave it. It'll give us protection until that drunken lot ashore get over their shame at losing their ship so easily, and spread the word."

He grinned without mirth. "We'll use it as a cloak to cover some nasty business of our own."

"Where, zur, beggin' yer pardon?"

Mainwaring glanced at Howe, the grin now real.

"Where? Why, Port Louis itself, Mr Hooke, wherever else?"

Caroline Grenville crouched by the entrance to Rigaud de la Roche-Bourbon's sleeping cabin, her ear pressed to the thin wood of the door. She listened, intent and trembling, to the breathing in the great cabin, where she imagined he lay sprawled on the deck's painted canvas or the settee that ran under the stern lights. It was the heavy breathing of a man sodden with drink, and gradually as she listened it deepened into a sonorous snore.

She let out a long, shaking breath, her face in her hands for a moment, trying to keep the panic from welling up within her. Her gown was virtually in rags, and with no comb or the simplest of toiletries, her hair hung in wisps round her temples and over her forehead, and her face was pale and smudged. The torn bodice of her gown had long ceased to be an effective covering, and as she sat taking stock of her situation she realised with a shiver that Roche-Bourbon's latest attentions had left her shamelessly exposed.

She shuddered as she thought again of him blundering into the little cabin in the dark of the night, his speech thick with drink, his normally precise attire askew, his actions clumsy and ineffectual as he had lurched towards where she lay cowering under the thin coverlet. He had fallen across the box bunk with a grunt and exuding alcohol fumes, wriggling round to force his weight atop her, sniggering inanely as he pawed at her breasts. She had cried out, twisting under him, fighting off his clutching hands, certain that this was the moment when he would take her in a horror of brutal drunkenness.

Suddenly he had pulled back from her blows, fallen awkwardly off the bunk, and had risen unsteadily to his feet, huge in the light of the doorway. As she had shrunk against the bulkhead he had stared at her, the dark eyes glittering for a moment in anything but drunken stupidity, a slow smile crossing his features.

Then he had spun, the velvet coattails swirling about him, and had gone out of the door, thrusting it shut behind him. Caroline had listened in breathless silence as she heard the key seemingly turn in the lock, and the shuffling steps as Roche-Bourbon crossed the cabin, to slump down with a contented grunt, his heels scraping on the painted canvas.

She grasped the door latch and turned it slowly. To her surprise and momentary terror it opened, the door swinging away with a creak and thumping against the bulkhead as she shrank back against the box bunk. For a moment she waited, sure the tall figure would arise and come to the door to finish what had been begun so many times. Then, her heart pounding, she crept to the doorway and peered through.

The great cabin was dark, the candles in the hanging lantern guttered out, and only the stars shining through the stern lights illuminated the figure that lay sprawled in the gloom over the settee like some great cat.

Her hand at her throat, Caroline Grenville stole into the room, her eyes wide and flicking whitely this way and that. She had no real idea of what she was seeking, only too aware that she was essentially trapped in a French warship whose officers acquiesced in their commander's mistreatment of her. A desperate resolution was beginning to form in her mind.

Her eyes moved from the slumped figure to the broad desk in the centre of the cabin. The light from the stern lights glinted on steel and as she moved closer she could see that the gleaming object was the barrel of a small, deadly-looking pistol.

With a glance at Roche-Bourbon she reached for the pistol, picking it up with slow care. Her heart was pounding as she felt the cold menace of the metal. Remembering what she had once been taught, she pulled the little weapon back to half-cock and checked the priming in the pan, easing the frizzen home noiselessly. Then she turned, staring with wide eyes at the dark, sprawled figure on the settee. She raised the pistol slowly, trembling a little, centring it on the sleeping face. For a moment her fingers tightened on the weapon, her heart racing.

Then she lowered it, a small, still voice seeming to speak within her.

Not yet, it said. *It must not look like murder. His men would kill me and their revenge would be terrible. Wait.*

Letting out a long, shuddering sigh, Caroline Grenville eased the weapon off full cock with her other hand, and lifted the muzzle. Holding the little weapon against her, she turned towards the desk, rearranging objects hurriedly to fill the gap left by the removal of the pistol. Then she backed slowly into the shadows until she reached the doorway of her prison. For a long moment she stared at the sprawled figure of Rigaud de la Roche-Bourbon.

The right time will come for this, said her mind again. *The right time, when I shall repay you – and stay alive.*

She turned and quietly shut the cabin door behind her.

Twenty-seven hours after her escape from the guns of the bay, *Hotspur* was just under a league off the eastern coast of Mauritius, having worked to the north in the darkness, weathered Cap Malheureux on the northern tip, and stretched away to the eastward until the backing of the wind to the north had given the ship a fair wind for the run south. Under reduced rig during the daylight hours, *Hotspur* had jogged slowly southward very much in the guise of a small East Indiaman inbound from Madras. Now as the inkiness of the second night began to lift, the graceful little brig was some six leagues to the north of Mahébourg, under topsails and jib alone. The wind was steady from the north, and the ship lifted and fell quietly along with a rhythmic rush at her bows, her canvas still grey curves in the pre-dawn light, the single lantern above the transom rail flickering above the burble and hiss of the wake.

Below, in *Hotspur*'s great cabin, Edward Mainwaring was peering intently down at a chart which was unrolled on the narrow trestle table which had passed for a desk in the simply-fitted little ship. Across from him, his expression equally intent, stood the slim figure of James Howe.

Mainwaring tapped the chart with one brown finger.

"There. There's where we'll begin, James."

"Mahébourg? But I thought the French would be gathering their squadron at Port Louis, if anywhere, sir?"

"They would, and likely are, James, but I have in mind doing a bit more than simply annoying the French. Their squadron could be interfered with in a number of ways, to try to keep it from falling on poor Peyton. One small gun brig can't do that alone, but more than one vessel could. Remember what we achieved in Toulon with that odd little collection of craft."

Howe's eyebrows rose. "You mean go after *prizes*, sir?"

"Yes, in fact."

Howe puffed out his cheeks. "They'd have to be small vessels, like this or smaller, sir. And we'd have no one to man them. I don't see how—"

Mainwaring held up a hand. "Trust me for the moment, James. In all truth, I don't see the course ahead clearly, either. Perhaps all we'll do is collect a poor effort at fireships. I don't know. But I *do* know that if we're to have any effect on the damned French, it's going to take more than one hull. I mean to get them."

"And then, sir?"

Mainwaring smiled crookedly. "And then we go by the feeling in our guts, James. I'm afraid I can offer little more than that."

Howe grinned back. "Not that we haven't followed you on less, sir. But I was thinking that ten six-pounders will do bloody little damage against a seventy-gunner."

"Aye. But if instead –" began Mainwaring.

There was a slap and thump of bare feet from the after companionway, and a knock sounded at Mainwaring's door.

"Come?"

The tousled blond head of one of the Hotspurs, whom Mainwaring identified after a moment as Macauley, thrust in through the door.

"Mr Hooke's pardon, sir, but you'd best come on deck. We've sighted a sail to loo'ard."

Mainwaring exchanged a look with Howe. "Perhaps our first prey, James." He nodded. "Very well, Macauley. Tell the master we'll join him directly."

"Aye, aye, sir!" said the man, and was gone.

Howe had moved to the narrow cot which was the only bed in the cabin. On it Stephen Pellowe lay in pale sleep under a coarse coverlet, and Howe touched his forehead gently.

"How is he, James? He was able to get down all the broth I had made for him."

"Asleep, and with little fever, sir. I think he's better. God grant the wound doesn't go putrid."

Mainwaring sighed, his eyes dark with concern. "Aye. And the sooner we get on with our business, the less he'll have to suffer. Join me on deck, James."

A moment later, Howe and Mainwaring were standing with spread feet on the spray-dappled windward side of the brig's quarterdeck. The wind had veered to the north-east, and *Hotspur* was on a broad reach as she bore off to the southward, lifting and rolling as the dark swells passed beneath her, the whitecaps beginning to wink here and there on the sea surface as the wind built with the slow coming of the day. A curling wave from time to time would dash against the brig's flank, and Mainwaring and Howe were soon sodden with the warm spray as they stood, peering into the dim distance to the leeward of the ship.

Isaiah Hooke, huge in tattered shirt and grimy petticoat

150

breeches, stood with the two officers, one burly paw pointing off.

"See there, zur. Just as that 'aze or squall lifted. Twin lateens, runnin' wing-an'-wing afore the wind. She'd be a Mahometan, zur."

Mainwaring stared, wiping the salt spray from his dripping face with one hand. It stung in his eyes, and he blinked. Then he saw it: a low, black hull with beautiful sheer and a strangely raked bow with a beaklike stempost, and two enormous, winglike lateens resembling pale scythes in the pre-dawn light, arching and graceful above the dark hull.

"Bit out of the way for an Arab, I'd think," said Howe, more to himself than anyone.

"Lessen 'e's a slaver, zur. A blackbirder."

"You'd think he'd be wary of the French," mused Mainwaring. Then his tone hardened. "Whatever his reason for being here, gentlemen, that is a ship. As I recall, one can handle lateens with damned few hands. Mr Hooke, call Rumford to us. I don't know if we can fight this fellow, but, by Christ, I mean us to try!"

"Zur!" croaked Hooke, knuckling a forelock and making off forward over the wet, canted deck. He was back in a moment with Rumford at his side.

"Mr Rumford, who's your gunner?" demanded Mainwaring.

"That was Whittaker, sir, but the Frogs did fer 'im. 'Im an' 'is mate, Starkey. Shot 'em like fish in a barrel, they did. 'Twere 'orrible, sir."

Mainwaring nodded, his face grave. "I see. I'm sorry, Rumford. But we've got to fight this ship if we've any chance of paying the swine back. What d'ye know of our guns, beyond what I've found?"

"Ten six-pounders is all, sir, for long guns, and smart as paint if well served. Them's in th' waist, five t' larboard an' five t' starb'd. There's four swivels, one-pounders, t' either side o' the' foredeck an' the quarterdeck 'ere, sir, in them strongbacks, but the Frogs must've struck them below."

"The magazine?"

"No proper one, sir. Just that room aft o' th' orlop for the casks an' fer fillin', sir."

"Good Christ!" muttered Mainwaring.

"Sorry, sir. We ain't no man-o'-war."

Mainwaring grinned at Rumford's hurt expression. "I understand, Mr Rumford. Forgive me. No slur was intended. What of small arms?"

"That chest I showed 'ee, sir. Twenty good Sea Service Bess firelocks, an' a brace or two o' pistols. The key'd be in the cabin, sir."

"I think I may have found it. Ought else? Cutlasses?"

"No, sir. Nought."

"Powder and shot?"

"Dunno, sir. Last time I was in there wiv Whittaker, on me rounds, like, there was a good twenty casks o' powder for the great guns, an' mayhap fifty rounds made up for the six-pounders and swivels, made an' rolled. Besides what we got in th' garlands, there, we'd 'ave close on six hunnert iron shot, sir."

"That's more reassuring. Did he say ought of musket cartridge?"

"Can't say, sir," said Rumford. "Directly we put Cape Colony astern the gunner was makin' firelock rounds; 'e may 'ave rolled an' made a score or so fer each Bess, sir."

Mainwaring grinned at Howe. "Sink me, James, if we can manage to fire the damned things with this corporal's guard we've got, we should be the terror of the seas," he said drily. He looked for a moment at the Arab vessel and then turned back to Rumford. "How many of your lads have done the exercise at the great guns, Mr Rumford?"

Rumford winced. "Barely 'alf, sir, not bein' a man-o'-war, an' such. But they're steady, no flinchin', an' all as will tail on t' a gun tackle wiv a will, or shoulder a firelock t' avenge a messmate's loss, sir."

Mainwaring nodded, his mind beginning to race. "I'm

sure they are, Mr Rumford. Now listen carefully, all of you. Mr Rumford, you're to pick the smallest possible crew of sailhandlers that you'd need to manage the ship under fighting sail, even if it means a foot race from one pin-rail to the next. Then send the rest to Mr Howe, and report yourself and your sailhandlers to Mr Hooke. Isaiah, you'll lead 'em, and carry out my orders for working the ship."

"Zur," rumbled Hooke.

"James, as soon as you've got your men from Mr Rumford here, blend in the Pallases with the Hotspurs amd report to me how many six-pounders you can man. Appoint gun captains and people to monkey up the cartridge. Take Sergeant Fell and put him in the magazine; he's steady and has done work like that before. When you're ready to stand by the guns, report to me, but under no circumstances open the gunports or run out. That we do at the last possible moment. Clear?"

"Aye, aye, sir!" Howe's eyes were alight. "And the small arms, sir?"

Mainwaring shook his head. "We can't afford the luxury of musketmen, James. But get into that arms chest and have muskets with cartridge boxes to hand behind the gun positions. The lads can go for them if we come to boarding distance."

"Sir."

"And one other thing, Mr Hooke. Keep Winton on the wheel as coxswain. He does his duty well."

Hooked nodded. "Aye, zur. 'E'll like that."

"I'm sure he will. Very well, then, questions?" said Mainwaring. "Good. How soon can you do this?"

"Fifteen to twenty minutes, and we'd be ready for the first round, I'd guess, sir," said Howe, after an exchange of glances with Hooke and Rumford.

"Not going to Quarters in a first-rate," said Mainwaring drily, "but never mind. If you can give us guns to fire in that time, I'll order a double tot o' spirits, if the buggers

153

left some good Jamaica rum in the ship! All we need is fighting spirit, gentlemen. You have your orders."

Twenty-five minutes later, *Hotspur* was as prepared to fight as could reasonably be expected given her few people, Mainwaring thought, his stomach beginning to flutter uncomfortably. He was pacing the quarterdeck barefoot, clad only in the remains of his ragged breeches and a checked shirt he had found in the chest of the Frenchman who had briefly occupied the great cabin before him. Ahead in the waist, two of the six-pounders were fully manned, but the remaining eight had been set up, with tackles and tools in place, the guns ready to be served by the two crews whom James Howe had set to run from gun to gun. It would not allow a full broadside; but it would allow all five guns per side to fire, and that was as much as Mainwaring could hope for. Behind Mainwaring, two squat and ugly little swivels sat unattended in their yokes and strongbacks, primed and loaded.

It will have to do, thought Mainwaring grimly. He turned from the waistdeck rail to where Winton stood in spread-footed attentiveness at the helm, Hooke beside his shoulder.

"Mr Hooke? Is there a glass in the drawer of the binnacle box?"

"Zur, the Frogs didn't make off wiv it." He pulled a leatherbound brass telescope from the drawer of the binnacle box and padded over to hand it to Mainwaring.

"Be charitable, Isaiah. They likely needed the thing." Mainwaring pulled open the long bring-'em-near and glanced up at the foretop lookout's perch.

"Foretop, there! How does she bear?"

"Dead abeam t' starboard, sir!" came the cry from aloft. "Steerin' th' same course we be, wing an' wing, sir!"

"D'ye see colours?"

A pause. "Nought but green pennants at the yard peaks, sir!"

Mainwaring spread his feet as *Hotspur* rolled slowly under

154

him and raised the glass. It took but a moment to steady the curiously flattened image across the distance.

"Can 'ee make 'er out, zur?" came Hooke's growl at his shoulder.

"Aye, she's an Arab, right enough. Turbans on the lot of 'em. Some gentlemen in finer robes aft. A clutch of Arab hands peering at us. A fair lot of people, Isaiah," breathed Mainwaring. "She'll be a fight to take."

"Gunports, zur?"

"Two. Perhaps three. But it's difficult to tell with these things. I've heard of *sambuks* – like a cutter or a pinnace – fairly a-bristle with ordnance, and big deep-sea dhows with little more than a wheel-lock or two. No way of telling with the poxed Arabs. They'll either blow you out of the water with enough broadside to sink a first-rate, or just pelt you with rocks and nightsoil. Only Christ knows when you'll face either."

Hooke's eyebrows rose. "Didn't know yew'd sailed Arab waters, zur?"

"Haven't, in fact. But there was an old man, Ezra Pennefather, who sailed in the *William and Anne* out of Old Town, and had made two voyages to the Zanzibar coast. Scared myself and the other lads that skylarked about the waterfront half to death with his tales." Mainwaring pursed his lips, and raised the glass again to peer through it. "The one thing he did make quite clear was that one should never assume the Arab is a coward." He paused. "That's damned odd."

"Zur?" said Hooke.

"I couldn't be certain, Isaiah, but I thought I saw a *blond* head appear above the bulwark for an instant."

Hooke spat into the sea. "Some poor bastard, took prisoner."

Mainwaring nodded, snapping shut the glass. "Aye, but that's of no matter now." He handed the glass to Hooke and cupped his hands, peering up at the foretop. "Aloft, there! Any changes o' course in the Arab?"

"No, sir! Like he was ploughin' a furrow, sir!"

Mainwaring nodded, his lips a tight line.

"Very well. Mr Hooke, sheets and braces, if you please. Stand by to alter course to starboard. We'll come to a broad reach. Winton, stand by. Now, two points to starboard!"

"Two points to starb'd, sir!" echoed Winton, his eyes bright with excitement, and turned the great double wheel with slow, steady power.

Hotspur lunged off to starboard, heeling as she came off her run, and the freshening wind caught her on her quarter. The brig's masts creaked against the wedges and partners, and the sheet and brace blocks rattled as Hooke's sailhandlers threw muscular effort into their work. The swells were growing now, and the ship's bows began to build a roaring white cloud of foam beneath the steeving jib-boom and the cutwater. Above the transom rail the white Bourbon ensign streamed out over the quarter rail in pure, snapping beauty that made Mainwaring look at it for an instant in honest respect.

But now *Hotspur*'s jib-boom end, beyond the still, hard arches of the jibs, was steadying on the distant and graceful shape of the Arab, and Mainwaring was spinning on Winton, barking, "Meet her! Not a point more, Winton! Steady as she bears, now!"

As Winton called out his acknowledgment, Hooke appeared in the waist from behind the longboat and bounded up the quarterdeck ladder.

"Sink me, zur, but she's a tidy little craft. Fair flies, she does, off th' wind."

Mainwaring grinned at him. "Aye, a ship with canvas lifting to a wind brings you to life well enough."

Hooke opened his mouth to speak when the foretop's voice rang down, high overhead.

"Deck, there! She's turnin', sir! Towards us!"

Mainwaring hung on to the windward rail as *Hotspur* heeled beneath him. He could see the Arab's aftermost lateen gybing over with a series of wavelike ripples in the

156

sail, the dhow heeling hard over to starboard as the huge yard came over. The image of the hull foreshortened as the dhow carried on through the turn, and in the next moment the craft had turned to bear directly for *Hotspur*, the two lateens like grey scythes above the narrow black shape of the hull. From the yard peaks, the long tendrils of the green pennants floated out to leeward, and a white line of foam boiled and flashed below the dhow's cutwater.

"Look at 'er come on, zur. Wants a scrap, that 'un."

"So it would appear," said Mainwaring tersely. He narrowed his eyes, calculating the distance off to the hurrying dhow, and the angle of the wind on the simple white pennant at *Hotspur*'s maintruck. He cupped his hands, looking forward.

"Mr Howe! Do not open your gunports and run out until the last possible moment, before you fire!"

"Aye, aye, sir!" came Howe's cry.

Beside Mainwaring, Hooke was looking puzzled. "Damn odd, says I," he muttered.

"What's that, Mr Hooke?"

"That Arab, sir. 'E's makin' fer us wiv no apparent fear, like. Even a little brig like this c'd throw a fair broadside, and w'd call fer some care. But 'e's showin' none, zur."

Mainwaring narrowed his eyes. "I've heard they can be fanatics. Overwhelming odds not necessarily a deterrent."

Hooke shook his head. "Dunno, zur. Seems t' me 'e's actin' more like 'e wants t' *speak* t' us, zur."

Mainwaring squinted at the dhow, seeing the heads of men working about the deck. There was no glint of steel, no evident arms, even at this distance. Then he glanced down at his clothing.

"Well, if they *do* want to speak to the Frenchman they may think still mans this ship – although Christ knows why – they'll be in for a shock at how we look. Surely it can't be possible that –"

"Look 'ee that, zur!" burst in Hooke. "One of 'em's up on the stempost, wavin' at us, zur!"

157

It was as Hooke said. A white-turbaned figure, in ballooning scarlet trousers, was astride the angled stempost of the dhow, riding it like a mount, waving bare, muscular arms in a gesture of anything but attack.

"By God, Isaiah, I think you're right!" Mainwaring breathed.

"Zur, one o' th' Frogs left a grey coat an' cocked 'at in th' cabin I've stowed me gear in. Might fit ye," said Hooke. "A ruzee dogurr, so t' speak?"

"A *ruse de guerre* indeed. And right you are, Mr Hooke. Get a man below for them, quickly. And stand by for some rapid sailhandling. Talk or fight, I want that bastard's ship!" Mainwaring cupped his hands, looking for Howe. "Mr Howe! Keep your lads down, out o' sight below the bulwarks! You lads on deck, act as if all is well!" He turned back to Hooke. "Now, Isaiah."

"Wot's yer plan, zur?"

"Practise my French, actually. They're coming on rather quickly, so you'd best see to that coat and hat!"

Ten minutes later, *Hotspur* had rounded up into the wind in a storm of rumpling canvas and slatting blocks, and now her foretopsail was flat aback, and the little brig was pitching slowly in the brightening sunlight, the wind moaning in her rigging, the whitecapped waves atop the longer swells curling in to splash and hiss along her flank. Edward Mainwaring, standing in cramped discomfort in a coat at least two sizes too small pulled on over his rags, and an equally small cocked hat crammed down on his head, stood shifting his weight from one bare foot to the other, wishing the pangs of hunger in his stomach would go away. He was watching the lean black shape of the dhow coming up steadily on the larboard side. The Arab vessel still bore directly for *Hotspur*, close enough now to see that the two green pennants floating gracefully out above the winging lateens carried gilt, curving inscriptions of some sort.

Mainwaring cupped his hands even as he was realising that the flutterings in his stomach had nothing at all to do with hunger. "Mr Howe," he intoned in a low but penetrating tone. "Move your crews to the *larboard* guns, if you please! Low and out of sight. Stand ready to open, run out, and fire in a clock's tick when I call."

Howe nodded, his face white with tension, and gave several terse, whispered orders. The two crews scuttled in a half-crouch across the waistdeck and stood by two of the six-pounders, the linstocks smoking ready in the gun captains' hands.

"'Ere 'e comes, zur!" called Hooke, by the wheel.

The dhow plunged towards them, a beautifully shaped vessel with sleek, deeply sheered hull and the cloudlike lateens floating above. When it was no more than two hundred yards off, it turned into the wind, the long, angled stempost lifting and lunging in the green swells, the great lateens rumpling and thumping, voices raised in a torrent to send dark-faced, turbaned men in loose-fitting robes to pull in rhythmic energy at the two great purchases that served as the dhow's fore and main sheets.

"Steady, lads, steady," said Mainwaring through his teeth, keeping his face impassive. "Not a move! Keep her into the wind as she lies, Winton!"

"Aye, sir!" breathed Winton, his face pale as marble.

"Look there now, zur," Hooke called. "One of 'em's speakin' to us!" He coughed. "D'ye speak their lingo, zur?"

Mainwaring managed a tight smile. "Enough French to get by. But if the bastard wants a chat in *Arabic* –"

A burly Arab wearing the same scarlet, voluminous pantaloons beneath a loose white kind of surcoat, and with a round white turban set atop a dark and bearded face, scrambled up on the rail towards *Hotspur*, hanging on to a shroud and balancing expertly as the dhow lifted and plunged under the booming, thumping lateens.

"*Messieurs les français!*" came the call, in French thickly-accented but understandable to Mainwaring's ear. "*Vous n'avez pas encore payé, hein? J'ai reçu ces misérables forçats anglais, mais vous me n'avez pas payé, comme le capitaine Roche-Bourbon m'a promis!*" He spread his hands and shrugged a Middle Eastern gesture of philosophical resignation. "*Et bien, quoi faire? Dois-je les tuer, tous?*"

"Dear merciful God!" breathed Mainwaring, turning pale.

"Zur?" Hooke was at his side.

"They've got English prisoners, Isaiah! Sold to 'em as slaves – no, they've been *paid* to take 'em as slaves!" Mainwaring shook his head. "By the *French!* By that bastard whose name I hoped I'd never hear again!"

"*What?*"

"God damn their bloody, pitiless souls!" Mainwaring raged. "Mr Howe! Uncover and run out! At their quarterdeck and rigging! *Fire as you bear!*"

Within an instant of Mainwaring's cry, the larboard gunport lids had slammed open, the gun trucks squealing as the men threw themselves against the side tackles. Barely a moment later, both six-pounders fired with an almost simultaneous ear-splitting bang, the flames licking out on ten-foot tongues from the muzzles.

As the gun's thunder punched at Mainwaring, he saw the first ball hit the dhow at the rail, almost precisely at the point where the Arab had been standing. The ball struck with a visible impact, a radiating halo of splinters and fragments bursting out in all directions, the Arab smashed away and back as if a child's doll kicked away in a tantrum. One red-clad leg, torn from the body, cartwheeled up to slap against the luffing main lateen, and slid down it leaving a long, red smear on the patched, stained canvas.

The second ball punched a gaping hole in the bulwarks, a few feet further aft from where the first ball had penetrated. It passed on its invisible path of destruction over the dhow's quarterdeck, to where two black crewmen in billowing white robes and little red skullcaps had stood, wrestling with the dhow's wheel. The ball felled them like a great fist, sending the bloody wreckage of their bodies cartwheeling across the deck to fetch up in a horrid welter against the far rail. Released from their grip, the dhow began to lurch its bows round towards *Hotspur*.

Oblivious to the shrieks and cries arising from the dhow, Mainwaring was punching the waistdeck rail, pointing with the other hand at the dhow.

"The other guns, James! *Fire*, damn you!"

Howe's two crews scrambled to the next aftermost six-pounders, and again the gunport lids thumped open, the guns' trucks squealing and rumbling as the guns were snouted out through the ports. Even as the men tailing on to the side tackles were giving them a last, grunting haul, the gun captains were crying "Clear!" and the linstocks were arcing down. The two guns fired again within an instant of each other, and again with the sharp, thunderclap reports the tongues of flame licked out, and billowing clouds of acrid smoke boiled up and away from *Hotspur*'s side, shredded away to leeward by the wind, obscuring for a moment the image of the dhow, all save the winglike arcs of the huge lateens above the roiling wall of smoke.

But now Hooke was pointing, his voice a bellow.

"She'll strike us, sartin, zur! Look there!"

Lunging through the swirling smoke, the great black beak of the dhow's stempost was suddenly there, lifting and plunging towards *Hotspur*'s side, the lateens filling out in suddenly still curves as the Arab vessel fell off the wind. The dhow would plunge its stempost into *Hotspur*'s side in moments, unless –

"Winton! Helm, there! Hard a-starboard! Lively, now!" barked Mainwaring. "Brace yourselves, lads!"

With frenzied effort, Winton spun the great wheel to starboard, the brass cap of one spoke flashing in the brilliant morning light. Hooke had understood Mainwaring's action, and even before Mainwaring could bark an order to him, the sailhandlers were hauling with desperate speed at the foretopsail braces and sheets. *Hotspur*'s slow footing ahead began to change to a turn to starboard. But the dhow was upon them, a shadow falling over the rail as the high, angled stempost lifted and then ground down upon the rail with a crash that sent a cloud of splinters and debris flying. The shock trembled the deck beneath Mainwaring's feet, and the hulls thumped and groaned as they ground together.

The impact of the hulls' collision sent Mainwaring staggering to one side, and he sprawled in the scuppers, his elbows and knees banging down hard on the decking. In an instant he was thrashing to his feet, a wild cry issuing from his throat.

"At 'em, lads! *Board! Board!*"

Flinging aside the awkward cocked hat, Mainwaring leaped for the rail, pulling himself up atop it by the main-topmast backstay, teetering there for a moment, and then leaping for the deck of the dhow. He was conscious of many things at once: *Hotspur* rolling and groaning beneath him, as if in pain, the lifting and falling expanse of the dhow's deck, with coils of rope, a bloody welter of debris, and a clutch of white-robed, scrambling bodies, mouths wide in shrieks and cries of anger or alarm, eyes finding Mainwaring with white-edged blazing anger; the enormous curves of the lateens overhead, luffing again with thunderous reports, the double sheets of the fore lateen writhing above the deck like mating pythons; smoke drifting and swirling over the scene – musket smoke? Was *Hotspur* afire? – and the flash and bang of small arms; and the realisation, as he leaped for the dhow's deck, that he was empty-handed.

Mainwaring landed with a heel-jarring jolt on the splintering planking, off-balance. He fell heavily on his side with a grunt, sending a white-clad figure that had been lunging at him off-balance in turn, and tumbling past him with a snarled oath. Mainwaring rolled to his knees, and then ducked his head, half-conscious of the whistling cut of a gleaming, half-moon-shaped blade inches from his face.

He sprang to his feet, his heart pounding, hearing a wild cacophony of Arabic cries, shrieks and bellows of rage, the clash and scrape of steel on steel, the thump and scuffle of struggling bodies above the grinding of the hulls and the booming whump a-whump of the luffing lateens overhead. Now there were other cries, English voices mingling with the Arabic.

A thickset, black-bearded figure was suddenly before Mainwaring, in scarlet pantaloons, his heavily-muscled torso bereft of shirt. The beard split in a toothy grimace of effort, and Mainwaring sensed rather than saw the scimitar cutting down vertically for the crown of his head, a blow that would have cloven him like an apple. With a gasp, Mainwaring twisted, hearing the blade hum past his ear, seeing the man overbalance forward with the force of his stroke. Mainwaring stepped into his fall, lifting his knee hard into the man's groin. A cough of air burst from the Arab's throat, and then Mainwaring butted the man with his own forehead, striking him just below the line of the white turban. Stars flashed for a moment in Mainwaring's eyes, but he saw the Arab stagger back, eyes blinking in porcine confusion, and Mainwaring was on him like a panther, driving his bunched fists in rapid, thudding blows into the man's mid-section. With a grunt the man fell away, his breath gone, the gleaming scimitar falling with a ring to the deck.

As Mainwaring scooped up the light blade and leaped forward over the man, who had sat down abruptly, eyes glazed, another came rushing for him, a gleaming-tipped half-pike centred on Mainwaring's chest. Catching only a glimpse of white robes and a beard distorted by a cry of rage, Mainwaring banged the lunging half-pike aside with a curving parry of the little sword, and then cut with it for the man's throat. He was astonished to see the turbaned head leap from the shoulders as the impact stung his wrist, the headless body tottering forward a step before collapsing, blood pulsing in a dark arc over the deck from the stump of the neck.

In the next instant two struggling bodies bludgeoned into

Mainwaring, a huge Arab locked in silent, deadly struggle with the marine sergeant, Fell. Mainwaring sank to one knee on the decking, slick now with blood, staring as he saw Fell, eyes ablaze with fighting fury, body the Arab back against the bulwark and then bury the point of a half-pike, its shaft gone and Fell wielding it like a dagger, into the man's belly. The Arab screamed horribly like a dying rabbit, and Fell swore in a sob of rage and revulsion, cuffing the dying wretch to the deck with his balled other fist.

Mainwaring fought to his feet, and Fell swung on him, eyes wild, the head of the dripping half-pike raised.

"*Steady*, Sergeant Fell!" cried Mainwaring.

Fell's eyes cleared, he blinked, and then leaned back against the rail, his breath coming in gasps.

"Aye, sir – no fear, sir!"

Mainwaring lurched off-balance against the rail as the dhow heaved under him, and he swung to look at the scene, sensing that the sounds of the struggle had suddenly died away. White-clad bodies, their robes dark with bloody stains, littered the deck, an English body here and there among them; a clutch of Arabs squatting in a knot by the break of the dhow's quarterdeck, watched by two panting, blood-smeared Hotspurs with muskets; a scimitar-wielding Jackman pushing more Arabs towards the gathered knot of prisoners; and *Hotspur*, drawn off a few feet, looking huge and reassuring as she rose and fell beside the dhow.

James Howe was slumped against the mainmast foot in exhaustion, his breath coming in great gasps. He was squinting up at the huge, rumpling lateen, the Arab scimitar in his hand and his arm up to the elbow a solid, dripping scarlet.

Mainwaring moved to him. "James? Damme, are ye –"

Howe shook his head, staring down at the gory blade. "No, sir. Not hurt. Just the damned blood. He squealed like a pig, and kept grabbing at me." Abruptly Howe

164

stumbled to the rail and was sick over the side, the sword clattering to his feet.

Mainwaring touched his shoulder and then turned away, feeling the churning in his own bowels. "Mr Hooke?" he croaked.

Hooke appeared from behind the dhow's idly spinning wheel, which had a very European look to it. He was unmarked save for a spatter of blood across his shirt front, and was carrying a belaying pin.

"Zur?"

Mainwaring pointed, feeling all at once desperately weak. "Get a man on that damned wheel, Isaiah. She'll tear *Hotspur*'s channels out of her if she broaches round. And I'll need you to put hands to those lateen halyards. That bloody luffing will shake the sticks out of her!"

"Aye, aye, zur," said Hooke, casting an anxious glance at Howe. "Mr 'Owe, zur. Is 'e –"

"Overcome for the moment only, Mr Hooke." Mainwaring saw Fell bending over some of the bodies, picking up a musket from beside a dead Hotspur.

"Sergeant Fell? What's the butcher's bill?"

Fell looked up. "Two, sir. Two of the Hotspurs, Bennett and Thompson. Both dead, sir."

"Wounded?"

"None, sir. Bit o' luck, sir."

"Quite," said Mainwaring. He peered at *Hotspur* again, feeling and hearing the thump and grind as the hulls closed once more. His throat was as parched as paper, and he swore.

"God damn the French! Mr Hooke, move quickly to get those lateens down, if you please!"

"Aye, zur. After, zur?"

"Lay out a towline for the present, Mr Hooke. We'll take her in tow while we assess the damage, if this wind builds no more. Sergeant Fell? You'll be responsible for those Arabs. Now, if we can get below and see to those prisoners –"

"Sir?" It was Howe, pale and shaken, but moving again and at the broad midships grating in the dhow's deck. He thrust aside the hunched body of an Arab and peered down through the grillwork. "You'd best look here, sir."

Mainwaring went down the short ladder to the waist, staggering a little as his feet slithered on a patch of blood. Then he looked down, beside Howe.

"Well, bugger me!" he breathed. A dozen pairs of eyes above tight, muzzling gags were watching him; eyes full of concern, anger, relief and excitement; pale eyes, some of startling blue.

"The swine had 'em bound and gagged, sir. Likely so they wouldn't call out to us," said Howe. "If the dhow had sunk, they'd have been finished."

Mainwaring stared down at the men on the deck below, trussed like so many hogs awaiting slaughter, men with the look of English seamen, burly, many fair-haired, in rags.

"Sergeant Fell?" called Mainwaring. "I think we have a place to put those Arab gentlemen. James, get those lads out, and quickly!"

Within an instant, in response to Howe's brisk order, Rumford and half a dozen other Hotspurs were cutting away at the lashings over the companionway door leading down to the middle of the vessel. Then they were off, and Rumford led a rush below. In the next moment they were amongst the imprisoned men, pulling away the gagging, cutting their bonds with quick sweeps of their knives, and exchanging greetings with cries of joy and gruff curses that passed for joy, and playful cuffs on the head.

Howe glanced at Mainwaring. "I think they're more of *Hotspur*'s people, sir."

"I have an odd feeling you're right, James," Mainwaring said with a laugh. "But what a pity that the woman who sailed with them couldn't be free as well."

"Lady Caroline, sir?"

"Yes. I prefer not to think what the damned French may

have done with her." He took a deep breath. "Come, James. Let's meet our new people."

Twenty minutes later, *Hotspur*, under the reduced sail of her spanker and headsails, was pitching slowly ahead into the brisk wind on a starboard tack, tightly close-hauled. Astern of her, the great double lateens lying with their yards in a rumpled mass on the deck, the dhow followed obediently in *Hotspur*'s wake, tugging to the towline that came over her bows past the jutting beak of the stempost and was strongly secured to the dhow's foretack timber-bitts. Amidships in the dhow, Edward Mainwaring steadied himself against the vessel's roll and pitch and gazed in amazement at the line of ragged and dirty – but very evidently cheerful – men who were appearing up the companionway, blinking at the sun and chafing their rope-burned wrists, to find themselves engulfed in back-thumping embraces by more of the Hotspurs.

"How many of 'em *are* there?" murmured Mainwaring to Hooke, who was standing beside him wearing a huge grin.

"Dunno, zur, nigh on fifty, belike. They're all seamen, by the look of 'em, zur. We've a proper ship's company now, I'm thinkin'."

Mainwaring shook his head in wonder. "Fifty! And the damned French were selling the poor bastards to the Arabs as slaves, rather than treating them as prisoners of war." He nodded as Howe approached, the returning colour now evident in his cheeks. "Well, James?"

Howe's grin equalled Hooke's. "They're English, all right, sir. Most of 'em are Hotspurs, and some are out of other English ships, mainly East Indiamen."

Mainwaring watched as more men appeared on deck, blinking like their predecessors. "How long had they been held? Did they say?"

"The big blond lad with the petticoat breeches said they'd been kept below most of the time since the Arabs plucked 'em out o' the water, sir. It was only the merchant lads that the French sold. The Hotspurs were being shot in the water by the French and managed to avoid the shot or feign death until the French were bored and sailed off. Then the Arabs came along and rescued them, so to speak." He coughed. "The East Indiamen, some of 'em, have been held for months. The French, or at least one Frenchman, has been dealing with the Arabs in prisoners for some time."

"Odd," said Mainwaring. "Other than the rags and dirt, they look fit enough."

"They are. The Arabs fed 'em tolerably well, they said, and let 'em move about the deck every day. I'd say it was a way of keeping the produce fresh for market, sir."

"Aptly put," said Mainwaring. "Well, then –"

"Beggin' yer pardon, zur," put in Hooke, "but if there's bread or biscuit, or whatnot, I'd like t' get b'low after it, zur. We've damned little vittles left in poor old *Hotspur*."

"Quite right, Mr Hooke. I forget that my own stomach growls too much from being empty as well. Carry on, and see what you can find." As Hooke loped away, Mainwaring turned back to James Howe. "D'ye think these lads will sail and fight, James? The Hotspurs will have a grudge to even, so I've no fear for them. But the East Indiamen?"

Howe's grin darkened somewhat. "I think we have no doubts in that regard, sir. They all say they've a score to settle with the French, and for the Arabs, they'd cheerfully slit their throats."

"Yes. Well, we can't have that. Take *Hotspur*'s longboat and strike in a cask o' water and some biscuit. Make certain the sailing rig is in order. Then send away those Arab gentlemen in her."

Howe's eyebrows rose. "Two hundred and fifty or three hundred leagues to the Zanzibar coast, sir. They'll be damned lucky to make it."

"They're getting more of a chance than a life of slavery

would have meant for these lads, James. Get 'em away, as quickly as you can." He paused. "One other disagreeable task, and then I'd be pleased if you'd have us pulled back to *Hotspur*, and you and Mr Hooke join me in the cabin. I shall need your advice."

"Aye, aye, sir. The other task, sir?"

Mainwaring looked at the heap of Arab dead, and the dark rivulets and bloodstains on the dhow's decking. "Those dead, James. Over the side with 'em. I should think our new messmates in particular would willingly carry out that undertaking."

"Sir," said Howe, without a flicker.

A turn of the glass later, Edward Mainwaring stood in *Hotspur*'s great cabin, his feet braced against the ship's pitching as he stared down at a French chart which was unrolled and held down by the dragoon sword on the cabin's small desk. On the other side of the desk stood James Howe and Isaiah Hooke, the latter casting quick glances out of the stern lights at the black hull of the dhow, lifting and plunging along in *Hotspur*'s wake. He was watching two men working on the enormous tack tackle of the dhow's foresail.

"If I may have your attention, gentlemen," said Mainwaring presently. "We are – here, about two leagues nor' nor'east of Pointe Desny, the southern cape of the island, and the southern arm of the bay that holds Mahébourg. We know the French will have gathered their ships at Port Louis – here, on the nor'west coast, where we came from. If they haven't sailed for the Coromandel yet, they will damned soon enough, before the monsoon makes it impossible." He thought for a moment. "The *Neptune* that did for us was, I thought, still in Port Louis harbour amidst a clutch of French East Indiamen being refitted as a naval squadron. That night you so gallantly stormed ashore to my rescue I hadn't had enough time to assess the ships there, but I think *Neptune* was among 'em, and they all appeared ready to sail."

"Not certain how you could have told, sir, with respect," said Howe.

"They were all riding very heavy and deep at jettyside, James, damned clear over the waterline wale, and that means vessels crammed with stores. Also they'd cast off their harbour furl and were simply clewed up with some gaskets loosely passed."

"'Ow many of 'em were there, zur?" asked Hooke.

"About seven sail, but only *Neptune* a line-o'-battle ship." He paused. "Stephen, as I recall, said that *Pallas* was virtually blown out of the water by a far bigger vessel, however, the one the French would need to give La Bourdonnais the edge over Peyton. Since they were split, with the body of the squadron at anchor or alongside while the big vessel was still at sea, that might mean La Bourdonnais' squadron could still be in Port-Royal."

"With all due respect, sir," said Howe, "they could just as easily be at sea. I'm afraid I don't –"

Mainwaring held up a hand. "Of course, James. Perhaps I'm not making much logical sense. Perhaps I should simply say that I have a kind of gut feeling: I think they're still there."

Hooke moved to lean against the cabin's box bunk, remembered at the last moment the sleeping form of Stephen Pellowe, and lurched himself upright again with a wince. "Either way, zur, ain't likely we'd bother the buggers wiv this ship. What d'ye plan, if ye don't mind me askin'? We've a ship, an' 'ands as can work th' ship, an' we've vittles, but we ain't got *Pallas*, zur."

"Quite right, Isaiah." Mainwaring pointed at the chart's outline of the Indian coast. "Somehow, somewhere, we have to impede or prevent the French from getting at Peyton. If they're away to sea already, there may be little more we can do beyond trying to find and follow 'em, and get to Peyton with word before they reach him." He leaned forward. "James, that dhow's a handy enough vessel and now we've got enough lads for full crews o' both ships. Could we shift four of the six-pounders to her?"

Howe thought. "They'd have to be rigged as weather-deck guns. She's not pierced for gunports, and the Arabs only had a swivel or two, beyond those odd-looking firelocks. Might make her a little tender, but it could be done. Two a side, in the waist."

"A better broadside than nothing."

"Aye, sir. Better than nothing."

"Very well, make it so, James. I'm giving you the dhow, as a prize command. You'll take Winton as your senior hand, and," and here he thought, "twenty hands, to give you gun crews and sailhandlers. That'd still leave you and Rumford enough hands for full watches in *Hotspur*, Isaiah?"

"Aye, zur, 'twould, an' we'd 'ave a few spare 'ands scullin' about."

"Good. Begin as quickly as you can to render her a ship you can fight and sail, James. And then we begin our campaign."

"Sir?" Howe looked puzzled.

"Prizes, James, prizes! We'll build a destructive little fighting squadron with some select prizes. Vessels we can manage, such as cutters or luggers, handy, quick vessels."

"I'm afoul o' yer compass 'eadin', zur," said Hooke. "Can't stop a whoreson French squadron wiv a clutch o' smacks, zur, beggin' yer pardon."

"Quite right, Isaiah. We'll sail for Mahébourg and Port Louis and see what opportunity gives us. Of course, we haven't the strength to take a large vessel, even an East Indiaman. We can't be a bull standing in front of a bull, but we can be flies around his flanks."

"Zur?"

"Flies that sting and bother, Isaiah. If we can find the French in Port Louis, we can stand off and run away from any effort to chase us down – that dhow flies like the bloody

171

wind, and even *Hotspur* here can pick up her skirts creditably – and try to go in after 'em, as we did with the French and Spanish squadrons in Toulon. You'll recall we made rather a mess there."

"Aye, but what if they *are* at sea, sir?" inquired Howe.

"One vessel, the quickest, will have to sail for the Coromandel and Peyton. I want it small enough not to drain away men, and large enough to arrive successfully. The rest of us will simply sail in pursuit of the bastards, and when we find 'em, harry 'em as best we can. There'll be night. There may be a chance to try a fireship attack. There'll be a chance they'll anchor or put in somewhere – Tromelin, the Madagascar coast, Diego Suarez, even the Seychelles – and give us the opportunity to go in at them, however we can manage it." Mainwaring thumped a fist on the table. "Somewhere, somehow, there'll be a chance, a chance to strike, and to repay!" He looked levelly at both men in turn. "Doing this will give our lads a sense that there's a chance, because there's always hope whenever action is being taken. We know we're in the middle of the bloody Indian Ocean with as much possibility of winning through as a ferret in a hog byre. But the lads won't dwell on that. They'll keep before them that they're not simply going to die in the hold of a French prison hulk or live a hell of slavery in some God-abandoned Arab sinkhole."

"Although perhaps it might be quieter there, and a chap could get some sleep. With respect, sir," came a sleepy voice from the box bunk.

"*Stephen!*"

In a bound Mainwaring was beside Pellowe, Hooke and Howe with him. Howe put a hand on the youth's forehead.

"No sign of fever, sir, none at all. He's over the worst."

"Sorry for having been such a beastly burden to you

all, sir," offered Pellowe, trying to sit up. "I'm afraid I've contributed very little to things."

Mainwaring exchanged a look with Howe and Hooke, and then smiled at Pellowe.

"On the contrary, Stephen. I think just now you've given us the best possible gift." He looked at the young man in mock seriousness. "And what about something good and filling from the galley fire, now?"

Pellowe grinned. "Thought you'd never ask, sir!"

6

Hotspur crept along through the evening gloom, half a league off the southern tip of Mauritius. Her canvas was reduced to the fore and main topsail, the spanker, and the jibs, and she ghosted through a smoke rising from the grey, breeze-ruffled sea like a faded watercolour image. A rain squall moments before had drenched the ship in a hissing downpour, and now the mustard and black colours of the hull gleamed in the half-light below the sodden canvas and the curling damp Bourbon ensign.

High in the foretop, Edward Mainwaring's feet slithered on the painted white wood of the crosstrees as he wrestled himself in a spasm of fear out around the futtock shrouds and into the top. Soon he was wedged in amongst the bar-taut welter of halyards and lifts, feeling the miserable drip of water down his back inside the torn shirt and uncomfortable French uniform coat. Fumbling in the tail pocket of the coat, he found the leatherbound sleeve of the glass and began a slow sweep of the dark, shadowed shore of the island, adjusting as *Hotspur* rolled slowly with a creak and low roar beneath him.

There was a shaking in the rigging, and with some scuffling and inventive curses James Howe pulled himself into the top and settled beside Mainwaring. A far cry from the elegantly wigged and suited officer of Mainwaring's first acquaintance some years before, Howe was now in the fo'c'sle glory of tar-smeared petticoat breeches, bare feet, a torn check shirt, and loosely-queued hair. He reached into his shirt and pulled out two substantial-looking French ship's biscuits, one of which he offered to Mainwaring.

"Here, sir. You've not eaten in hours and nor have

I. Damned sight better bread than the square shot we make."

Mainwaring lowered the glass and took the biscuit. The crust was hard enough, but after a jaw-straining assault, the interior proved chewable and remarkably tasty.

"Indeed," said Mainwaring, cheeks a-bulge. "I'm obliged, James. How's Stephen?"

"Ramping about his cabin and insisting he's fit to stand a watch. And eating anything he can get his hands on. He'd have gone for the net bag holding one of the messes' duff if Yeo hadn't rescued it. I expect he'll be gnawing leather next."

"D'ye think he's fit to take the deck?"

"He's well enough to try, sir. Depending on what happens within the next few hours, I'd let him. I'll have to get back to the dhow in a moment – Winton's still having trouble with the tiller tackle – and that'd give you relief on watch besides Mr Hooke."

"Aye. Very well, I'll let Stephen take the first if we stand down from Quarters. By the by, we must give your command a name. Simply calling her 'the dhow' or, as the lads have put it, 'the A-rab scow', isn't quite good enough for a prize of the Navy of His Britannic Majesty George the Second, I should think."

"Indeed, sir. Hard to know what to call a dhow, sir."

Mainwaring looked aft to where the dhow, its lateens pulling gently, slipped along in *Hotspur*'s wake. "She's graceful enough. I'd like to call her the *Anne*."

"*Anne*, sir? I don't –" Then Howe grinned. "Of course, sir. *Anne* it is."

"Thank you, James. No doubt Their Lordships will not approve of either the ship or the name, if it ever reaches their ears, but I rather like the sound of it."

"Aye, sir, I'm proud to command her. That is, if we can set that bloody tackle to rights."

Mainwaring stuffed the last of the biscuit into his mouth and pulled open the glass. He pressed it against the splintery, tarred column of a topmast shroud and centred the field on the Mauritius shore once more.

"Ah," he exclaimed presently.

"Sir?" Howe knew the tone.

"A lugger, James. By God, a lugger. Yard-headed fore and main, and those odd yard-headed topsails. A bowsprit like a lance. Only thing that could catch her would be your *Anne*. She's putting out, likely to steer round to Port Louis, and there's nothing about her to say she's a fisherman." He snapped shut the glass. "You'd best get to your boat and back into *Anne*, James. Steer for an interception of that lugger. We'll come up as quickly as we can and try to trap her between the shore and us. It's just the sort of small, handy vessel we need, James."

"Aye, aye, sir!" With a topman's agility he was out over the top and down the ratlines, with Mainwaring following a moment later.

As Mainwaring bounded on to *Hotspur*'s quarterdeck, hands in the waist were already casting off Howe's boatrope and his small boat flashed by the brig's stern, her four oars dipping rapidly as Howe barked at his boat's crew.

"Mr Hooke! The lugger. D'ye see her, inshore, there?"

"Aye, zur! D'ye mean t' chase 'er?" asked Hooke from beside the wheel. "She'd show 'er skirts t'us, quick, zur."

"Not if Mr Howe can cut off her escape, Isaiah. He's going to range in ahead of us and try to cross her bows, hold her while we close from astern, and leave her only the shore – or surrender." Mainwaring had begun to pace the windward side of the quarterdeck excitedly, and he realised with a start that he had been without shoes for so long that he almost could not imagine hearing boots ring on the decking as he walked.

Hooke murmured something to the helmsman, a thickset Welshman named Jones, and then looked astern.

"The A-rab – er, Mr 'Owe – is standin' in t'meet 'er, zur, by th' look of it."

Mainwaring nodded. "Good. By the by, I've named the prize as the *Anne*."

Hooke's eyebrows raised, and then he beamed. "Smart as a new-scraped carrot, that name, zur. Beggin' yer pardon."

Mainwaring grinned. "I agree, Isaiah!" He padded up to the transom rail and peered at *Anne*. The dhow had hoisted aboard Howe's little jolly boat with astonishing quickness, and even as Mainwaring watched, the hands were hauling at the enormous fore and main sheet tackles, and as two men spun the great wheel over – its tackle problem obviously in hand – the dhow curtseyed round to starboard on to a reach, the lateens winging out into full, womanly curves, and accelerated visibly past *Hotspur*'s quarter, the bow wave suddenly white and leaping under the black, angling stempost. As the Arab craft swept by, Mainwaring could see Howe standing spread-legged on his quarterdeck, looking up at the streaming green pennants. Howe saw him and waved. Mainwaring lifted his own arm and waved in return, feeling a surge of affection for the spare, determined and loyal figure.

He turned and moved to the inshore rail, unlimbering the glass once more. At deck level less of the lugger's hull was visible, but the image was nonetheless clear in the twilight: ivory-grey sails in a pretty pattern, moving against the dark backdrop of the island's forested shore. The lugger's course appeared to be south-west, a run before a sharper breeze close in by the land; *Anne* was standing in on a beam reach, already heeling well over, the graceful green pennants floating out together from the lateen peaks, and was steering west by nor'west, it appeared, to intercept the lugger. For *Hotspur* to come up as quickly as possible to the point of interception, accepting no dramatic course change, it would require –

"Mr Hooke!" Mainwaring turned to move forward, thrusting the glass shut again and pocketing it.

"Zur?"

"Haul your wind, if you please, Mr Hooke. Hands to the

177

braces and sheets. Bring her to starboard, broad reach or higher, as we'll be steering due west."

Hooke glanced at the binnacle card and then took a deep breath. "Aye, aye, zur!" he boomed, and the twilight air was soon rent with his barking calls that brought the hands at the pinrails and fiferails to action instantly.

"Helm, there!" called Mainwaring. "Starboard, two points. Steer due west."

Jones spun the wheel, his dark locks blowing about his forehead. "Starboard two points, steer due west, aye, aye, sir!" His soft Welsh lilt reminded Mainwaring with a momentary pang of another Welshman, Williams, now dead, who had been a liked and capable part of Mainwaring's 'people' what seemed like centuries ago.

Hotspur turned, her blocks creaking and rattling, the yards rumbling round in their jeers, the sea hissing in her wake as she heeled to the wind and began to move towards the dark, distant shore, with *Anne*'s double-winged shape hurrying on ahead.

Mainwaring moved to the waistdeck rail, looking forward to where Hooke was seeing to the belaying of the jib sheets. Hooke caught his eye and came aft, looking proprietorially at the gun crews, whose captains were instructing them to cast off the guns' vent covers and check once again for any gun tool laid out in the wrong order, and blowing on the glowing match in their linstocks. *Hotspur* had been at Quarters for most of the day, and Hooke's feet crunched as he crossed the sand littering the gun-deck area.

"Gun crews ready, zur. Larb'd an' starb'd batteries, three guns a broadside, an' them swivels on th' quarterdeck, zur."

"Very good. Send someone below for Mr Pellowe, Isaiah. If he's well enough, I should like him to command both batteries in the waist. You're to concentrate on sail-handling. Have the runner tell Mr Pellowe that he's not to open gunports and run out until I give the word. We'll need all the surprise we can get."

178

"Aye, zur!" Hooke sent a man from the nearest gun scrambling below with the message to Pellowe and then went along the line of guns, speaking in a low voice to each gun captain in turn. Hooke was a strange-looking figure in his ragged assortment of clothing, and Mainwaring thought again how odd they must look in comparison to when *Pallas* first sailed for the Indian Ocean. In his own case he was barefoot, in torn breeches and a cast-off seaman's shirt, his shoulders squeezed into a too-small French officer's coat only for the use of the pockets, and with no hat. His hair was pulled loosely back and secured with a piece of tarred marline, and with over two weeks' growth of stubble on his chin and bowels rumbling with costive problems he knew that he, and all the others, both felt and looked more like thieves and pirates than officers and men of the Royal Navy.

Hooke bounded up to the quarterdeck. "Look thar, zur. Them green pennants on *Anne* must be some kind o' signal. Were I in a coastal lugger, an' a whoreson A-rab came thunderin' along t' pass th' time o' day, I'd be crammin' on every stitch o' canvas I 'ad, zur, an' sayin' me Papist beads. But the lugger ain't even turned an 'air, in a manner o' speakin', zur."

Mainwaring pulled out the glass again and peered shoreward, crouching to see under the foot of the forecourse. "You're right, Isaiah. *Anne* will intercept him nicely at this rate, and there's no sail change, no alteration of course, as if he thinks *Anne* wants to speak to him."

"Christ, zur, were *all* the Froggies in on this 'ere trade in slaves?"

Mainwaring lowered the glass and bit his lip thoughtfully. "Damned if I know, Isaiah. But there must be some explanation of why they seem to have no fear of the dhow, or why the dhow had no fear of us, when she thought we were French, unless it's due to –"

"*Anne*'s opened fire, zur!" burst out Hooke.

Mainwaring snapped his head up as two sharp reports reached his ears, the deep thump of ship's guns heard over water. Two puffs of smoke were curling over *Anne*'s hurrying black hull, and two glittering little geysers, like fingers of crystal, had shot up just off the lugger's bows.

"Good shooting, James!" breathed Mainwaring.

"Lugger's turnin' away, zur! Look there! The bugger's wearin' round! Hell, 'e could tear th' sticks out uv 'er, all-standin' that fashion!"

Mainwaring centred the round field of the glass on the lugger, which was half-obscured by *Anne*'s closer form. The lugger's yard-headed sails crumpled briefly as the low, sleek vessel turned away, and then filled with an almost audible whump on the other side as the wind came on the beam, and the lugger heeled dramatically on the same tack as the pursuing *Anne*. There was a pink flash from the latter, a thump and puff of smoke, and another crystal finger shot up just off the lugger's weather quarter.

"Mr 'Owe's got one o' them guns rigged as a bow chaser, zur!"

"Aye, but can he hold her until we get to him, is the question, Isaiah!"

Mainwaring looked aloft; the topman Slade had climbed into the foretop, where Mainwaring had been minutes before.

"Foretop, there!" Mainwaring called, through cupped hands. "Can ye make out how close inshore the lugger is?"

There was a pause, and then Slade's Cockney tones rang down, high over the wind. "Deck, there! 'E ain't 'ardly got any sea room, sir! Only upwind, is all!"

"Precisely where we're steering," said Mainwaring, as much to himself as to Hooke. Then he turned to the master. "Can ye set more canvas, if you please, Mr Hooke? Tops'ls and heads'ls aren't quick enough, if we're not to lose him!"

"Aye, zur!" responded Hooke. "For'rard, there, Mr Rumford, if ye please! Set the t'gallants an' th' forecourse! Lively, now!"

With a rush men were at the fore and main shrouds, scrambling up the ratlines, or at the pinrails putting hands to the topgallant sheets and braces. Slade and Sawyer, hooting calls back and forth to one another that Hooke was wise enough to let pass, raced each other to the topgallant footropes, with a few others casting off the gaskets and overhauling the buntlines, then pushing the gathered roll of canvas off the yard so that it ballooned out, luffing and shaking their precarious perch. Then they scrambled in to the top, Hooke's bellows chasing them, and the men at the halyards below grunted the yards up, the topgallants filling out hard and clean as the halyards were sweated home and the sheet slack taken in.

"A touch on your fore lee t'gallant brace! Enough, an' belay!" barked Hooke.

Under Mainwaring's feet, *Hotspur* lifted ahead noticeably, and began to heel more dramatically to the power of the wind, even stronger aloft at topgallant height than could be felt on deck. The sea began to roar steadily along her leeward side, and the men grinned and nodded at one another in excitement and satisfaction as they went about their work.

Hooke regained the quarterdeck as Mainwaring was standing beside Jones, his eyes on the binnacle card.

"Can ye hold her, Jones?" asked Mainwaring.

"Aye, sir, that I can. She's flying, look you, sir!"

Mainwaring grinned at the Welshman and nodded to Hooke. "Well done, Mr Hooke. We've made two knots more, by the feel of her."

Hooke squinted forward. "Aye, zur. Can't say if we're going t' catch th' bugger, zur. 'E's footin' ahead uv us, t' my eye."

Mainwaring followed Hooke's gaze. Far off the larboard bow, *Anne*, on almost a parallel course to *Hotspur*, had clearly closed any escape for the lugger to leeward. Dead ahead lay the dark, surf-crashed shore of Mauritius. But just off the brig's leeward bow, the lugger was close-hauled now, heeling dramatically, obviously fighting to win ground up to weather of the inrushing *Hotspur* before the latter closed the gap. And the angle on the bow of the lugger was narrowing rapidly.

"God damn and blast! You're right, Isaiah. Are we close enough for guns?"

"Dunno, zur. Damned near, if not."

Mainwaring cupped his hands. "Steph – er, Mr Pellowe! For'rard, there!"

Stephen Pellowe, his blond locks startling in the dim light, stood up from behind one of the long six-pounders. "Sir?"

"Stand by to fire, larboard battery, as your guns bear! Maximum elevation, mind! Pull the bloody quoin blocks clear!"

"Aye, aye, sir!" cried Pellowe, eyes bright. His features were still pale, but he was moving with reassuring energy and conviction. "Larboard battery!" he barked to his crews. "Up gunport lids! Stand to your tackles! *Run out!*"

"Mr Hooke!" Mainwaring called as the gun trucks rumbled and squealed. "We're rounding up to fire! Stand by your sheets and braces!" He turned to Jones. "Ready, all! Down helm! Bring her into the wind!"

Hotspur heeled dramatically as Jones spun the great wheel. The canvas aloft suddenly became a luffing, thumping thunder that shook the deck under Mainwaring's feet, and with a crump like a gunshot the brig's foretopsail went hard aback on the foretopmast and the air was alive with snaking and writhing sheets and tacklines.

"As you bear," Pellowe was crying. "*Fire!*"

With a rippling blast that rent the air with twenty-foot tongues of pink flame, the larboard battery fired, almost in the same instant. The vents huffed like miniature volcanic bursts, and from the side of the ship the sudden, rolling wall of smoke gouted out and away, obscuring for a moment the hurrying image of the lugger. Then it was swept away, and round the lugger the silver fingers of the shots' fall leapt up.

Pellowe was shouting, his voice cracking in emotion.

"Christ, we got her! Look, sir!"

Mainwaring craned to see, bracing as *Hotspur* pitched under him. As if in strangely slowed motion, the lugger's main topmast canted forward, the broad yard-headed topsail collapsing with it, a welter of wreckage and lines falling to the ship's side to splash and trail into the sea. Ripples shook through the lugger's surviving canvas, a moment before so still with power.

"She's roundin' up, zur," came Hooke's cry.

"Fall off, Mr Hooke," bellowed Mainwaring. "This is not the time to be in irons! Back those headsails, there! Flat 'em out to starboard! Mind your helm as she makes sternway, Jones!" He slapped the waistdeck rail in frustration. "Come on, come on," he muttered through clenched teeth.

Then *Hotspur* was off the wind, the headsails filling again on the larboard side, and Hooke's cry of "Let go and haul!" sent the foretopsail yard rumbling round, the topsail itself bellying out with a crack into a satisfying, still curve. *Hotspur* leaped ahead again as Jones steadied the brig's wheel to Mainwaring's commands, the black, reaching finger of the jib-boom centred again on the stricken lugger.

"Another pull of that bowline, Jackman!" Hooke raved. "Steady it out! Lord thunderin' Jesus, did ye never tail on t'a fall b'fore? *Haul!*"

Mainwaring knelt to see forward under the foot of the forecourse. As if to read his mind, Slade's voice came echoing down from aloft.

"Deck, there! The lugger, sir, lost 'is foretopm'st as well. Triatic stay gave way, sir!"

Mainwaring cupped his hands against the wind. "Mr Pellowe, give your lads a well done! Ye've shot well, it seems." He leaped down into the waist, seeing the pleased grins as he ran forward and vaulted on to the foredeck, almost falling flat on his face over the obstacle of the windward jib sheet before catching himself on the starboard knight-head. Hooke was in the bows, astride the bowsprit for a better view, one hand clutching at the gammoning for support as *Hotspur* lifted and plunged with a roar under him.

"Look, zur!" he was exulting. "All in irons, b'God! Driftin', an' not a Chinaman's chance o' puttin' 'er t' rights afore we comes up!"

Mainwaring cuffed a patter of spray from his face. "Aye, best we'd –" He stopped. "What in the name of Christ –"

Hotspur was rushing in so quickly that the stricken lugger was no more than half a mile away, with *Anne* hardening up to a close-hauled starboard tack a quarter of a mile to leeward of the lugger. Behind, the dark face of Mauritius loomed like a broad, black canvas against which the shape of the lugger was painted in pale colours.

And on that shape figures were appearing, figures that clustered at the rails, swarming up on to the ship's sides.

"Sweet Jesus!" gasped Hooke. "They're leavin' 'er! The Frogs are jumpin' from 'er, zur!"

"Christ grant the poor bastards can swim!" murmured Mainwaring. He watched in horrified fascination as man after man fell from the lugger's side to thresh in the dark sea, until soon a trail of figures marked by dark heads or the white dot of faces straggled in towards the island shore.

Mainwaring turned to look at *Anne* as she knifed in towards the lugger with astounding speed, the twin lateens still and taut in their curves, the bow wave a continual boil of white under her stempost as the dhow lifted and fell through the seas.

"She'll reach the lugger before we do, Isaiah," he said. "Look at them go over the side. Christ, we'll have to get someone into her, double quick, to keep her from –"

"She's on fire, sir!" burst out Pellowe from where he stood spread-legged on the brig's midships rail, one hand locked in the rigging for balance. "In the lugger, sir! I can see smoke round her counter!"

"Damn!" Mainwaring sprang on top of a cathead foot,

184

straining to see. Pellowe was right; grey tendrils of smoke were curling above the swimmers' heads and drifting away low over the sea face.

"A hit in the stern when we fired, sir. Or something came amiss below decks when the rigging gave way," came Pellowe's call.

Mainwaring was squinting, judging the distances as *Hotspur* swept in. A determination was forming in his mind: he would not lose the lugger without a struggle. They were barely five hundred yards off and closing rapidly. Mainwaring pounded the rail, trying to focus his mind.

"Mr Hooke! We'll have to bear up, to weather. Stay well to windward of her. Any closer than a pistol shot and that fire could set in us!"

Hooke scrambled aft from his perch on the jib-boom, his quickness as ever astonishing given his size. "What d'ye plan, zur? She's lost t'us, t' my mind!"

Mainwaring's eyes were twin points of steel. "Send down Slade and Sawyer to me. Larboard side, amidships. Steer us across her bows, well to windward, and then tack. If ye'll drop down into her, wear ship astern of her before you fetch up in shoal water!" *Hotspur* was rushing closer now, the lugger small and almost dainty in comparison, thick grey smoke roiling out of her stern. They were no more than four hundred yards away, and the individual panels of the snow-white flax sails of the lugger stood out in delicate relief, like sheets of mica, against the dark and shadowed Mauritius shore.

Hooke stared for an instant, no more, and then moved, a bellow sending Slade and Sawyer racing each other down backstays to the deck as Mainwaring ran aft to join them in the waist. *Hotspur* closed on the lugger, all eyes aboard the brig fixed with seamen's dread on the smoke that streamed away in a choking trail to leeward, and which was now enveloping *Anne*'s hull, the twin lateens slicing along above it in an oddly disembodied way.

"A pistol shot above her, mind, Mr Hooke," repeated

Mainwaring, over his shoulder. "Then keep clear till you see a signal from me"

Hooke had regained the quarterdeck. "*Signal*, zur? What –"

But Mainwaring was paying no attention. He had swung to face the two little topmen, as alike in their wiry competence as two peas in a pod.

"Will ye swim with me, lads?" he demanded, stripping off the French coat.

"To 'er, sir?" asked Slade. "Aye, sir, lessen' ye feel th' fire's too –" Mainwaring's expression stopped him.

"All right," said Mainwaring. "Listen carefully. We've a chance to save her. I don't think that's a serious fire, for all the smoke. We'll try to go aboard where the foretopmast wreckage is trailing alongside. If I'm right and we can put the fire out, she's ours. If not, it'll be over the side with us, to be picked up! Clear?"

"Aye, sir!" the two men chorused, with a gap-toothed mutual grin.

"Then come on!"

With a bound, Mainwaring was up teetering on the rail, just as the stricken lugger drew abeam. The sea seemed very far below him, but then his nerve stiffened as he felt Sawyer and Slade arrive beside him. He took a deep breath, and with an arcing dive launched himself into the dark water below.

When he struck, the water was a cold wall, the shock of it unexpected in the tropic heat. As he sank down, Mainwaring felt he had plunged too deeply into a bottomless, inky well of chill from which he would never be able to surface. His lungs bursting, he began to claw his way upward, until with a sobbing gasp he shot out of the water to shoulder height, surrounded by the sudden roaring of *Hotspur*'s passage, the hissing foam of her mid-wave churning round and over him. He coughed and spat, kicking in the water to get clear, and twisted to see the lugger, bigger than he expected, pitching beyond a heaving surface of whitecapped waves and their underlying swells that were now far larger than they had seemed from the brig's deck. With a curse at his own foolhardiness, Mainwaring struck out towards the lugger, vaguely aware of another figure splashing along beside him. He swam with blind effort, coughing and gasping as wavelets and boiling foam washed over him. Kicking furiously, his heart pounding in his ears, he felt with each stroke smaller and more desperate as he realised the power in the confused waters that gripped him.

Then abruptly he was thrusting his hands into a snaked mass of rigging and cordage, and he looked up to find the pitching rail of the lugger six feet above him, and a tangled welter of crumpled canvas, line and splintered spar trailing down to him. He felt rather than heard Slade and Sawyer arrive beside him, and he began to claw at the shifting mass of wreckage, trying to find a grip or a line that held and did not give way when he hung his weight on it.

"Here, sir." Sawyer was puffing. "Topm'st backstay!" In the next minute, the wiry Vineyarder was struggling out of the water, rising like a dripping ferret from the waves, his feet kicking as he struggled up the mass of wreckage along the tarred black line of the backstay. Mainwaring splashed over underneath him and clutched the backstay, feeling its hard, canvas-parcelled surface over which a smear of tar had been coated.

Then Sawyer was at the main channels, teetering on them over Mainwaring's head, and Mainwaring reached up, taking a fierce grip on the stay. He had a vague sense of Slade cursing colourfully below him as he hauled himself up, his arms knotted with effort.

And then he was there, scrabbling to get a foothold on the channel, peering wild-eyed over the pitching deck of the lugger. It was bare save for the figure of Sawyer who was running aft to the lugger's tiller bar. From the companion-way just forward of the tiller a wisp of smoke was curling, a strange contrast to the roiling line of smoke that rolled away aft from the lugger's stern.

Mainwaring vaulted over the rail, his feet slithering on the decking, and ran to the companionway. A quick glance shoreward revealed the cluster of swimming heads of the lugger's crew, and off the lugger's larboard bows *Hotspur* was rounding up into the wind to come about, stately and magnificent in her relative stillness.

"Sawyer!" called Mainwaring above the boom and thump of the canvas overhead. "Keep her on the wind as best you can. We're going below to see to that fire. If it grows worse before we return on deck, get clear!"

"Aye, sir!" cried Sawyer, wrestling with the swinging tiller bar.

Slade slapped up beside Mainwaring, dripping and panting. "Luck was wiv us, sir, no mistake. Look there!" He pointed over the side, and Mainwaring peered down past the roil of wreckage to see a pod of some half-dozen sea snakes, each at least four feet in length, swimming past where moments before the men had been.

"One nip from those, an' we'd –" began Slade.

Mainwaring shuddered, but he grasped the little man's arm, the gesture silencing him. Mainwaring pulled out his own shirttail and began to tear a hand-wide strip from the bottom of the wet, ragged cloth. "Make a mask for yourself, like this! Then follow me!"

He wrapped the wet strip across his nose and mouth, knotting it behind his head. As soon as he saw that Slade had done the same, Mainwaring sucked in a deep breath through the cloth, and plunged down the companionway ladder.

Thumping down in a dark passageway leading aft that reeked of smoke but was oddly clear of all but a slight haze, he ran aft until he fetched up before the aft cabin door. A touch on the wood proved it to be cool.

Very well, said Mainwaring to himself. He stepped back a pace, bumping into Slade as he did so, and then with a grunt drove his shoulder against the door. With a crash the splintering wood gave way, and Mainwaring tumbled into the great cabin of the lugger, his head just missing contact with the low-beamed deckhead before he sprawled on the painted canvas deck.

"What the deuced –" he began, as he scrambled to his feet. The cabin was hazy with smoke, but there were no flames. Instead, the stern lights had been smashed open, and from three small barrels set on the deck before them a reeking cloud of foul smoke was boiling up, to be carried through the stern lights and drift away over the sea.

"Look out, sir!" came Slade's warning, and Mainwaring spun in time to see the bare-chested figure of a seaman, cutlass blade agleam in one hand, burst out of the quarter-gallery door towards Mainwaring. But before the latter could act, Slade had flashed past and hit the man in a running tackle, both men gasping with the impact. They crashed to the deck against one of the smoke barrels, and for a moment a violent, silent struggle ensued until Slade's knife flashed in the smoky gloom, and the attacker screamed briefly before slumping back, still.

Slade rose, coughing, wiping the little blade on the man's tar-stained striped trousers.

"Not werry 'ospitable, th' buggerin' Frogs, be they, sir?" he said with a gap-toothed grin.

"Quite," agreed Mainwaring, through tight lips. "My thanks again, Slade. These damned smoke pots, now!"

Mainwaring seized a tall iron lantern stand that was clamped to a bulkhead and wrenched it free. With all his strength he smashed away at the woodwork of the stern lights until he had broken open a wide enough passage for the barrels. Then, with his coughing almost uncontrollable, he flung down the stand and lifted one of the barrels, staggering to the opening and thrusting the barrel through into the sea, to be followed quickly by the other two. With a grimace of effort Slade wrestled the body of the Frenchman to the opening and bundled him through as well, grunting in satisfaction as he heard the splash below.

"It'll – take a bit for – this to clear," coughed Mainwaring. "Back on deck!"

When they regained the upper deck, their eyes streaming and throats aflame, they found Sawyer in a deathgrip on the tiller bar, but the lugger still hove to into the wind, lifting and thumping down under them in the swells, the rigging wreckage creaking and scraping along her side, the canvas aloft banging and rumpling with head-rattling force.

"Hold her, Sawyer!" barked Mainwaring. "There's no fire danger. It was a trick, and a poor one. Slade! We'll lower the heads'ls and the fore, first. That'll keep her head to wind."

"Aye, sir!" The Cockney was pointing. "Look, sir, *Hotspur*'s hove to, and she's sending a boat!"

Mainwaring swung round. His quick glance took in the brig, foretopsail aback, riding easily about a cable off the lugger's bows; a jolly boat, with Hooke at the helm, dancing over the dark swells towards the lugger; and astern, *Anne* hove to as well no more than a pistol shot away, the remnants of the smoke swirling round her huge, brailed-in lateens.

"Always pleasant to have a party," murmured Mainwaring, and he ran forward, with Slade at his heels. In a moment they had searched out the halyards for the lugger's two jibs in the mass of lines at the rail, and threw off their coils before hauling them down with brisk heaves. Then it was a dive to the pinrails for the throat and peak halyards of the foresail, an anxious glance aloft to see if the collapsing topsail wreckage had done any damage. None was apparent, and with quick-footed movements to stay clear of the yard as it fell, the two men soon had the foresail collapsed in a ballooning tentlike gather on the foredeck.

Sawyer was yelping from aft. "That's done it, sir! Ridin' east, she is, now!"

A thumping alongside told of the arrival of *Hotspur*'s boat, and in another moment Hooke was wrestling himself over the rail, a clutch of Hotspurs and Pallases behind him, gazing about at the empty length of the lugger's gear-strewn deck, the rumpled mass of the foresail and the trailing gear overside, the luffing and rumpling main, and Sawyer, spread-footed at the tiller bar, grinning at them in delight.

Hooke moved to Mainwaring, eyeing the sodden, shortened shirt which now bared his midriff.

"Ye be goin' t' rags by degrees, zur, beggin' yer pardon."

"How astute of you, Isaiah, damn your impertinence. No doubt I shall be naked by the time we finish this business. Glad you're here."

"Aye, zur. Wot th' deuce was –" Hooke gestured to the last of the smoke, drifting now behind *Anne*.

Mainwaring shook his head. "Christ only knows, Isaiah. They fled the ship as if it were afire, but then we only found smoke pots in the cabin, with some unfortunate Frenchman who was either left behind to keep the lugger to windward after we sheered off, afraid of the fire – I presume that was their intention – or who didn't fancy a swim. Slade did for the fellow."

"What next, then, zur? That tops'l damage ain't too severe, t' first glance."

"Aye," said Mainwaring. "Set your lads to work on that foretopmast. If we remain hove to here, we should drift out to sea unless the wind backs on us. Should give us a hour or two of work before it'll be too difficult to see."

"Zur." Hooke looked skyward. "Summat odd about them clouds, zur. Like a storm fetchin' up all th' way from the Chinee Sea. Don't like it, zur."

"All the more reason to work roundly. Jury rig the foretopmast to hoist the topsail, or sail without it if you must. You'll have to do some carpentry on the stern lights. And send a lad to look at her below decks, and assess her guns. We must know if she can fight, and all I see so far are these swivels."

Hooke rubbed his hands, as if preparing for hard labour. "Aye, zur. Then –"

Mainwaring grinned. "Then, Mr Hooke, you'll need to

pick your prize crew. You'll take command of the lugger as prize master."

Hooke's eyebrows rose in pleasure. "I'm obliged, zur," he rumbled.

Mainwaring nodded, looking up at the darkening, steely clouds. He shivered in his wet rags, in spite of the heat.

"Not at all, Mr Hooke. I have the same odd feeling you do about those clouds. We may have something else to battle with besides the damned French as we bring this business to an end." He laughed with little mirth. "You may have cause not to thank me for your new responsibility!"

One hundred and twenty miles south-south-west of Mauritius, the captain of the sturdy East Indiaman *St George*, forty-four guns, paced his quarterdeck and looked anxiously from the snapping striped ensign above his head to the dark arch of cloud that lined the north-eastern horizon. *St George* was beating well to windward under her working canvas, and her captain looked again at the arch and wondered if he needed to have the hands called to take in *St George*'s topgallants. He knew he would have to make the decision within the turn of the glass, but years of voyaging in the Indian Ocean brought a caution to him that led him to cup his hands and call to his sailing master in the vessel's waist.

"Mr Harris! I'll have the t'gallants handed and sent down, if ye please!"

Footsteps sounded behind the captain, and he turned to see a tall, white-haired gentleman in plain cocked hat and billowing boat cloak standing on the leeward side and eyeing him with quiet concern.

"May I join you to windward, Captain?" asked the man.

"Of course, Sir Richard."

"Are you expecting heavy weather, Captain Eversham?" inquired the man, as he climbed the slope of the quarterdeck.

"I don't like the look of that arch, to be frank, Sir

192

Richard," replied the captain, nodding towards the northern horizon. "It could be the edge of the first of the monsoon nor'easterly gales, and I intend to take no unnecessary risk."

"Quite prudent, I am sure." Sir Richard Brixham paused. "What effect do you think this may have on our efforts to reach Port Louis?"

The captain of the *St George* was a direct man. "When we sailed under your charter three months ago, Sir Richard, I told you that it was unlikely we'd get anything but a storm of ball and shot for our trouble if we put into Port-Royal in an effort to talk to this Frenchman, La Bourdonnais. I'd wager even less for your chances of actually seeing the fellow, who in any event is likely off to do devilment with our people on the Coromandel." He pursed his lips. "This may delay us for weeks, or be followed by a southerly that will fetch us up at Mauritius within two days. With the wind in this quarter we've a chance to raise the island within three. I can't say. We've been damned lucky to make as good a passage out as we have."

"We know, Captain. Believe me that it is recognised and appreciated."

Eversham's expression softened, and he stepped closer to Brixham. "Look here, Sir Richard. Your youngster's ship clearly did not report to Commodore Peyton, as our consul at Istanbul transmitted through his intelligences overland. A long passage, the perils of the sea, French action – the likelihood is that both he, and his ship, are lost, what?"

"I will not believe that for a moment, Captain Eversham!"

Both men turned to see a woman standing at the companionway which led below. She was not tall, but carried her strong and generously curved body in an upright and alert way that suggested energy and strength. About her a blue cloak, lined with brilliant scarlet, swirled and billowed, opening now and then to reveal an unexpected costume of a simple man's shirt, tucked into dark

193

corduroy breeches, in turn above polished boots that would have done credit to a cornet of light horse. But there was nothing masculine about her; the shirt clung to her full, rounded breasts, and the figure that filled the breeches did not have the narrow angularity of a man. Her face was sunbrowned, not at all the pale mask of a salon creature, and the wide-set eyes that were fixed with such clarity on Captain Eversham had a sea-blue intensity. It was a face of beauty enhanced by strength, with broad cheekbones and a full mouth which showed the promise of a sunlit, wide smile, but which now was set in determination. Her hair was brown and kissed into lighter tints by the sun, and its short, unpowdered curls danced against her cheeks as the wind sent the cape into more flaring lifts and curvings.

"I must believe what I *feel*, Captain," she went on. "Edward Mainwaring is part of me; part of my life. I simply know that he is alive, and I intend to ascertain that in one manner or another!" She moved to the two men, looking from one to the other with conviction. "You must press on. We must not turn away, not when we are so near, and after so very long a voyage!"

Richard Brixham smiled at Eversham. "My daughter is a woman of extraordinary conviction, Captain," he began.

"That is most evident," said Eversham, not unkindly.

"And she has the equally extraordinary facility of being found to be right when all apparent facts dictate otherwise." He looked at the young woman with an expression of infinite affection. "Her mother was like that. So I must add my voice to hers. Regardless of that approaching monsoon arch, or the undoubted treachery of the French, Captain Eversham, we must pursue our mission to its end."

Eversham nodded, looking again at the approaching line of cloud. He sighed, but then smiled.

"Very well, Sir Richard. You are, after all, paying the charter."

Sir Richard Brixham turned to his daughter and put an arm around her.

"You are still convinced, my dear? Of what you feel? That we should be here, doing this?"

Anne Brixham looked up at her father, and gave him a dazzling smile.

"Dear Father, as I love you, I have never felt surer of anything. We must – *I* must – be here for Edward, in some way." She looked out over the sea northward.

"And I will not fail him!" she said.

The day, when it dawned, would have had its usual brilliant sun rising over Le Pouce and Montagne Longue, to bathe the green slopes of Mauritius and the red-tile rooftops of Port Louis with a golden light. But the dark, boiling clouds that swept in from the north-east shut out that golden light, and sent instead sheets of silver rain pelting down over the sodden land, and whipped it over the huddled buildings before a searching, hard-edged wind. The same wind roared out over the sea, thrusting ahead of it all the way from the Indian coast a line of rolling grey swells topped by white-frothed waves that soon broke into long streaks of foam, turning the blue-green sea into a grey and white heaving wasteland in which swell after swell chased one another off to the south-west.

Ten miles off the western coast of Mauritius, their prows pointing determinedly towards the distant Port Louis, Edward Mainwaring's little squadron was struggling in towards the hidden dark hump of the island on a larboard tack. It had got under way near midnight once Isaiah Hooke had finished his repairs to the lugger's foretopmast. During the night, as the wind had continued to increase under the strange black arches of cloud, Mainwaring had led his ships westward, steering away from the coast to give them sea room should the wind back or veer unexpectedly. But it had not, and now dawn found all three ships, separated by no more than a quarter-mile between them, forging bravely into the building seas and oddly ominous wind.

On *Hotspur*'s quarterdeck, Edward Mainwaring stood in

a barefooted wide stance at the weather rail. He was wearing the too-small French coat, its lapels buttoned over, but was bareheaded, his hair still gathered in its simple queue. He cuffed the spray and rainwater from his dripping, stubbled face and nodded to Elusha Rumford, now *Hotspur*'s acting master, as the latter rolled aft.

"She should drive easier now, sir," said Rumford, the noise of sea and wind causing him to raise his voice more than usual. He was drenched to the skin, even with the protection of a ragged oilskin jacket, and wisps of hair were plastered across his face and cheeks. "I've taken a double reef in the fore an' main tops'ls, an' a double reef in th' spanker. For'rard, she's carryin' nought but the foretopm'st stays'l. Should be all she can carry for now, sir!"

"Aye, aye," acknowledged Mainwaring. "She feels more comfortable. Well done, Mr Rumford! What's her state below?"

"Tolerable enough, sir. Bit more o' water in th' wells than I'd like t' see, and wiv th' deck caulkin' shrivellin' in th' sun, she's a tad wet on th' messdeck. No cause fer alarm, sir – yet."

"Very well. Keep me informed. Helm, there! Ship's head?"

The windward of the two helmsmen – for Rumford had wisely put two men on the double wheel before the wind had begun to rise – wiped his dripping face and peered at the binnacle.

"Ship's head steady on due east, sir!"

Mainwaring nodded, knowing he meant a figure-eight lurching and circling of the bowsprit whose mean heading was due east. He steadied himself as *Hotspur* banged down with a thump and shudder into a grey swell, instinctively lowering his head as a cloud of spray burst up above the weather bow and rattled its way aft, drenching any figure on deck.

"Very good," he said, spitting. "Mr Rumford! If my last look at the chart was correct, my reckoning would be that we are perhaps three leagues off Port Louis, or a touch north, and I have it in mind that the French will have possibly put to sea to avoid being shut up in port. Double the lookouts, if ye please, and keep a sharp eye for 'em!"

"Aye, sir!" said Rumford, knuckling his dripping brow. His bellow down the companionway soon had men scrambling aloft up the weather rigging, pulling themselves into the swinging tops to join others already there, hanging on motionless while the ship rolled, then scrambling upward as she came upright.

Mainwaring braced his back against the rail and looked away off the larboard quarter to where Hooke's lugger was lifting and plunging along, five hundred yards away. The low, rakish craft was under double-reefed fore and main lugsails, the peculiar little mizzen, normally set on a small mast almost at the transom, and sheeted to a boomkin, not set at all. Hooke had also struck the vessel's topsails and flying jib, but even under this reduced rig, with the bare black poles of the topmasts projecting like slim foil blades into the grey sky, the lugger was boiling along at a remarkable rate of knots.

On *Hotspur's* starboard quarter, at about the same distance from the brig, the *Anne* dhow was displaying the wisdom of her Red Sea builders. Her huge lateens were crumpled down into a rough, loose-footed reef that gave her the look of a gull rumpling its folded wings while squatting on a windswept beach. Mainwaring wondered how James Howe had managed to effect the reef, for he had little knowledge of the towering Arab rig. Howe had evidently devised some method, for *Anne* was beating with only a slight heel, the flared bows of the dhow lifting steadily over the swells, the black-angled stempost appearing through the clouds of spray like an admonishing finger. From the lateens' yardarms the green pennants snapped in iron-rod stiffness, their ends whipped ragged by the wind.

"Tidy little squadron, sir, if I may say," grinned Rumford, appearing up the waistdeck ladder.

"Aye. Did ye pass the word to Mr Pellowe to ensure his gun captains had their vent covers and tompions in place?"

"'E'd already seen t' it, sir. If ye don't mind me sayin', sir, 'e'll make a fine career o' things. Plucky lad, an' th' lads'll follow 'im."

Mainwaring nodded. "I know. Refresh my memory, Mr Rumford. Did Mr Hooke find any additional weapons in the lugger? I was trying to decipher the damned French chart."

"Besides th' swivels, just a single four-pounder, sir, struck into the 'old for ballast. Mr Hooke told me they found powder an' ball fer it, an' 'e was aimin' t' rig it in th' bows, as a chaser, like."

"Good. Something to do damage with, at least. If Mr Howe's six-pounders serve him well –"

"They will, sir, beggin' yer pardon. Lookin' through th' glass I saw 'im securin' 'em on th' weather deck amidships, in th' waist, sir. 'E's got two a side, wiv closin' gunports rigged out through th' bulwarks."

"Has he, by God!" grinned Mainwaring. He realised at that moment that the dull ache in his stomach was not because of the constriction of the coat, but meant that he had not eaten since the swim to the lugger, and that the meal then had been a crusty and stale fist of bread.

"Mr Rumford, I'm reluctant to leave the deck in this weather, and with sighting the enemy shore so imminent, but I'll bloody well pass out if I don't gnaw on something. Could ye send a lad below to –"

"Deck, there! Deck!" The voice from the brig's foretop cracked in excitement. "Ships, sir! Ships! Look at 'em!"

Mainwaring sprang to the weather rail, the hair on the back of his neck tingling in spite of the rain and wind. He cupped his hands.

"Where away? Speak, damn your eyes!"

"Sorry, sir! Ahead, sir, dead on the bows, against the island! I count four, no, *five* sail, sir! Christ, one's a whoreson line-o'-battle ship, sure, sir!"

Mainwaring's heart was pounding in his throat as he peered forward, squinting against the stinging rain. For a moment he could see nothing but shifting curtains of rain, swirling across the wind-riven surface of the sea.

Then he saw them. The faint grey of the mountainous outline of Mauritius, barely discernible in the driving mist and rain. And before it, spread out in a line against the grey of the island, the dark, sinister shape of ships' hulls, like shadowed ghosts.

"The Frogs are out, sir," murmured Rumford at his side.

Hotspur lifted and thumped down with a force that staggered Mainwaring, and he had to turn away for an instant as a blinding cloud of spray burst over the bows and lashed back over the dark, slick deck.

"Aye, and they're steering to get sea room, Mr Rumford! Steering north-west, if I'm not mistaken. Damn! We're going to lose them at sea, in this!"

Mainwaring found he had to shout to make himself heard even a short distance from Rumford, and that *Hotspur* was beginning to pound with even greater force.

"What of the wind? What d'ye sense, Mr Rumford?"

"It's risin', sir! There's somethin' odd about it, that I c'n feel in me bones, sir. An' she's backin' t' th' nor'west. The Frog'll not hold that course long."

Mainwaring clutched at the rail as *Hotspur* heeled sickeningly and then lunged upright, her foredeck streaming. Behind him, Mainwaring could hear the men at the wheel cursing with their effort.

"Aye!" he cried. "They'll have to run off to the south, or round into the lee of the island. The southerly turn is the one we've got to prevent."

Rumford cuffed at his dripping face, staggering a little. "Wiv respect, sir, seekin' a lee t' shelter us might be wisest fer us, too, sir, the way this wind's buildin'."

"Rumford, listen to me," Mainwaring said, taking a step towards the sailing master. "If the French do get free of here without our having struck at them or hindering them

199

in some way, however futile it may be ultimately, they *will* make good their descent on the Coromandel, and on Peyton! D'ye think your lost lads would want that? I know the men I lost in *Pallas* would not! Even if it costs us our lives, we must do what we can against them! D'ye not see, man!"

Rumford nodded, grimacing as a sheet of spray rattled over them with the stinging intensity of hailstones.

"Aye, sir, I follow ye. But Christ, we'll be like throwin' pebbles at a plough horse, sir!"

"More like horseflies, Mr Rumford, and they can sting!" cried Mainwaring, as *Hotspur* leaped and plunged with a shudder under him. "D'ye have those English colours handy?"

"Aye, sir! An' I made sure Mr Howe an' Mr Hooke took some wiv 'em, sir."

"Well done. Get ours up, then, and lively! If we're going to die in this, by God, I'll do it under my own colours!" He spat out a mouthful of salt water, feeling a wild irresponsibility bubbling up within him. "Helm, there! No nearer to windward! Take that second mountain peak, there, as a mark. Ye'll need to down slack on your braces in a moment, Mr Rumford!"

"What are ye doin', sir?"

Mainwaring twisted his shoulder to take the impact of another cloud of spray, and turned back, dripping and spitting. "God damn the bloody spray! The wind's nor'westerly, aye? The French are not beating out to sea, to my eye!" He pointed at the distant dark shapes above which ghostly white canvas was now visible, rumpling and ballooning. "Look at 'em! Broadside on to us, and steering *north*, larboard tack! If they're not steering to weather Cap Malheureux, I'll warrant they'll make for the only other possible shelter on the nor'west coast!"

"Ye think they're going fer shelter, sir? I don't –" began Rumford.

"The fleet in being, Rumford! They never risk their ships

unless they must! They'll go for shelter, right enough!"

Rumford stared. "Well, bugger me, sir. They'll be putting in t' th' bay where yew found *us*!"

"Aye, that's my thought. But if the wind doesn't veer the way I think it will, they'll weather the cape, and be gone!"

Hotspur heeled with a roar, a cloud of spray bursting up round her catheads, Rumford and Mainwaring clutching at the rail as it drenched them.

"I think ye need not worry on that score, sir!" cried Rumford. "Sink me, but it feels like she's backin', right enough!"

Mainwaring swung, putting his face to the wind, and then squinting up at the bar-stiff masthead pennant.

"Christ, Rumford, you're right! That'll deny them Cap Malheureux!"

Mainwaring looked anxiously aloft. "We'll steer for the lead ship, now. You'll need your lads at the sheets and braces. Are we carrying too much?" he cried, over the thunder and roar.

"Aye, sir! The wind's built another notch! Foretops'l, double-reefed, an' foretopm'st stays'l, is all I'll keep. I'd strike the rest, sir. She'll be damned near still flyin' as fast as she's able, sir. This be damned near a whole gale, now!"

"Very well, make it so, and get that ensign up! If we drive her under, let her die an English ship," Mainwaring cried. "Ye'll want more lads on the wheel!"

"Aye, sir!" boomed Rumford, and staggered forward.

Mainwaring turned and grasped the transom rail, peering through the driving rain and mist. The wind was breaking the wave crests, streaking them into long paths of foam. *Anne* was down to only the fore lateen, a tiny triangle of white above the dark hull, but was lifting and plunging gamely along, the dhow hull still equal to the challenge. The lugger as well was down to the foresail, but it was evident that the sleek, fine-lined vessel was struggling in the building seas and wind, for each foaming swell that burst over her windward bow threatened to bury her entirely, the black hull and its delicate, almost fragile jib-boom surfacing after agonising moments. But as the brilliant red of the English ensign rose on the staff beside Mainwaring, he noted with a burst of pride that brave scraps of red were soon whipping in the gale from the yard-arm peaks of both the lugger and the dhow.

Good lads, said Mainwaring inwardly. *Good lads!*

Ahead in the ship, Rumford was bellowing at a clutch of drenched, wet-rat seamen struggling at the pinrail with the lee braces, only to bark a sudden warning and join them in a leap for the rigging as a white foaming wall of water burst over the bows and roared aft to the mainmast foot. The men clung like gibbons on a branch until the water sluiced away, and then were slithering back to their work, their curses carrying over the wind to Mainwaring's ears.

He squinted ahead, trying to make out the position of the French ships. A curtain of rain had closed over them, but there was a tickling at the back of his neck. As if to read his mind, the voice of the foretop lookout, clinging with his mate to his wildly swinging perch, pierced down to Mainwaring through the wind roar.

"Deck, there! They're turning, sir!"

"*Damn!*" Mainwaring checked himself, cupping his hands to focus his voice. "Deck, aye! What course, now?"

"Sir, they're turnin', inshore, like! One o' th' leadin' ships 'as lost 'er topm'st, I think. The gale's driven them in."

"Can ye make out their heading clearly, man? Where do they steer?"

A pause. "Inshore is all, sir! They'll not weather th' 'eadland, stake me divvy o' duff on it!"

Mainwaring grinned at the man, and gave him a wave, as Rumford slithered and lurched his way back on to the quarterdeck.

"She's lyin' a tad easier now, sir! Are ye still steerin' fer the lead Frenchman?"

"Aye!" said Mainwaring. "But it seems we've got

Captain Monsoon sailing with us, Mr Rumford! He's dismasted one of the Frenchmen, a t'gallant mast, possibly, and they're steering inshore."

Hotspur took a wild plunge that sent green water smashing like a curving glass wall over the windward rail amidships, and an arm of hurtling water struck Mainwaring and knocked him into a sitting position with his back against the binnacle box. He fought to his feet, cursing until he heard the smothered laughter of the four men at *Hotspur*'s wheel, and his curse changed to a grin.

"Proper rinse ye got that time, sir!" offered Rumford.

"Thank you, Mr Rumford, God damn and blast your pox-ridden soul! How far off are we? And how far off are the whoreson French?" Mainwaring rung out the tails of the French coat, adding another ingenious oath he remembered from Hooke's endless inventory.

Rumford was squinting into the rain. "You were right, sir! The lead ship's disappearin' in behind that bay's northern point, th' wind'ard one, an' th' rest are followin' 'er in. An' we're no more'n a league off, now, sir."

"Think the buggers have seen us?"

"Likely, sir, though they may not 'ave made out our colours afore they put in. An' likely they'd think we were theirs from what they was up to afore."

Mainwaring nodded, spitting off to leeward. He was beginning to shiver in the drenching wet, and salt spray was burning in the many days' stubble that darkened his chin. "Aye, they'll have little to think we're English. Only fools or suicidal madmen would sail in at them in a protected anchorage, given their weight o' broadside. A brig, a lugger and a God-damned dhow against a seventy-gunner and six other ships – the stuff of idiocy. Which is precisely what we're going to do."

"Like fools and madmen, sir?"

"Like fools and madmen, Mr Rumford!"

Mainwaring peered at the lugger and cuffed a drip of water from his nose. "Can ye remember what signal I agreed on with Mr Hooke, for action? I can't bloody think, now!"

Rumford hunched his shoulders as a cloud of spray hissed over them, shaking his head and spitting like a hound coming out of a bog. "No, sir. Sweet duckfooted Jesus, if ye'll pardon me sayin' so, ain't no need fer buggerin' *signals*, sir! If we be fixin' t' fling ourselves on 'em like rats on a bulldog, why, steer for 'em, says I, an' Mr Hooke and Mr Howe'll do th' same! Wiv respect."

"Sink me, Rumford, you've a practical mind. Very well. Likely a gun now would just alert the French we're about to come gnawing at their shins. A pox on signals. Tell Mr Pellowe to double-shot both batteries, if they can serve 'em in this sea, and have some lads break out those firelocks. And send a man to get that bloody great dragoon blade o' mine." He spat to leeward. "We'll just hope Mr Hooke and Mr Howe know what we're about!"

"Aye, sir," grinned Rumford, "no fear, they will." He staggered off forward, slithering on the streaming decking.

Mainwaring vaulted up into the weather rigging, fixing a grip of steel on the main shrouds' shear pole to keep from being flung into the sea. He held up his free arm to protect his face against the pelting rain which stung like insect bites, and squinted over it to the scene forward.

As if on cue, the rain parted and he could see the line of French warships, clearly outlined against the shape of the island. Their canvas was luffing and ballooning aloft as they moved in stately slowness behind the point of the northern – and now windward – arm of the tree-lined bay, rounding up to anchor in the same sheltered waters where Mainwaring had taken *Hotspur*. Already the leading ships were turning to the hawsers, canvas disappearing from their yards, their motion eased and still as they came to rest one by one in the refuge of the bay.

Ye think to lie there till it's done, said Mainwaring to himself as *Hotspur*, plunging alarmingly into a cloud of spray, shuddered under him. *But ye'll not lie still, nor undisturbed, by God!*

Hotspur rose, waterfalls of foam pouring from her bows, and Mainwaring could see Pellowe in the waist struggling with the gunners over their weapons, water sloshing and foaming about their ankles. The likelihood of a dry match in these conditions was poor; if only some ingenious bugger would rig up a gun lock on ships' guns.

Mainwaring shifted his gaze ahead; the brig was no more than a quarter of a mile off the headland. On her present course, if he judged the leeway rightly, she would pass with the headland close aboard her windward side before shooting in to the calmer waters of the bay. The land would hide her hull at least until the very last moment. He was watching the largest of the French ships, with the dark, massive bulk of a seventy-four, vanish behind the point, followed by the last vessel, a brig or snow. That meant *Hotspur*, *Anne* and the lugger would approach unseen for the last of their run in, and would burst out into the inner bay and the anchorage still virtually at full speed – and barely a musket shot from the first of the anchored ships.

Hardly time to think, Mainwaring realised, looking again at the spray-wreathed and pitching dhow and lugger. *They'll have to fight their own fight, make their own decisions. Not like Toulon.*

Rumford's feet slapped to a halt beside him. "No more'n fifteen minutes till we're in, sir. Mr Pellowe's says to tell ye th' guns are primed an' loaded, an' 'e'll run out directly ye give th' word, but 'e can't promise they'll fire in this. What d'ye plan, sir?"

Mainwaring raised his voice as the wind howled anew in the thrumming rigging beside them.

"We'll steer for the largest ship, Mr Rumford. Once round the headland, I'll trouble you to let fall the main tops'l for a last lifting push. We'll steer for her, and range in alongside, so I'll ask as well that ye put men at bow and stern with grapnels. We'll give 'em a broadside, if the damned guns will take light, even if it is nothing more than a pinprick to them. Then we board her and do as much damage as we can before the bastards get us!"

Rumford glanced at the men at the helm, who seemed to know that a silent question was being asked. Their faces like stone, they nodded.

"Aye, aye, sir," said Rumford, looking Mainwaring in the eye. "If that's what ye will, that's what we'll do, sir. Little else t' look for'rard to. An' none o' th' lads fancy t' lose their parts an' be a girl-voiced slave t' some buggerin' A-rab!"

"Very well," said Mainwaring, a great calm seeming to rise from within him. The image of Anne Brixham's face floated for a moment before him, and the evergreen, crystal-sharp coastline of New England. "Pass the word to all the lads, Mr Rumford. We fight to the last. To the bloody last!"

With the wind roaring like a great bow in the rigging, *Hotspur* drove on in a welter of foam and spray towards the headland, behind which the thin, black vertical lines of the French topgallant masts were faintly visible through the swirling mist and rain. Above *Hotspur*, the red blaze of the English ensign stood out in brilliant colour against the dark, mixed grey of the sea and sky. And astern of the brig, still holding their own, the dhow and lugger plunged in after them, the ensigns bright and brave above their taut, reefed canvas with their dark water stains, and the spray-wreathed hulls.

Mainwaring lurched over to stand by the men at the double wheel as *Hotspur* surged in towards the point. He called small steering changes into the senior man's ear to keep the brig just off the lighter water that marked the shallows, but close enough aboard the point so that Mainwaring could see the wall of individual trees, bowing and curving as the wind tore at them. Now *Hotspur*'s men were all on deck; one man coming aft to present Mainwaring gravely with his heavy dragoon sword; Pellowe's gunners clustered motionless round their guns; Rumford's sailhandlers at the pin- and fiferails, a few ready to race aloft and loose the topsail; and all eyes on the rapidly approaching low point, so clear and so close, bracing themselves against *Hotspur*'s still-violent motion as the sea roared steadily under her bows in a white wave, and she rushed in, closer to the looming shore, with the French squadron – and death, sure and certain – waiting beyond.

It would only be a moment more . . .

Then Fell, the marine sergeant, was pointing and shouting from his post on the foredeck.

"*There*, sir! Christ, *look* at 'em!"

With the wind tearing at her canvas, *Hotspur* swept in past the headland and its narrow beach against which the gale-driven surf was roaring no more than a pistol shot away. Then she was shooting into the bay, the waters suddenly still even as the boom of the surf sounded beyond the point, and the air full of drifting mist from its crash. Before the rushing brig, the panorama of the anchored French squadron unfolded in sudden and startling detail.

"Look at th' damage!" Rumford was exulting. "Aye, Cap'n Monsoon did fer 'em, sure!"

The waters of the bay, though sheltered to a degree from the driving force of the gale and the lift of the oceanic swell, were still swept over by curls and eddies of the gale. In a broad semi-circle the French ships were anchored, bows turning to wind as they fetched up on their hawsers. But it was not the orderly anchorage of a naval squadron with its ships tucking their canvas up into the tidy rolls of a harbour furl; the foretopmast injury to one of the ships that Mainwaring had seen from afar was only part of the damage the French ships had suffered. As Mainwaring stared at them in astonishment, it was clear that virtually every one of the French ships had suffered some hurt to rigging and spar. Here a topsail yard hung crookedly from its lifts; there a jib-boom trailed into the water, torn curls of spritsail and headsail rippling and thumping as men punched and clutched at it. One of the smaller vessels, a brig, had lost both topmasts, giving it the forlorn, bald-headed look of a damaged shelf model. That *Hotspur*, the lugger and *Anne* had managed to preserve their own rigging and remain seaworthy as well was equally astonishing.

Hotspur was sweeping fully into the bay, her canvas still majestically drawing, her speed increasing in towards the anchored line of ships as the retarding effect of the great swells vanished.

Mainwaring sprang to stand beside the wheel, scanning round him at the line of ships, his mind racing. There were five smaller vessels, ships and a brig, and a man-o'-war which he recognised grimly as *Neptune*, his adversary and the prison then of Caroline Grenville. But his eyes were fixed now on the huge, towering shape that was anchored astern of *Neptune*: a mustard and blue hull like a fortress wall, and a lofty, undamaged rig, Bourbon ensigns streaming from the staff and truck.

"The seventy-four, by God!" Mainwaring breathed. "*Steer for her, lads!*"

Rumford was calling to him from the waist, his voice cracking in excitement. "The lugger's through, sir! An' Mr 'Owe, just astern of 'im! Christ, look at 'em come!"

Mainwaring swung round to look. The lugger was in behind the point, knifing with incredible speed through the level waters of the bay, canvas rising again in rhythmic hauls up the masts as Hooke added a few knots to his attack speed. The quickness of the low hull under its arcing canvas was breathtaking. Mainwaring could make out Hooke, a bulky figure on the low quarterdeck, pointing ahead, soundless orders rolling over the lugger's decks to drive the frenzied hauling at the halyards and sheets.

"'E's steerin' for th' frigate, sir!" Rumford cried. "That's a bucko lad!"

Already the lugger had sheered away on her own course, her long black jib-boom arrowing for the tan bulk of *Neptune*. Now something else was happening; something that made Mainwaring's throat catch in sudden emotion.

"Lord Jesus, sir!" blurted out one of the helmsmen beside him. "Mr Hooke's set her afire, sir!"

Mainwaring stared as a puff of smoke appeared up the lugger's fore companionway, joined in the next moment by smoke pouring suddenly up the after one, to stream forward around the dark vessel like a cloaking shawl, its wisps reaching for *Neptune*.

"The *Anne*'s through!" came a cry from the foretop. "She's steerin' for them two rafted t'gether, sir!"

But now the French were reacting. In the anchored, damaged ships, figures were running, voices raised in alarm and orders. From *Neptune*, towards which the lugger raced, the sound of gun trucks rumbling and squealing sounded over the howl of the wind. Gunports opened, a ripple of red-lidded black eyes appearing in the tan-coloured wall of the frigate's side. Then a ragged broadside thundered out, the reports sharp and penetrating, the gun flashes pink tongues of flame, smoke bursting ahead of them to roil up and back over the frigate's side. A forest of glittering, fingerlike shot splashes leaped up around the lugger, collapsing back in a curtain of spray as the lugger rushed on through it.

Mainwaring peered ahead. Before *Hotspur*, barely two hundred yards away, the wall of the seventy-four loomed. No gunports had opened yet, but as *Hotspur* rushed in, rapidly moving figures and faces were visible over the rail high above, white, palette-knife daubs of faces marked by dark mouths opened in orders, or agape in anger or astonishment.

As *Hotspur* rushed in, the British ensign rippling above her stern, Rumford was bounding up to the quarterdeck, pointing forward.

"The bastard hasn't opened his gunports, yet, sir! We may get in to him afore he does! What d'ye want –"

"*Alongside!*" cried Mainwaring. "Hold your course till the last, then hard over your helm, and smash in alongside him. No grapnels, as the wind'll hold us. If the rigs tangle, so much the better. When we hit, pass the word for the lads to board, any way they can." His eyes met Rumford's meaningfully. "Then it'll be each man's fate to himself."

"Aye, sir!" Rumford barked. Then he stared at Mainwaring. "We be goin' t' die, ain't we, sir?"

"Yes, we are, Mr Rumford. Take my hand. But when you close with 'em, take some with you! Make them *pay!*" He and Rumford shared a brief, strong grip, and then Mainwaring was springing to the waistdeck rail, to see Pellowe looking up at him in wide-eyed expectancy.

"One round, whatever side we put to him, Stephen! Then board him, and God protect you!"

Pellowe's look over the distance was steady and clear. "Aye, aye, sir. God protect *you*, sir!"

Mainwaring thrust the dragoon sword into the back of his belt. His stomach was knotted almost painfully tight and his legs were trembling uncontrollably. But instead of a paralysing fear rising within him at what lay ahead – a fear he had dreaded almost more than the prospect of death – he felt a strange calm. His quick glance took in the shapes of the lugger and the dhow, their smallness suddenly poignant, and the image of Anne Brixham's face floated again before his eyes which seemed instinctively to mist over with tears. The knot of pain within his chest became almost unbearable and a sob burst from his lips which he hid within a sudden cough, and he shook his head, spitting theatrically over the rail, fighting to win back his self-control.

He looked up, cuffing away the tears that streamed down his cheeks. The enormous wall of the seventy-four was one hundred yards away. Now fifty. Now thirty.

"Stand ready, lads!" Mainwaring cried.

"Deck, there!" The foretop's voice was almost a shriek. "The dhow's afire, too, sir! Mr Howe's goin' for th' head o' the' line, as a fireship, sir! There's – *Christ save us!*"

Something in the man's tone snapped Mainwaring's head up. "What is it, man!"

"A frigate, sir! English colours, at th' bay mouth, sir! Jesus, she's –"

The world abruptly exploded in a thunderclap of sound and a vast wall of flame that illuminated *Hotspur* in a garish, lurid light. The roar of the wind, the incredulous shriek of the lookout, the creak and groan of *Hotspur*, the thudding of Mainwaring's heart in his ears, all vanished in a staggering concussion. Mainwaring felt himself struck in the chest as if by a giant fist, tumbling head over heels to slam painfully against the transom bulkhead, the hilt of the dragoon sword hard against his back as he fell. The air was suddenly thick and dark, almost a yellowish colour, and was full of floating debris and wreckage. As he struck the deck, Mainwaring's eyes found *Hotspur*'s double wheel, which disintegrated as he watched into a radiating halo of flying fragments and splinters, the figures of the men who had been standing at it moments ago smashed away into nothing save a bloody smear on the decking. Mainwaring stared in horror as a dismembered arm, a tattoo vivid on the hairy forearm, arced towards him from somewhere forward and thudded against his chest before spinning away, a spray of warm blood spattering his face.

With a cry he fought to his feet, unable to see in an enveloping cloud of choking smoke, swirling low over the deck. Above him was a cracking, grinding chaos of collapsing rigging and splintering masts and yards, sensed rather than seen, and now he was conscious of a mass of rigging, snarled and slack lines, and curtained, ballooning canvas, low over the quarterdeck. He could dimly perceive figures moving and struggling in the smoke, and voices ahead were shouting orders or crying out in alarm and pain. Then a dark mass was blotting out the light ahead and to the starboard side – *the French seventy-four*, cried his mind – before *Hotspur* thudded with a rending impact into that dark wall, and the air was rent once more with the moan of creaking, groaning wood, with splintering and snapping, and with the shrieks and cries of men. The force of the ships' collision threw Mainwaring to his knees again, but he scrambled upright, intent on that wall of wood. He stumbled forward, coughing and hacking, ducking beneath a huge, shattered length of spar that he realised was part of the brig's main gaff.

Now he was at the rail and mounting it, the mustard-coloured side of the French seventy-four lifting and falling before him, the sea between the ships a frothed mass below the groaning timbers. Figures lurched past or bumped into him, and all about him was a dark, twisted roil of wreckage, enveloped in the choking fog of gunsmoke, lit here and there by the flicker of fire. The eddying storm of noise rose again: men's voices, in cries for help, in screams of agony, in bellows of anger; pounding and banging, as of steel on steel; and a deep, sonorous, almost inaudible *basso-profundo* rumble of pain that Mainwaring realised was coming from the hull of *Hotspur* itself.

Mainwaring steadied himself for a moment on the rail, gauging the distance to that lifting, falling wall and the line of battens that ran up its side. He leapt across, ignoring the pain in elbows and knees as he struck, his fingers and toes scrabbling monkeylike for a grip on the slick, salt-gritty painted wood. To one side the dark cave of a gunport gaped, but he scrambled on, up the slope of the ship's tumble-home, a strange reckless wildness beginning to rise in him.

Then he was at the entry port, and levering himself through, his heart pounding in his throat as he scrambled to his feet and pulled the dragoon sword from his belt. Over the enormous deck before him swirled the same choking, yellow smoke, engulfing the forms of a mass of struggling men, almost indistinguishable from one another except for the grey coats of *Troupes de la Marine*, and now the red flash of one English marine's coat, marking Fell or one of the other surviving marines. The Hotspurs had reached the seventy-four's deck virtually all at once, hurling themselves into the packed mass of men there.

Mainwaring looked wildly around, trying to get his

bearings, when a blow to the side of the head sent stars spinning in front of his eyes. He fell in a rolling tumble, something within him keeping an icy, raging control, and he coiled back up into a low crouch to meet his attacker, a thickset French seaman whose swarthy face was twisted in a snarl. The man, clad in a striped shirt and tar-stained trousers, lunged at Mainwaring with the bluntly formidable end of a gunner's handspike, arrowing for Mainwaring's chest.

With his free hand, Mainwaring fisted aside the in-rushing blow, his knuckles banging painfully against the wood of the shaft. Then he rose, stepping in, cutting down with a vicious blow of the dragoon blade. The gleaming steel sank into the Frenchman's neck where it joined his shoulder, and a scarlet cloud misted up round his throat. The man screamed, clutching with his bare hands at the bloody blade, the gun tool falling with a clatter to the deck.

With a curse Mainwaring kicked the man back and away, wrenching the blade free. He spun, looking for the quarter-deck, his mind fixed on the ensign staff and the white Bourbon ensign that streamed over the bloody struggle. A cloud of smoke swirled clear, and he saw some twenty feet away the steps of the short ladder leading to the quarterdeck. He sprinted for it, shouldering aside two men struggling silently, their hands locked on each other's throats. He dodged to one side as a French officer in the blue and grey of the *Troupes de la Marine* cut down at his head with a hanger, the lace at the man's wrist gleaming incongruously in the dark, grim light. The blade whistled past Main-waring's ear, and he dropped the slender man with a short, sharp blow of his free fist. Reaching the ladder, he was up it and on to the quarterdeck, running for the ensign staff. A seaman in a torn check shirt emerged from behind the seventy-four's mizzen foot, a cutlass held high above a face twisting in a grimace. Mainwaring threw up the dragoon sword into the guard position, the Frenchman's blade ring-ing against it like a hammer on a bell, and then drove a kick into the man's groin with the hard ball of his bare foot. The man gasped, his face suddenly grey, and fell away.

With an exultant cry, Mainwaring reached the ensign staff, looking up at the huge white ensign, streaming and curling, beautiful and hated all at once. He swung a cut of the dragoon blade at the short halyard, and as the steel dug into the varnished wood the great ensign suddenly collapsed in great folds around him.

Then he was staggering away, unable to withhold a cry of pain at the vicious cut which sliced to the bone through his left shoulder. The blood surged from the wound, warm and sticky, down his suddenly useless arm, and he slumped back against the transom rail feeling nausea and faintness as the ensign's folds swirled like sheeting around him. For a moment he was wreathed in smoke, and then it parted.

To reveal a tall, darkly handsome figure of an officer, in impeccable scarlet velvet and snowy lace, black hair queued back neatly, and glittering black eyes fixing Mainwaring with a look of sneering triumph. His right hand grasped the slowly circling sword whose blade gleamed in brilliant colour with Mainwaring's blood.

Mainwaring stared at the face, disbelief slowly moving to cold, trembling anger, not believing entirely that it was *that* face, so hated, so remembered. But then realising it was so.

"*You!*" he breathed. "It *was* you! The shooting of my men, the selling to the slave traders! All of it!"

"Been keeping track of us, have you?" said the Chevalier Rigaud de la Roche-Bourbon. "I must admit to equal astonishment in finding you in all this. How a colonial fishpot boy does rise, hmm? The kind of contemptible mock heroics we see here seem to be the sort of thing you prefer. Certainly leaves you looking ragged and dirty, however. Whoever could your tailor be?" The blade circled, drawing Mainwaring's eyes to its point as if hypnotised. Roche-Bourbon stepped closer.

"I should have killed you, of course, in that wretched little hut in Panama. You have cost me so much since then. Quite the ubiquitous little hero, in fact."

Mainwaring felt the hot ribbon of blood coursing down his arm and dripping to the deck, landing on his bare feet in heavy drops, and he swayed, his vision blurring.

"The woman – Lady Caroline – what have you done with her?"

"You know of *her*?" Roche-Bourbon snickered, the black eyes glittering unblinkingly at Mainwaring. "She proved to be a delightful toy. Her skin is milk-white, you know. Shows the welts admirably. I've enjoyed mounting her, and giving her pain has been such a delight."

A red haze seemed to form around Mainwaring's vision. "You bastard!" he whispered, and took an uncertain step towards Roche-Bourbon.

"Oh, so it is to be *now*, then?" smiled Roche-Bourbon. "So be it!" He stepped forward with catlike quickness, the gory blade whistling for Mainwaring's neck. But the fighting rage within Mainwaring had returned, augmented by some deeper, elemental anger, and a revulsion against all that the scarlet-clad figure represented. With an unheeding cry he brought the dragoon sword up into a ringing parry that caused a flicker of surprise to cross Roche-Bourbon's handsome features.

Then Mainwaring was at him, cutting again and again in savage hammerblows of the dragoon sword, forcing the Frenchman to recoil, step after step, able only to parry the furious, clanging blows that Mainwaring was delivering in a final outburst of loathing and disgust.

"For all – you've killed – and all – you've hurt! You bloody – foul – disgusting –" Mainwaring raged. Now more memories joined his rage: Anne Brixham, strapped naked by thongs to the deckhead and moments away from screaming torture; twisted and maimed bodies on the beach of an island off the Panama coast; the wailing women and terrified children of a fishing village on the shores of Toulon

215

harbour; the men of *Pallas*, dying in the water as they pleaded for mercy. "Now – you will – *pay!*"

Mainwaring's blows whistled in with blinding speed, savage impacts that drove the now-pale Frenchman back until he was against the rail at the top of the ladder leading to the waist. Mainwaring coiled himself to deliver the final blow that would smash down through Roche-Bourbon's guard, to cleave into his skull.

But in the split-second before Mainwaring's blade struck, Roche-Bourbon spun away with uncanny speed, and Mainwaring's blade came down with painful force to impact in a ringing contact with the rail. The blade leaped from Mainwaring's hands, his arm shot full of a lancing pain. At that instant, a length of heavy line, the tail of a halyard, whipped through the air, to strike like a lash on Mainwaring's wounded shoulder. With a cry, he staggered back, the nausea and pain engulfing him, and he looked wildly round for Roche-Bourbon, only to sink to his knees as his vision went grey.

The scarlet figure was before him, the gleaming boots inches from his eyes, the cold gaze mocking, the handsome face once again in the assured smile.

"Die knowing you've failed, you fool. *Die knowing that!*" And he raised his sword for a killing thrust.

Mainwaring struggled to rise, to meet the blow with a last, determined surge of effort. But he did not feel the burning thrust of a steel blade. Instead a pistol's report rang out, sharp and painfully loud nearby. He stared up as Roche-Bourbon's face, still frozen in the mocking smile, was marked by a small blue hole in the middle of his forehead.

With a strangled sound in his throat, the scarlet figure tottered backwards, the bloody sword falling to the deck, until his knees struck the top of the companionway rail. Without a murmur, the Chevalier Rigaud de la Roche-Bourbon toppled down the ladder, hit the waistdeck rail with a horrid thud, and fell on over the side into the sea.

Edward Mainwaring rose, staggering, to his feet, staring

at where Roche-Bourbon had vanished. He sensed the quiet that had fallen over the seventy-four's deck, that even the wind's howl seemed mute. He could see Isaiah Hooke – what the devil was Hooke doing here? – beaming up at him from a knot of grinning men in the seventy-four's waist.

Then he turned, the grey at the edge of his vision beginning to close in, looking off to where the *Neptune*, locked in fiery death with the lugger, was sending a black pyre of smoke roiling away to leeward, her yards flaming crucifixes above the black billows; to where the *Anne*, not afire, but lying alongside two other French vessels, with English colours streaming not only from her but the two French ships, cheers echoing over the wind from men on their decks; to the bay mouth, where a beautiful frigate under the colours of the English East India Company lay hove to, her broadside trained in readiness at the remaining French ships.

And to where, at the top of the far-side waistdeck ladder, a motionless Caroline Grenville stood, her gown torn and tattered, her face pale and bruised from beating. Her eyes shone with relief and triumph, and they were fixed on the spot where Roche-Bourbon had toppled to his watery grave, the smoking little pistol hanging limp in her fingers.

Mainwaring's eyes met hers, and a slow smile crossed his face.

"Thank you, Lady Caroline," he breathed.

And knew no more.

Epilogue

My dear Sir John,

I am sure you are no more surprised and pleased than I at the turn of Events which Sir Richard Brixham may have communicated to you upon his return from the Indian Ocean; the details of which I am sure you will be delighted to learn, and which have brought, amongst other things, a return upon our Investment in his charter Vessel far in excess of anything we might have imagined, and which has changed the affair from the willing support of a friend and associate to a most profitable Enterprise.

You will have been aware that the Provincial naval officer, Captain Mainwaring, who has succeeded in the past without recourse to any significant interest save the momentary one of His Majesty, was sent out in the *Pallas* frigate to assist Commodore Peyton on the Coromandel; the which he carried out so successfully when all had thought him lost, so as to capture or destroy the squadron assembled at Mauritius by M. la Bourdonnais, thereby saving Peyton and obliging M. la Bourdonnais to procure another.

All this through a daring and extraordinary Attack upon the anchored French, conducted with a peculiar little Squadron, occasioned by the loss of Captain Mainwaring's own ship, for which the Court of Inquiry has exonerated him, and ably supported by the East Indiaman *St George*, Captain Eversham arriving on the scene in the nick of time. That Captain Mainwaring's betrothed, Miss Brixham, was the chief cause of the *St George*'s charter, and her role in capturing, with some of the *St George*'s people, one of the anchored French, is verified, and is the talk of all.

Captain Mainwaring's associates in the other vessels escaped death or injury, by the Grace of God, and are returned with him in the *St George* & to much huzzahs. More extraordinary is the release of Lady Caroline Grenville, thought lost, who was released from infamous conduct at the hands of the French by Captain Mainwaring's attack, and has been fulsome in his praise since her restoration to her family. To this is added the astounding quantity of prize money arising from the French bullion taken by Captain Mainwaring in *Achille*, in which Captain Mainwaring and his people, by Order of His Majesty, are to share handsomely.

Sir Richard is quite beside himself with joy, for not only is he at once worth far more than you can imagine, but Captain Mainwaring and Miss Brixham are to be married immediately. In addition, it is all around St James' that Captain Mainwaring is to be knighted, and given a governorship in the American Colonies, he being of that Place, possibly in the Carolinas or Rhode Island. One might think that would end the whole delicious matter, but we may not have heard the last of Captain Sir Edward Mainwaring, as sufficiently exciting as the news has been to date . . .